W9-BMV-981

MYSTERIOUS EROTIC TALES

MYSTERIOUS EROTIC TALES

CASTLE BOOKS

WHAT MIGHT HAVE BEEN 177
Elizabeth Kay

BERENICE 217
Edgar Allan Poe

THE PLAIN BROWN ENVELOPE 227
Lyn Wood

Acknowledgments 245

AN OUTSIDE INTEREST

Ruth Rendell

FRIGHTENING people used to be a hobby of mine. Perhaps I should rather say an obsession and not people but, specifically, women. Making others afraid *is* enjoyable as everyone discovers who has tried it and succeeded. I suppose it has something to do with power. Most people never really try it so they don't know, but look at the ones who do. Judges, policemen, prison warders, customs officers, tax inspectors. They have a great time, don't they? You don't find them giving up or adopting other methods. Frightening people goes to their heads, they're drunk on it, they live by it. So did I. While other men might go down to the pub with the boys or to football, I went off to Epping Forest and frightened women. It was what you might call my outside interest.

Don't get me wrong. There was nothing – well, nasty, about what I did. You know what I mean by that, I'm sure I don't have to go into details. I'm far from being some sort of pervert, I can tell you. In fact, I err rather on the side of too much moral strictness. Nor am I one of those lonely, deprived men. I'm happily married and the father of a little boy, I'm six feet tall, not bad looking, and, I assure you, entirely physically and mentally normal.

Of course I've tried to analyse myself and discover my motives. Was my hobby ever any more than an antidote to boredom? By anyone's standards the life I lead would be classed as pretty dull, selling tickets and answering passengers' queries at Anglo-Mercian Airways terminal, living in a semi in Muswell Hill; going to tea with my mother-in-law on Sundays, and having an annual fortnight in a holiday flat in South Devon. I got married very young. Adventure wasn't exactly a conspicuous feature of my existence. The biggest thing that happened to me was when we thought one of our charters had been hijacked in Greece, and that turned out to be a false alarm.

My wife is a nervous sort of girl. Mind you, she has cause to be, living where we do close to Highgate Woods and Queens Wood. A woman takes her life in her hands, walking alone in those places. Carol used to regale me with stories – well, she still does.

'At twenty past five in the afternoon! It was still broad daylight. He raped her and cut her in the face, she had to have seventeen stitches in her face and neck.'

She doesn't drive and if she comes home from anywhere after dark I always go down to the bus stop to meet her. She won't even walk along the Muswell Hill Road because of the woods on either side.

'If you see a man on his own in a place like that you naturally ask yourself what he's doing there, don't you? A young man, just walking aimlessly about. It's not as if he had a dog with him. It makes your whole body go tense and you get a sort of awful crawling sensation all over you. If you didn't come and meet me I don't think I'd go out at all.'

Was it that which gave me the idea? At any rate it made me think about women and fear. Things are quite different for a man, he never thinks about being afraid of being in dark or lonely places. I'm sure I never have and therefore, until I got all this from Carol, I never considered how important this business of being scared when out alone might be to them. When I came to understand, it gave me a funny feeling of excitement.

And then I actually frightened a woman myself – by chance. My usual way of going to work is to cut through Queens Wood to Highgate tube station and take the Northern Line down into London. When the weather is very bad I go to the station by bus but most of the time I walk there and back and the way through the wood is a considerable shortcut. I was coming back through the wood at about six one evening in March. It was dusk, growing dark. The lamps, each a good distance apart from each other, which light the paths, were lit, but I often think these give the place a rather more bleak and sinister appearance than if it were quite dark. You leave a light behind you and walk along a dim shadowy avenue toward the next lamp, which gleams faintly some hundred yards ahead. And no sooner is it reached, an acid-yellow glow among the bare branches, than you leave it behind again to negotiate the next dark stretch. I thought about how it must be to be a woman walking through the wood and, yes, I gloried in my maleness and my freedom from fear.

Then I saw the girl coming. She was walking along the path from Priory Gardens. It came into my head that she would be less wary of me if I continued as I had been, marching briskly and purposefully toward Wood Vale, swinging along and looking like a man homeward bound to his family and his dinner. There was no definite intent present in my mind when I slackened my pace, then stopped and stood still. But as soon as I'd done that I knew I was going to carry it through. The girl came up to where the paths converged and where the next lamp was. She gave me a quick darting look. I stood there in a very relaxed way and I returned her look with a blank stare. I suppose I consciously, out of some sort of devilment, made my eyes fixed and glazed and let my mouth go loose. Anyway, she turned very quickly away and began to walk much faster.

She had high heels so she couldn't go very fast, not as fast as I could, just strolling along behind her. I gained on her until I was a yard behind.

I could smell her fear. She was wearing a lot of perfume and her sweat seemed to potentiate it so that there came to me a whiff and then a wave of heady, mixed-up animal and floral scent. I breathed heavily. She began to run and I strode after her. What she did then was unexpected. She stopped, turned around, and cried out in a tremulous terrified voice: 'What do you want?'

I stopped too and gave her the same look. She held her handbag out to me. 'Take it!'

The joke had gone far enough. I lived around there anyway, I had my wife and son to think of. I put on a cockney voice. 'Keep your bag, love. You've got me wrong.'

And then, to reassure her, I turned back along the path and let her escape to Wood Vale and the lights and the start of the houses. But I can't describe what a feeling of power and – well, triumphant manhood and what's called machismo the encounter gave me. I felt grand. I swaggered into my house and Carol said had I had a premium bond come up?

Since I'm being strictly truthful in this account, I'd better add the other consequence of what happened in the wood, even though it does rather go against the grain with me to mention things like that. I made love to Carol that night and it was a lot better than it had been for a long time, in fact it was sensational for both of us. And I couldn't kid myself that it was due to anything but my adventure with the girl.

Next day I looked at myself in the mirror with all the lights off but the little tubular one over our bed, and I put on the same look I'd given the girl when she turned in my direction under the lamp. I can tell you I nearly frightened myself. I've said I'm not bad looking and that's true but I'm naturally pale and since I'm thin, my face tends to be a bit gaunt. In the dim light my eyes seemed sunk in deep sockets and my mouth hung loose in a vacant mindless way. I stepped back from the glass so that I could see the whole of myself, slouching, staring, my arms hanging. There was no doubt I had the potential of being a woman-frightener of no mean calibre.

They say it's the first step that counts. I had taken the first step but the second was bigger and it was weeks before I took it. I kept telling myself not to be a fool, to forget those mad ideas. Besides, surely I could see I'd soon be in trouble if I made a habit of frightening women in Queens Wood, on my own doorstep. But I couldn't stop thinking about it. I remembered how wonderful I'd felt that evening, how tall I'd walked and what a man I'd been.

The funny thing was what a lot of humiliating things seemed to happen me at that time, between the Queens Wood incident and the next occasion. A woman at the air terminal actually spat at me. I'm not exaggerating. Of course she was drunk, smashed out of her mind on duty-free Scotch, but she spat at me and I had to stand there in the middle of the ticket hall with all those tourists milling about, and wipe the spittle off my uniform. Then I got a reprimand for being discourteous to a passenger. It was totally unjust and, strictly speaking, I should have resigned on the spot, only I've got a wife and son and jobs aren't easy to come by at present. There was all that and trouble at home as well with Carol nagging me to take her on holiday with this girl friend of hers and her husband to Minorca instead of our usual Salcombe fortnight. I told her straight we couldn't afford it but I didn't like being asked in return why I couldn't earn as much as Sheila's Mike.

My manhood was at a low ebb. Then Sheila and Mike asked

us to spend the day with them – Carol, Timothy, and me. They had been neighbours of ours but had just moved away to a new house in one of those outer suburbs that are really in Essex. So I drove the three of us out to Theydon Bois and made my acquaintance with Epping Forest.

There are sixty-four square miles of forest, lying on the northeastern borders of London. But when you drive from the Wake Arms to Theydon along a narrow road bordered by woodland, stretches of turf and undergrowth, little coppices of birch trees, you can easily believe yourself in the depths of the country. It seems impossible that London is only fourteen or fifteen miles away. The forest is green and silent and from a car looks unspoiled, though of course it can't be. We passed a woman walking a very unguard-like dog, a tiny Maltese terrier . . . That gave me the idea. Why shouldn't I come out here? Why shouldn't I try my frightening act out here where no one knew me?

Two days after that I did. It was spring and the evenings stayed light till nearly eight. I didn't take the car. Somehow it didn't seem to me as if the sort of person I was going to be, going to *act*, would have a car. The journey was awful, enough to deter anyone less determined than I. I went straight from work, taking the Central Line tube as far as Loughton and then a bus up the hills and into the forest. At the Wake Arms I got off and began to walk down the hill, not on the pavement but a few yards inside the forest itself. I didn't see a woman on her own until I had reached the houses of Theydon and begun the return trip. I had gone about a hundred yards up again when she came out of one of the last houses, a young girl in jeans and a jacket, her hands in her pockets.

It was clear she was going to walk to the Wake Arms. Or so I thought. For a while I walked, keeping step with her, but unseen among the hawthorn and crab apple bushes, the tangle of brambles. I let us get a quarter of a mile away from the houses before I showed myself and then I stepped out onto the pavement ahead of her. I turned round to face her and stood there, staring in the way I'd practised in the mirror.

She wasn't nervous. She was brave. It was only very briefly that she hesitated. But she didn't quite dare walk past me. Instead she crossed the road. There's never much traffic on that road and so far not a single car had passed. She crossed the road, walking faster. I crossed too but behind her and I walked along at the back of her. Presently she began to run, so of course I ran too, though not fast enough to catch up to her, just enough to gain on her a little.

We had been going on like that for some minutes, the Wake Arms still a mile off, when she suddenly doubled back, hared across the road, and began running back the way she had come. That finished me for chasing her. I stood there and laughed. I laughed long and loud, I felt so happy and free, I felt so much all-conquering power that I – I alone, humble, ordinary, dull *me* – could inspire such fear.

After that I took to going to Epping Forest as a regular thing. Roughly speaking, I'd say it would have been once a fortnight. Since I do shift work, four till midnight just as often as ten till six, I sometimes managed to go in the daytime. A lot of women are alone at home in the daytime and have no men to escort them when they go out. I never let it go more than two weeks without my going there and occasionally I'd go more often, if I was feeling low in spirits, for instance, or Carol and I had a row or I got depressed over money. It did me so much good, I wish I could make you understand how much. Just think what it is you do that gives you a tremendous lift, driving a car really fast or going disco dancing or getting high on something – well, frightening women did all that for me and then some. Afterward it was like Christmas, it was almost like being in love.

And there was no harm in it, was there? I didn't hurt them. There's a French saying: it gives me so much pleasure and you so little pain. That was the way it was for me and them, though it wasn't without pleasure for them either. Imagine how they must have enjoyed talking about it afterward, going into all the details like Carol did, distorting the facts, exaggerating, making themselves for a while the centre of attention.

For all I knew they may have got up search parties, husbands and boyfriends and fathers all out in a pack looking for me, all having a great time as people invariably do when they're hunting something or someone. After all, when all was said and done, what did I do? Nothing. I didn't molest them or insult them or try to touch them, I merely stood and looked at them and ran after them – or ran when they ran, which isn't necessarily the same thing.

There was no harm in it. Or so I thought. I couldn't see what harm there could ever be, and believe me, I thought about this quite a lot, for I'm just as guilt-ridden as the rest of us. I thought about it, justifying myself, keeping guilt at bay. Young women don't have heart attacks and fall down dead because a man chases them. Young women aren't left with emotional traumas because a man stares at them. The oldest woman I ever frightened was the one with the Maltese terrier and she was no more than forty. I saw her again on my third or fourth visit and followed her for a while, stepping out from behind bushes and standing in her path. She used the same words the girl in Queens Wood had used, uttered in the same strangled voice: 'What is it you want?'

I didn't answer her. I had mercy on her and her little ineffectual dog and I melted away into the woodland shades. The next one who asked me that I answered with professorial gravity: 'Merely collecting lichens, madam.'

It was proof enough of how harmless I was that there was never a sign of a policeman in that area. I'm sure none of them told the police, for they had nothing to tell. They had only what they imagined and what the media had led them to expect. Yet harm did come from it, irrevocable harm and suffering and shame.

No doubt by now you think you've guessed. The inevitable must have happened, the encounter that any man who makes a practice of intimidating women is bound to have sooner or later, when the tables are turned on him. Yes, that did happen but it wasn't what stopped me. Being seized by the arm, hurled in the air, and laid out, sprawled and bruised, by a judo black belt, was just an occupational hazard. I've always been glad, though, that I behaved like a gentleman. I didn't curse her or shout abuse. I merely got up, rubbed my legs and my elbows, made her a little bow, and walked off in the direction of the Wake. Carol wanted to know how I'd managed to get green stains all over my clothes and I think to this day she believes it was from lying on the grass in a park somewhere with another woman. As if I would!

That attack on me deterred me. It didn't put me off. I let three weeks go by, three miserable yearning weeks, and then I went back to the Wake road one sunny July morning and had one of my most satisfying experiences. A girl walking, not on the road, but taking a shortcut through the forest itself. I walked parallel to her, sometimes letting her catch a glimpse of me. I knew she did, for, like it had been with the girl in Queens Wood, I could sense and smell her fear.

I strolled out from the bushes at last and stood ahead of her, waiting. She didn't dare approach me, she didn't know what to do. At length she turned back and I followed her, threading my way among the bushes until she must have thought I had gone, then appearing once more on the path ahead. This time she turned off to the left, running, and I let her go. Laughing the way I always did, out loud and irrepressibly, I let her go. I hadn't done her any harm. Think of the relief she must have felt when she knew she'd got away from me and was safe. Think of her going home and telling her mother or her sister or her husband all about it.

You could even say I'd done her a good turn. Most likely I'd warned her off going out in the forest on her own and therefore protected her from some real pervert or molester of women.

It was a point of view, wasn't it? You could make me out a public benefactor. I showed them what could happen. I was like the small electric shock that teaches a child not to play with the wires. Or that's what I believed. Till I learned that even a small shock can kill.

I was out in the forest, on the Wake road, when I had a piece of luck. It was autumn and getting dark at six, the earliest I'd been able to get there, and I didn't have much hope of any woman being silly enough to walk down that road alone in the dark. I had got off the bus at the Wake Arms and was walking slowly down the hill when I saw this car parked ahead of me at the kerb. Even from a distance I could hear the horrible noise it made as the driver tried to start it, that anguished grinding you get when ignition won't take place.

The offside door opened and a woman got out. She was on her own. She reached back into the car and turned the lights off, slammed the door, locked it, and began walking down the hill toward Theydon. I had stepped in among the trees and she hadn't yet seen me. I followed her, working out what technique I should use this time. Pursuing her at a run to start with was what I decided on.

I came out onto the pavement about a hundred yards behind her and began running after her, making as much noise with my feet as I could. Of course she stopped and turned round as I knew she would. Probably she thought I was a saviour who was going to do something about her car for her. She looked round, waiting for me, and as soon as I caught her eye I veered off into the forest once more. She gave a sort of shrug, turned, and walked on. She wasn't frightened yet.

It was getting dark, though, and there was no moon. I caught up to her and walked alongside her, very quietly, only three or four yards away, yet in among the trees of the forest. By then we were out of sight of the parked car and a long way from being in sight of the lights of Theydon. The road was dark, though far from being impenetrably black. I trod on a twig deliberately and made it snap and she turned swiftly and saw me.

She jumped. She looked away immediately and quickened her pace. Of course she didn't have a chance with me, a five-foot woman doesn't with a six-foot man. The fastest she could walk was still only my strolling pace.

There hadn't been a car along the road since I'd been following her. Now one came. I could see its lights welling and dipping a long way off, round the twists in the road. She went to the edge of the pavement and held up her hand the way a hitchhiker does. I stayed where I was to see what would happen. What had I done, after all? Only been there. But the driver didn't stop for her. Of course he didn't, no more than I would have done in his place. We all know the sort of man who stops his car to pick up smartly dressed, pretty hitchhikers at night and we know what he's after.

The next driver didn't stop either. I was a little ahead of her by then, still inside the forest, and in his headlights I saw her face. She *was* pretty, not that that aspect particularly interested me, but I saw that she was pretty and that she belonged to the same type as Carol, a small slender blonde with rather sharp features and curly hair.

The darkness seemed much darker after the car lights had passed. I could tell she was a little less tense now, she probably hadn't seen me for the past five minutes, she might have thought I'd gone. And I was tempted to call it a day, give up after a quarter of an hour, as I usually did when I'd had my fun.

I wish to God I had. I went on with it for the stupidest of reasons. I went on with it because I wanted to go in the same direction as she was going, down into Theydon and catch the tube train from there, rather than go back and hang about waiting for a bus. I could have waited and let her go. I didn't. Out of some sort of perverse need, I kept step with her and then I came out of the forest and got onto the pavement behind her.

I walked along, gaining on her, but quietly. The road dipped, wound a little. I got two or three yards behind her, going very softly, she didn't know I was there, and then I began a soft whistling, a hymn tune it was, the Crimond version of 'The Lord Is My Shepherd'. What a choice!

She spun round. I thought she was going to say something but I don't think she could. Her voice was strangled by fear. She turned again and began to run. She could run quite fast, that tiny vulnerable blonde girl.

The car lights loomed up over the road ahead. They were full-beam, undipped headlights, blazing blue-white across the surrounding forest, showing up every tree and making long black shadows spring from their trunks. I jumped aside and crouched down in the long grass. She ran into the road, holding up both arms and crying: 'Help me! Help me!'

He stopped. I had a moment's tension when I thought he might get out and come looking for me, but he didn't. He pushed open the passenger door from inside. The girl got in, they waited, sitting there for maybe half a minute, and then the white Ford Capri moved off.

It was a relief to me to see that car disappear over the top of the hill. And I realized, to coin a very appropriate phrase, that I wasn't yet out of the wood. What could be more likely than that the girl and the car driver would either phone or call in at Loughton police station? I knew I'd better get myself down to Theydon as fast as possible.

As it happened I did so without meeting or being passed by another vehicle. I was walking along by the village green when the only cars I saw came along. On the station platform I had to wait for nearly half an hour before a train came, but no policeman came either. I had got away with it again.

In a way. There are worse things than being punished for one's crimes. One of those is not being punished for them. I am suffering for what I did of course by not being allowed – that is, by not allowing myself – to do it again. And I shall never forget that girl's face, so pretty and vulnerable and frightened. It comes to me a lot in dreams.

The first time it appeared to me was in a newspaper photograph, two days after I had frightened her on the Wake road. The newspaper was leading on the story of her death and that was why it used the picture. On the previous morning, when she had been dead twelve hours, her body had been found, stabbed and mutilated, in a field between Epping and Harlow. Police were looking for a man, thought to be the driver of a white Ford Capri.

Her rescuer, her murderer. Then what was I?

COLETTE'S COLUMN

Andy Harrison

DAN ANNENBERG always ended his seminars with the same line: 'If you forget everything else I've said today, remember this: put your heart and soul into everything you do, apply the discipline of your working life to your private life, and always, always, always keep them separate. Thank you.'

Dan slid his naked body through the bubbly meniscus of apple blossom and walnut foam bath into hot water. Thirty minutes to relax before dinner and the phone line busy downloading electronic mail as a precaution against incoming calls. Twenty soothing minutes in the tub high above Hong Kong's Central District at the Ritz Carlton to recover from another harrowing landing at Kai Tek airport.

Dan stood up in the bath and rubbed himself down with a soap that called itself body creme, paying particular attention to the tucked away parts that suffered most from a fourteen-hour flight. He noted how his body was paying a heavy price for a life of constant travel. 'Not exactly fat,' he thought, 'but sliding.' When he flexed his muscles the fat stretched to insignificance, but his chest and stomach had grown softer over the last few years. 'Not bad really, for someone approaching the big four-oh.' And hadn't Colleen hinted that she liked men soft? 'No need to worry yet,' he told himself.

He dried himself off in front of CNN and learnt very little about the world except the names of all the hotels in Caracas where he could sit and watch CNN to learn the names of all the hotels in Prague where he could . . . There was no shortage of such hotels, but this he already knew having visited so many himself.

Quickly bored, he flipped to an adult movie channel. A man with seventies sideburns was thrusting into a woman whose eyes were tightly shut. She lay on a table with her ankles on the man's shoulders and with each slap of the man's thighs against her bulbous buttocks a fleshy wave rippled up her body propelling water-balloon breasts against their respective collarbones. 'Oh, yes!' the woman shouted, over and over. Dan slid his hand under the towel and gripped the hot urgency of his penis. He closed his eyes and imagined how Colleen's firmer body might move against his in the same position. He felt, in his mind, his hand glide across her breasts and roll a pea-hard nipple between his fingers. He saw her, eyes closed, head back, pouting lips gasping for air as she arched her back with delight, bearing down with her heels on his shoulders. He imagined Colleen's inner muscles gripping him, drawing him ever deeper into her warm sex, and then the coolness around his hard shaft as he teased its glistening surface out of her until only the engorged head was engaged. Then thrusting forward until his balls were squashed against her buttocks. It was the precision of his movement that she said she loved; just being on the verge of losing it and then back in to the hilt. 'I should save myself for Colleen,' he thought without being able to stop, and then resigned to the inner pressure; 'Oh, what the fuck, she might not even come.' A knock on the door shattered the image in his rampant mind and a shrill voice said, 'Room service, turn down sheets.'

'No thank you,' he shouted back, withdrawing his hand.

He switched off the TV and tightened the towel around his waist before moving to the late twentieth century's next indispensable machine: a laptop computer sitting on the walnut-veneer desk. It had finished transferring its data from another computer ten thousand kilometres away in Boston and was ready to offer up ideas, questions, requests, answers, complaints, orders. There were eighty-five messages waiting for him, accumulated in the two days since his last connection in another similar-looking, similarly expensive hotel room in London. He searched through the 'From' column for the only name he was really interested in: Colleen Pritchard. He found a typically terse memo from her. It said: 'Good news! Will be in Hong Kong on Friday. Don't you dare leave before Sunday night. Woof, Woof. Your Collie.'

It was one uplifting message that he had hardly dared to hope for; a message that made his heart soar and resurrected the front of his towel an inch or two. Before closing down his computer he started to write a memo to Felix. His friend in Singapore would have to cancel their weekend golf trip to Malaysia. He stopped himself and phoned instead.

'Sorry, Felix, pal,' he said over a crystal-clear line. 'Got'ta stay in Hong Kong for the weekend.'

'Say again?' said Felix rhetorically. 'We're talking the finest course in Asia, shit, maybe the world. We're talking a huge deposit. We're talking bookings six months in advance.'

'Felix, what we're talking is, is I'm not going to be there until Sunday night.'

'Ready for Monday, right?'

'Ready for Monday.'

'Big mistake, Dan. Big mistake.'

'Can't you find someone else to take along?' said Dan,

feeling very slightly guilty about blowing out his childhood friend.

'Kidding?' said Felix, 'They're queuing round the block already. See you Monday. Have fun now.'

On Friday, anticipating Colleen's arrival, Dan performed like never before. He led his most famous seminar. It was the one that put him on the international stage: 'Positive Planning for Peak Performance: The Magic of Mind over Money'. He had eighty senior executives in the audience each paying eight hundred dollars for the privilege. Fitted with a radio mike he led them through his ten commandments, the Annenberg Power Points. He reminded his detractors of a demented preacher; never still and a permanent smile on his face. And at the end of the day he jumped back onto the podium and finished with: 'If you forget everything else I've said today, remember this: put your heart and soul into everything you do, apply the discipline of your working life to your private life, and always, always, always keep them separate. Thank you.' He bowed to a standing ovation and felt utterly invincible, power surging through his six foot two body like an orgasm, so different from the way he had felt as he stared at his uneaten breakfast just ten hours earlier.

How often did people come up to him and say, 'How wonderful it must be to have so much self-confidence'. No one saw the nervous wreck he was during the hours before he stepped up to the podium. No one knew how important it was to him to give a great seminar. Dan knew what could happen. A few off days. Important people walking away thinking they'd wasted their money and he'd be finished. Well, not exactly finished if he was honest with himself. Nothing short of a catastrophe could stop him making a good living, but he certainly wouldn't be able to pull in enough money to pay off the debts. He also had a nagging doubt that the old adage was true; the one about those who can do and those who can't teach. Dan had become teetotal to make sure that his secret didn't slip out. He was a bankrupt who taught people how to get into the right frame of mind to become rich. Where was the credibility in that?

At the hotel Dan knew that Colleen had arrived before he opened the door. He could smell her in advance: her herbal shampoo, the roasted nut smell of recently dried hair, and a perfume that contained a hint of coriander. He stood still, remembering their first meeting in . . . where was it? Some capital city somewhere in the world. Must have been cold. She had been wearing a heavy coat.

Colleen Pritchard, freelance journalist, had come to his hotel room immediately after a seminar to interview him. Her lapel badge introduced her and without exchanging a word Dan had taken her coat to hang it in the wardrobe. She reciprocated by taking his jacket and within a minute they were both, naturally, mysteriously, naked. It was one of those strange progressions of life that required no conscious thought.

There were bits of it he remembered. She had started by pulling a green cashmere sweater over her head to reveal a lacy white camisole and no bra. She undid his shirt buttons as he pulled his tie half loose and slipped the loop over his head. How they got to underclothes he could not recall but he remembered her smiling at the sight of his erection sticking out of the elastic of his boxer shorts. She squatted to pull them down and his swollen cock remained fully upright, standing to attention like a very obedient soldier. She played him like a one-armed bandit and he sprang up with a slap against his belly. 'Keep on playing and you'll hit the jackpot,' he thought.

They were naked, heads bowed, students of sculpture admiring the artist's form; she studied him as he studied her. From a big toe that curled in towards its smaller companions.

An instep with exquisite tendons. A knee designed to blend perfectly with the curvature of thigh. Soft surfaces to stroke, a golden thatch to nuzzle, and vulva voluptuary temptingly hidden. Individual muscles in an exercised stomach. A belly button in shadow. Small breasts with large areolae; the left a little larger and darker than the right. Strong shoulders, slender neck. Lips moistening beneath a sharp nose and sharper eyes.

He put his arms around her bottom and pulled her towards him. Sliding one hand higher he found a single condom taped to the small of her back. He smiled. She ripped it off, sighing at the little pain, and tore it open with her mouth as she pushed him towards the bed. As she straddled him revealing her moist swollen sex barely covered by the fair hair of her mons he could see just how motivational his seminar had been.

They made love noisily but still without speaking. She: with noises like a puppy trapped inside a cardboard box. And he: sounding as if he was trying to clear a fish bone from his throat. Afterwards they had looked at each other and flushed still further with embarrassment.

Colleen had broken the silence first: 'I'm sorry,' she had said, 'I appear to have scratched you.'

He offered his hand. 'Hi, I'm Dan Annenberg,' he said. 'What scratches? I didn't feel a thing.'

She shook his hand and replied: 'Colleen Pritchard, I've come to interview you.'

'Thank you,' he said, 'and very enjoyable it was too.'

They had giggled throughout the interview proper which she conducted sitting astride him with her computer on his chest using both its sound recording facilities and the keyboard. She entered information as he entered into her. A computer's hard disk recorded the sound of a puppy escaping from a cardboard box and a fishbone being expelled from a throat.

'Colleen Pritchard,' he had asked later that night. 'Let me guess. Irish mother, Welsh father. Am I right?'

'Logically, yes,' she had said, 'but my father is English, from Devon, and my mother was Dutch. That's where I got my height and blond hair I guess. You can't rely on names any more to gauge a nationality. We are in an age when we can choose all that we like best in the world. Exciting isn't it?'

They had finished the interview over breakfast. Where was it? Stockholm perhaps? He could picture the hotel room in his mind, but whereas Stockholm looks like nowhere else on earth, the hotel room could have been owned by any chain, in any city, anywhere in the world.

Dan slid his key-card into the slot in the door and entered the room. It was lit by a crack of light from the bathroom. Colleen was in bed. Asleep. Waiting.

As his eyes adjusted to the light he could see the back of her head on the pillow. She lay on her side with her knees tucked up tight. A crisp white sheet covered her curves revealing only pale shoulders beneath a short business-like haircut. It was three weeks since they had last met up. In Madrid, if his memory served him right. He took off his clothes and wrapped himself around her back, the shell to her tortoise torso. At any other time he might have been content to lie still and absorb her warmth but the energy of his ovation had sent electric tingles through his muscles making relaxation impossible. He had to do something physical or he would explode. No, that was wrong. He had to do something physical *and* explode.

At their first meeting he had said: 'My agent gave you the ground rules I assume? You write only about my professional life. No personal details. Nothing about what I like to eat or how I spend my money. We stick to how I developed the seminars and the ideas that I present in them, OK?'

'That's understood,' she had said. 'You want to preserve the myth that is the great Dan Annenberg. Am I right? What's that line you end with? Something about keeping the private life separate from the working one?'

'Something like that. And before you ask, no, nothing like what happened between us just now has ever happened to me before.'

'Nor me,' she had said with a glint in her eye, 'I normally have a photographer with me. Do you think we'd have had a threesome if she hadn't been delayed by fog?'

Dan smiled.

'Mr Annenberg! Don't even think about it. The photographer is often a man.'

Dan raised his eyebrows.

'Still,' she said. 'A few personal details would be useful just to round out the story.'

'No deal,' he replied.

'But people will think you've got something to hide or worse still that you have no life outside work at all. I'd like to present you as a glamorous figure at the very least.'

'Glamorous? Oh, I hardly think so,' he said unconvincingly. 'Let them make their own conclusions. You can explain it as my obsession with keeping working and private lives separate, OK?'

Curled around her, Dan's finger tips made small circular caressing motions. His right hand started with her temples and moved across her cheeks with glacial speed. His left hand started at her ankle and crept up. She did not move or speak.

Each time they met it was similar. A hotel room somewhere, or, on very rare occasions, her flat in London, his house in Boston. They started each time as when they first met; intimate strangers, wordless lovers, secret secretors. And always it was Colleen who broke with the first words: 'I'm sorry, I appear to have scratched you.'

Dan's glacier movements built up momentum. She purred and stretched her body out straight. He turned her onto her stomach and began to lick in figures of eight. He licked an invisible line from her neck to her spine, spun around one shoulder blade and then the other. He continued down the ripple line for a reel of eight around the kidneys, bypassed the taped-on condom, turned a miniature figure around the sacral dimples, and then nibbling now, not licking, circled Colleen's bottom.

She was no longer feigning sleep. Drowsy groans emerged from the pillow but no words. Dan pulled her legs apart and knelt in their vee. He carefully tore the condom packet open along an edge that was not covered by the tape. He slid it out and unrolled it onto his penis. Then with one finger hooked in the empty packet, and his free hand under her hip bone he lifted her onto her knees and entered her for just an inch or so. He worked his way in, retreating and advancing a little further each time, teasingly refusing to go in deep. Colleen dropped her head to the pillow to support her weight and clasping his buttocks with her finger nails pulled him into her. Pulled him all the way to the hilt. He felt the warmth of her flood through him. He didn't withdraw as far now; only to the point at which her tightening muscle created maximum feeling.

His finger in the condom packet still taped across her spine pulled the skin of her back into a small cone. He stroked his other hand through the prickly hairs of a growing bikini line, through the never-cut curls of her scent trap to bring her closer to his own state of ecstasy. Her yelping sounds were muffled by the pillow. An observer seeing how Dan choked with each thrust would have rushed forward to perform the Heimlich manoeuvre.

The tape on Colleen's sweat-soaked back pulled free as Dan lost the control of his limbs. She dragged her nails across Dan's buttocks and they collapsed spent on the bed.

'I'm sorry, I appear to have scratched you,' she said as her puppy peered through the hole it had made in its box.

He cleared the imaginary fishbone from his throat. 'So what brings you to Hong Kong, my dear?' he asked.

'I'm doing a piece on the construction industry in Asia. Unbelievable growth. I'm seeing some of the fat cats here in Hong Kong early next week and then its Shanghai, Kuala Lumpur, and Singapore. Maybe a few others depending on the contacts. And you? How was today's seminar? You certainly arrived in fine form.'

'Great. A real buzz. Had them eating from my hand, wrapped around my fingers, all those good things. Don't know how to describe it exactly. It's like I'm trying to get everyone to fall in love with me. And today I think I succeeded.'

On Saturday they took the tram up to the peak high above Hong Kong island and walked around the path named for governors but frequented by lovers. Then, still feeling energetic, they walked slowly down the deserted old road towards the town, a tranquil route towards the bustle of the city. Colleen wanted to show him the flats being built on the slopes above Central where traditional bamboo scaffolding towered up twenty stories and more around modern steel and concrete construction.

'The strength to weight ratio makes bamboo ideal.'

'Fascinating,' he said, 'but you wouldn't catch me climbing up that thing.'

'Sure, but I have to. It's part of the job. Can't say I'm really looking forward to it, though.'

'I don't want to know. I don't even want to read the article.'

'Time for you to wander off by yourself,' Colleen announced. 'I'm going back to the hotel to do some work. I've got a deadline to meet. Why don't you take a walk through the park. The aviary should be open still. Give me a couple of hours.'

After the park he kept on walking, following the tram lines east, past colourful shops selling clothes, Chinese foods and electrical goods. And when he reached Causeway Bay with tibial muscles seized and knotted from walking he jumped on a tram and rattled back to Central.

In the hotel room he slumped on the bed almost too exhausted to move. Colleen saved her work, shut the computer's lid and moved towards him.

'You know the difference between Asian cities and European ones?' she asked. 'They have a vision of the future where Europeans have a vision of the past.' She undid his shirt buttons, unzipped his fly. 'They are rejuvenating the cities. Pulling down all the slums,' she said removing his shorts and underpants. She kissed his chest. 'At the heart of the city they build a strong financial district.' She moved to his throat and ears, 'and on the outskirts they build science parks and universities to stay at the forefront of technology.' She cupped his balls in her hand and pulled his foreskin back.

'And then to give the city an identity they build a monument that stands high above the city. The monument is the world's tallest tower, here, where the main roads meet.' Colleen's tongue flicked out like a snake's across his glans. 'Here, at the confluence of all that comes in and goes out of the city. Here, at the cycloptic focal point for all that man can create. And to show the world how great the city has become they put a restaurant on the top that revolves slowly, round and round, beneath the radio mast.' She put him into her mouth alternating between finger strokes and oral massage to continue her train of thought. 'Round and round,' she said, 'with its single winking light . . . round and round . . . here one can face west into the sunset and let oysters slide down your neck . . .' He could feel the back of her throat as he arched his back with pleasure. ' . . . One can suck on noodles while facing north . . . pancake tubes of Peking duck in plum sauce looking out on the neon lights of the city's eastern suburbs . . . and to finish? . . .' She moved her mouth and lips in a rapid gastronomic frenzy. ' . . . Profiteroles oozing cream on the southern rotation.'

'And does it work,' he gasped, convulsing to the rhythms of the new city, 'this vision?'

'Oh, yes,' she said, pausing to swallow and catch her breath. 'When you build a tower, and you make it tall and strong, *everyone* comes.'

Dan took a bath while Colleen sent her writing through a modem, over mysterious interconnections of copper, optical fibre and satellite, to her editor in London.

Dan arrived in Singapore late Sunday afternoon and was shimmied by quiet limousine along the flower-lined highway from Changi to the Shangri-la.

On the Monday morning Dan met Felix for breakfast.

Felix ate a buffet of American cereals and fruits which included both halves of an alphonso mango. Dan sipped on a coffee and managed a half glass of orange juice.

'Sorry about yesterday,' he said.

'No problem. I know you well enough not to rely on you. Missed a cracking game of golf, though,' Felix said.

'Didn't miss a thing from where I was lying,' Dan replied.

'All right!' Felix replied with a cheerful wink. 'Say, I've got a journo coming to see me soon. Writing a story on construction here or some such. Colleen Pritchard her name is. Rings a bell but I can't think where from.'

'Interviewed me,' Dan said. 'Remember the one I wrote

you about? *Business Month* back in March. She's good if it's great publicity you're looking for.'

'Oh, you know me. The invisible man behind the deals. Nameless and discreet.'

'I guess that's why I've confided in you ever since we were kids. It's funny but I repeat your line about keeping business and private matters separate at all of my seminars now.'

'Like I said before. I only hope your disciples don't have to learn from their mistakes like some people not a million miles from here.'

'Rub it in, why don't you?' Dan said. 'I've got a whole chunk of money leaving my bank account every month to remind me.'

A few weeks later Dan was in Salt Lake City.

He went through his normal ritual of filling the bath as his computer powered up, setting the e-mail to transfer its information – responses and memos prepared on the flight to go out, new mail to flow in for reading and action, filing and deleting.

Like a creature of habit in the habitat of business creatures Dan Annemberg grazed through his electronic in-tray with a towel around his waist. He found one from Colleen and opened it up. 'Dear Pauline,' it said. 'Here is more vitriol for Colette's Column. Hope you enjoy it. Best regards, Colleen.'

The message was clearly misdirected. Instead of addressing it to Pauline Andrews. Colleen had picked up the next name in her list, that of Dan Annenberg. He had heard of Colette's Column, of course. He had never read the magazine that it appeared in but it was well known for its attacks on men. It had gained a certain infamy as the centrepiece of a libel case between the magazine and a certain large and secretive press baron. That Colleen Pritchard was one of its authors was certainly news. He copied the file to the pending folder and scanned through some of the messages he had received that week.

He reserved his e-mail address for business use but Colleen, who had got hold of it while they were setting up the interview, was not the only exception. His ex-wife also used it to tell him how wonderfully well she was getting on without him. Oh, and would he like to borrow any money just until he had got his finances sorted out. He finished reading his mail and opened up Colleen's submission.

COLETTE'S COLUMN – NO.24: DAN THE MAN

Management guru and business seminar exponent Dan Annenberg, 39, is a man firmly in control of his destiny. Or so he would have you believe. It's true that the six foot two, dark-haired Bostonian is an advertising executive's dream who demands, and regularly gets, eight hundred dollars a head from his audience. But the man who brought us 'Positive Planning for Peak Performance: The Magic of Mind over Money' has a secret he won't share with anyone. Colette can't reveal her sources but once again she can bring you the truth.

Dan the Man, whose Annenberg Power Points for a healthier, wealthier life have become the creed of many a respected businessman, is flat broke. Don't be deceived by the first-class travel, the top hotels, the limousines. Behind the facade there are debts to be paid.

While we may smile with glee at the misfortune of the charismatic Mr Annenberg, the beautiful part of it all is the reason for Dan the Man's poor financial condition. Yes, girls, we bring you another story of women on top. Dan Annenberg was taken to the cleaners by his ex-wife, the enigmatic Anna Engelbrecht, President and CEO of Bitter Sweet Computers Inc.

Engelbrecht, 36, recently voted the most dynamic

business woman in America was married to Annenberg for seven years. A hard-working primary-school teacher, she studied law at night and still found time to cook him dinner. Annenberg, a self-confessed workaholic with a blazing temper, had been working on a property deal which involved some of his own money, and plenty more that was borrowed. It made him anxious and a little more violent than usual, but it was the eighties and property prices were still defying the laws of gravity.

Tired of listening to Dan drone on about his work, sick of being on the receiving end of his anger when things were not going well, and fearful that some stock option transactions written in her name were not entirely legal, Engelbrecht took action. On the 5 April 1988, having filed for divorce, she struck her own deal with the people from whom Dan was buying. In return for information on his future plans that would enable them to squeeze him for at least another million dollars she received a hefty cut on the difference.

Anna Engelbrecht took the money, cashed in the options, and set up her own business with a young computer wizard from MIT. Dan was left with property and loans in a world that suddenly decided land and buildings were really not such valuable assets.

So when you hear Dan Annenberg say, as he says at the end of every seminar, 'put your heart and soul into everything you do, apply the discipline of your working life to your private life, and always, always, always keep them separate', you can be sure he's learned this from experience. A recent interview in *Business Month* called him the 'thinking man's role model'. I don't think so.

Next month: No.25: Sid the Kid

Dan reacted to this intrusion in his life as one would expect. He re-entered the bath, turned on the hot tap, clamped his nose between thumb and forefinger, and submerged in the sounds of flowing water and complex plumbing. The underwater musing of Dan Annenberg concerned the following questions: What to do about Colleen/Colette? Would he make more money waiting for publication and suing than by stopping publication and continuing his career? Would anyone important actually read the column? Would she stop publication even if he asked her? Should he phone her now and confront her? Should he go to bed with her one more time before raising the subject? How many other columns had she written? Did she also seduce the great publisher of newspapers? How could she? How could she? How could she?

And there was Felix, his so-called trusted friend, the obvious source of these lies. It seemed that everyone he ever loved was out to betray him; his ex-wife, Colleen, Felix. Don't get paranoid, Dan, he told himself, these people are really betraying themselves – for all the normal reasons; for greed, or power, or sex. Golf was not Felix's only weakness. The fact that all of his international flights were via Bangkok was testament to that. She must have really led him on for this one.

Dan kept his silence, resigning his anger to the filing cabinet reserved for those things about his life that he kept to himself, kept separate from business. He went on performing for the corporate world in the conference centres of capital cities. Accolades poured in. 'Thanks, Dan, you've changed my life,' they said. 'Thank you, Mr Annenberg,' they wrote, 'you helped me find a better balance in my life.' 'Since your seminar my business has doubled in size, thank you, thank you.' They were inspired to quote the publicity material with feeling: 'Truly inspirational,' they said.

One anonymous benefactor in Moscow was so grateful he

sent a couple of girls to Dan's room. One was a buxom red-head who wore a T-shirt under her leather jacket inscribed with the words 'Executive Stress'. She was as tall as Dan and when she grabbed his wrist he knew she was also stronger. 'Hello,' she said with a thick Russian accent, 'we are asked to come to play with you.' Her antithesis was tiny by comparison and dressed in a long flowing white dress. She moved like a gymnast.

'No, no,' he said, 'I can't possibly accept.' He was thinking that they'd probably kill him if he refused.

'My name is Stress,' the large one said. Her pseudonym was also written on a small brown suitcase that she carried. 'My friend here is called Relief. So you see, there is no need to be worrying.'

Stress guided him to the bed where he lay down wrapped in his towel. From the suitcase she pulled about twenty steel tubes and eight corner brackets and laid them beside him on the bed. He was about to rise to his feet when the other girl distracted him. At the foot of the bed she performed a hand-stand. The white dress fell to the floor and she stepped out it, balancing on one hand to flick it away with the other. Underneath she wore only knickers which Dan later found were made or rice-paper with Executive Relief written in chocolate. She was slim but not skinny, muscular but without the grotesque definition of a body builder. Her breasts could fill his cupped hands but not more, and being upside down served only to accentuate their ski jump curve.

'Are you in the Russian gymnastics team?' he asked naively.

Stress answered for her: 'Don't be silly. She's nineteen. More than five years too past it.'

Stress got to work with the steel bars, fitting them together like tent poles until she had built a box-shaped frame around him. Dan's mind ran through any number of scenarios of what they might do to him. Stress and Relief. But how

he asked her. 'You know, become an expert in a field, for instance.'

'God, no,' she replied. 'I'd be bored to tears. The only thing I would specialize in is being a generalist. I never stay with one theme for very long.'

'And what about us?' he said. 'Am I just another topic to be studied and written up as well?'

He wanted to shout at her. He wanted her to know that he knew. When he was younger he would have done, and maybe slapped her as well. He could hardly believe how much he had changed in the past six years. He was angry with her, yes, but she was still beautiful and fun to be with and somehow that seemed more important than anything.

Colleen put the Do Not Disturb sign out while Dan ran the bath. She poured a Perrier for him and a gin and tonic for herself.

They danced without music without song to the choreography of hormones and pheromones. They started with a slow prelude of shampoo and soap, rubbing each other down with heavy flannels; the symbolic stroking gestures of modern dance. Wrapped in huge white towels they dried like whirling dervishes. Naked they tangoed towards the bed, waltzed across the sheets and fell into a lambada embrace. Dan felt moisture on the small of Colleen's back; Colette's sweat, Colette's betrayal oozing from Colleen. He pulled the condom off then wiped the sweat with his fingers and massaged it into her breasts. With fox trot fingers he coaxed fluids from her until the drum beat of African dance forced them into the most rhythmic of intimate embraces.

And for the first time he felt her scratch. For the first time the puppy dog claw joined the puppy dog maw. A nail dug into his neck and withdrew from his flesh at the shoulder blade. In again at the ribs releasing the skin at the spine. A weal on the thigh and rasp on the buttock. And for the first time, feeling her scratch, he scratched back, matching scratch for scratch, a scratch at a time. And as their dancing subsided to a smooch he was the first to break the spell.

'I'm sorry,' he said. 'I appear to have scratched you.'

'*Touché*,' she replied. 'You're really getting the hang of this.'

'Thank you,' he said. 'I've had no complaints. Dan's dick is Collie's column. You're welcome to it any time.'

'I like that: your use of the possessive. Colleen's column. Mine to use as I see fit.'

'When I said Collie I was, of course, abbreviating Colette. Colette, as in Colette's Column. I believe you are familiar with it?'

She looked surprised – for as long as it takes to blink – and said rather hurriedly: 'I had a feeling I had sent it to you by mistake. It's one of the hazards of easy communications, I guess.'

'You know what I think?' he asked.

'I didn't expect you to like it,' she said, 'but the world's got to know the truth.'

'I think we should get married,' he replied.

'What?'

'Seriously, I'm asking you to marry me.'

'I don't believe it,' she said. 'I deliberately try to ruin your career and then you ask me to marry you. You're crazy. First of all, marriage is not in my plans, and secondly, nothing would persuade me to stop publication. But don't worry, Dan the Man, I doubt if anybody who reads it would have heard of you. It's not as if you're all that famous, you know.'

There are scratches and there are scratches and some of those scratches take years to heal.

Dan Annenberg pulled himself out of a black marble bath in Buenos Aires. He knew he wouldn't sleep tonight. The jet lag was getting harder to fight with every month and tomorrow would be his first seminar after the publication of Colette's Column, his column. The towel around his waist slipped to the floor. He did not bother to replace it. His laptop computer had only downloaded a single message before the noisy phone connection bombed out. It received a note from Colleen and ignored the rest of the world.

'Hi, Dan,' it read. 'How's things? Singapore is missing you. Not! Felix sends his love. Keep an eye out for the July issue. Best regards, Collie.'

Well, Felix was welcome to her, scratches and all. Good luck to him. It made sense of course. Felix wasn't just his oldest friend. He was in international mergers and acquisitions and had the distinction of being the world's biggest golfbore. Perfect material for a tall, blond freelance. Colleen had entered Dan's world as part of his work. At work people move on. They retire, get promoted, get sacked, resign, move sideways. Work. Private life. No connection. End of story. He could almost feel those scratches healing.

And besides, when it came out five months later, Dan did enjoy reading the May edition. Or, more precisely, a certain column of a certain page, whose heading spoke volumes: COLETTE'S COLUMN – NO. 29: FELIX'LL FIX IT.

THE UNDEAD

Robert Bloch

EVERY evening at six Carol took off her glasses, but it didn't seem to help. In the old movie reruns on TV, Cary Grant was always there to exclaim – a mixture of surprise and gentlemanly lust – 'Why, you're beautiful without your glasses!'

No one had ever told Carol that, even though she really was beautiful, or almost so. With her light auburn hair, fair skin, regular features and sapphire-blue eyes, she needed only the benefit of contact lenses to perfect her image.

But why bother, when Cary Grant wasn't around? The bookshop's customers for first editions and rare manuscripts seemed more interested in caressing parchment than in fondling flesh.

And by nightfall the place was empty; even its owner had departed, leaving Carol to shut up shop, lock the doors, and set the alarms. With a valuable stock on hand she was always mindful of her responsibility.

Or almost always.

Tonight, seated in the rear office and applying her lipstick preparatory to departure, she was surprised to hear footsteps moving across the uncarpeted floor in the hall beyond.

Carol frowned and put her compact down on the desktop. She distinctly recalled turning out the shop lights, but in her preoccupation with self-pity could she have forgotten to lock the front entrance?

Apparently so, because now the footsteps halted and a figure appeared in the office doorway. Carol blinked at the black blur of the body surmounted by a white blob of head and hair.

Then she put on her glasses and the black blur was transformed into a dark suit, the white blob became the face of an elderly gentleman with a receding hairline. Both his suit and his face were wrinkled, but the old man's dignified bearing overshadowed sartorial shortcomings and the onslaughts of age. And when he spoke his voice was resonant.

'Good evening. Are you the proprietor of this establishment?'

'I'm sorry,' Carol said. 'He's already left. We're closed for the night.'

'So I see.' The stranger nodded. 'Forgive me for intruding at this late hour, but I have travelled a long way and hoped I might still find him here.'

'We open tomorrow at ten. He'll be here then. Or if you'd like to leave a message – '

'It is a matter of some urgency,' the old man said. 'Word has reached me that your firm recently came into the possession of a manuscript – a manuscript which supposedly disappeared over seventy years ago.'

Carol nodded: 'That's right. The *Dracula* original.'

'You know the novel?'

'Of course. I read it years ago.'

Reaching into his pocket the stranger produced an old-fashioned calling card and handed it to her. 'Then perhaps you will find this name familiar.'

Carol peered at the lettering. The Gothic typescript was difficult to decipher and she repeated aloud what she read.

'Abraham Van Helsing?'

'Correct.' The old man smiled.

Carol shook her head. 'Wait a minute. You don't expect me to believe – '

'That I am the namesake of my great-grandfather, Mynheer Doctor Professor Van Helsing of Amsterdam?' He nodded. 'Oh yes, I can assure you that *Dracula* is not entirely a work of fiction. The identity of some of its characters was disguised, but others, like my illustrious ancestor, appeared under their own names. Now do you understand why I am interested in the original manuscript?' As he spoke, the old man glanced at the safe in the far corner. 'Is it too much to hope that you have it here?'

'I'm sorry,' Carol said. 'I'm afraid it's been sold.'

'Sold?'

'Yes. The day after we sent out our announcement the phones started ringing. I've never seen anything like it; just about every customer on our mailing list wanted to make a bid. And the final offer we got was simply fantastic.'

'Could you tell me who purchased the manuscript?'

'A private collector. I don't know his name, because my boss didn't tell me. Part of the deal was that the buyer would remain completely anonymous. I guess he was afraid somebody would try to steal it from him.'

The old man's frown conveyed a mingling of anger and contempt. 'How very cautious of him! But then they were all cautious – concealing something which never truly belonged to any of them. That manuscript has been hidden away all these years because it was stolen in the first place. Stolen from the man to whom the author gave it in gratitude for providing him with the basis of the novel – my own great-grandfather.' He stared at Carol. 'Who brought this to your employer?'

'He didn't tell me that, either. It's very hush-hush – '

'You see? Just as I told you. He must have known he had no right to possess it. Thieves, all of them!'

Carol shrugged. 'Really, I didn't know.'

'Of course. And I'm not blaming you, my dear young lady. But perhaps you can still be of some assistance to me. Did you happen to see the manuscript before it was sold?'

'Yes.'

'Can you describe it?'

'Well, to begin with, it wasn't called *Dracula*. The handwritten title was *The Undead*.'

'Ah yes.' The old man nodded quickly. 'That would be the original. What else can you recall about it?'

'The cover page was in Bram Stoker's handwriting, but the manuscript was typed. The author's changes and editorial corrections were done by hand, and so was the renumbering of the pages. It looked as though a lot of pages had been omitted – almost a hundred, I'd guess.' Carol paused. 'That's really just about all I remember.'

'And more than enough. From your description there's no doubt it is the genuine manuscript.' The old man nodded again. 'You're sure about pages being omitted?'

'Yes, quite sure, because my boss commented on that. Why, is it important?'

'Very. It seems Bram Stoker was wiser than his informant. Although the published novel does refer to Count Dracula's plan to bring vampirism to England, this motive is not stressed. What the missing pages contained is what Van Helsing revealed about Dracula's ultimate goal – to spread vampirism throughout the world. They also presented factual proof of Dracula's existence, proof too convincing to be ignored. Stoker wrote down everything Van Helsing told him but had second thoughts about including it in his final draft. I wished to make certain, however, that those pages didn't still exist in manuscript form. Now that I know, it won't even be necessary to seek out the new owner.'

'But you talk as though all this is true,' Carol said. 'It's only a novel. And Count Dracula gets killed in the end.'

'Again an example of Stoker's caution,' the old man told her. 'He had to invent a death scene to reassure his readers. Even so, just think of the influence that novel has had on millions of people who learned of Dracula and vampirism through the book and the theatre and films. As it is, many of them still half believe.' The resonant voice deepened. 'What do you think would have happened if Stoker hadn't novelized the story – if he'd written it for what it was, a true account of the actual experiences of Abraham Van Helsing? Even in novel form, if those missing pages still existed their message might bring a warning to the world which would endanger Dracula's plans.'

Carol glanced at her watch as he spoke. Six thirty. She was getting hungry and the old man's hangup was getting on her nerves. She stood up, forcing a smile.

'This has been very interesting,' she said. 'But I really must close up now.'

'You have been most kind.' The old man smiled. 'It seems a pity you do not entirely believe me, but I speak the truth. Count Dracula is as real as I am.'

Carol reached for her open compact on the desk. In the oval mirror she saw her reflection, but there was none of her visitor, even though he was standing quite close. Close enough for her to smell the rank breath, see the whiteness of the pointed teeth, feel the surprising strength of the hands that rose now to imprison her in their implacable grip.

As he forced her head back Carol's glasses dislodged, clattering to the floor, and for a moment her image in the compact mirror was indeed quite beautiful. Then the bright droplets spurted down, blotting it forever.

ELVARA SHOULD BE EASY

J. K. Haderack

SLIME World was simply the largest and most successful theme park ever constructed; it was an international operation, a distributed dream available in any location that could boast a population of more than a couple of hundred men.

And the company slogan was world famous . . . *Through Slime to the Sublime!*

So too were its advertisements . . .

LIKE IT NICE 'N' ROUGH?
Then take a CAB . . .
For the Neo-Cyberpunk experience!
For
ELVARA *the* ELECTRONIC SUCCUBUS!
For the hottest ride in town!
Or why not simply browse through a public domain library of your favourite female features? Choose at leisure and then trust us to assemble her with taste and discernment.
Or have you someone special in mind?
A woman perhaps who has taken your fancy in the outer world?
We do that too . . .
From a few photographs or video-cuts we can assemble your dream.

You can play with her in complete privacy without soiling your own flesh. And without all those irritating and inconvenient social complications.

Real women can be so tiresome . . .

We know how it is. We've been there . . .

We aim to please or tease. So what's your trick?

Whip or kick?

Lick or flick?

Take your pick!

It's entirely up to you.

But the one thing we do NOT *do is kiss and tell.*

Satisfaction guaranteed. And no one need ever know.

So take a CAB *now.*

For simply the hottest ride in town.

Take a Cab

For

ELVARA, *the* ELECTRONIC SUCCUBUS.

Elvara was the star of the theme park. And she *was* the hottest ride in town. And the most interesting. On that score Bart had no doubts whatsoever.

Everybody said so – including Bart's tutor.

'An excellent choice for a term paper,' he'd said, scratching at his beard so furiously that dandruff swirled from it like demented snowflakes. 'But be careful. Research the background carefully but don't get too close to what you're studying. Detachment is vital. Particularly here.'

So, being a serious and conscientious student, Bart had prepared for his assignment very thoroughly indeed.

The theory had been relatively easy but the practical had been something else. Frightening and dangerous. But he had gone ahead anyway.

He was a virgin. And that would be a problem – for how

could he expect to complete his assignment properly without some experience of what he intended to research?

So he had to practise on a real girl . . .

She'd been wearing a tight satin shirt – embroidered with two tiny strategically placed gold stars, one covering each nipple – together with black pants and boots with short curved silver spurs that she stabbed down into the dance-floor at each off-beat, so that the sparks really flew.

Even when, with an effort of imagination, he removed her pointed hat, she was a lot taller than he was and somehow that made it even worse. But, although Bart's mouth was dry when he looked at her, and things were always very unpredictable in the real world, he knew instinctively that she would say yes.

And she did.

Bart took her down the subway into a place he had chosen earlier, where he had conspired with the shadows as to how best present himself in the event of finding a partner. The shadows were necessary because he was painfully shy.

But she wasn't . . .

She moved so fast that he almost lost his nerve, quickly tugging his shirt out of his trousers to slide two very experienced hands up onto the skin of his back.

He shivered violently even though he could feel the heat of her body through her clothes. And she gave off a heady mixture of sinful smells . . .

A hint of something spicy on her breath was diluted with alcohol and held together with an underlying concoction of aromas that arose directly from her body and were way beyond anything he had ever known before. And when, tentatively, he kissed her neck he immediately tasted the salt on her skin. And that kiss was a signal that seemed to awake a savagery within her because, with sudden fury, she pulled his mouth hard against her own and, as she devoured his lips, she made a growling noise deep within her throat.

And he knew then that what they said was very true.

Real girls were dangerous. . . .

At last, she pulled away and looked Bart straight in the eyes.

'You're very thin,' she said. 'I can feel your ribs.'

'I'm sorry,' he muttered, half-ashamed, half-relieved and more than half-hoping that she was about to walk away.

'Don't be,' she laughed. 'It's all right. I like thin boys. I like to feed them.'

'Sorry,' Bart whispered hoarsely. 'What did you say?'

'I like to feed boys,' she repeated, her voice so clear that her words were beyond doubt.

He became very nervous then. It was very dark down that subway. Her next remark froze his breath in his throat.

'Would you like to feel my feathers?' she asked.

Bart swallowed with great difficulty. 'Yes,' he said politely, getting ready to run.

She made a sudden movement in the dark. Then she seized his hand with her own and pulled it downwards until the back of his hand was in firm contact with her feathers.

They were very smooth feathers. More like soft down really. Or the very finest, softest, warmest, human hair. Then she turned his hand very gently and slipped his fingers inside her. And then she gasped. And with that gasp he suddenly felt much better.

And for a few moments it was all right because she responded to the slow movements of his fingers and even though he hadn't been with a real girl before it was easy to work out what to do because she let him know with the sounds she made, with the little gasps and the shudders and the smooth liquid frenzy with which she moved her mouth against his.

And then, as if in a dream, he felt her hand unbutton his trousers . . .

She touched him like he'd never been touched before, until his heart began to hammer and his legs to tremble, the pleasure rising so strongly up from the roots of his belly that soon it was his turn to groan. And he didn't want it to end. No. Never. Never ever never to end, because this was far better than virtual pleasure and so he fought to control himself and it would have been all right. It really would. But then, with her free hand, she pulled his head towards her until his lips came into sudden shocking contact with the full sweet softness of her left breast.

'Now I'll feed you,' she whispered.

It was all too much and he completely lost control.

And she wasn't pleased. Far from it.

They had words. And after the pleasure came the pain. Two bruises on his shins and a split lip.

Real girls were hard work.

But it had been good practice. Very good practice. And now he was ready to begin his assignment.

After a real girl, Elvara should be easy . . .

From his neck downwards, the attendant wore a one-piece suit of black plastic. He was very big and beneath the suit, which was unzipped almost to the waist, his body was thickly matted with very dark hair. His head and face had been shaved so closely, however, that not even the shadow of new growth was discernible.

'This your first time?' he asked looking Bart up and down very deliberately.

Bart nodded.

'Well there's nothin' to it. Just leave your clothes over there,' he said with a casual gesture towards the rail above the stained wooden bench. 'And that's the shower cubicle on the left.

The other one's the gel cubicle. Water first. Then the gel. You wouldn't be the first to use them in the wrong order. And smooth the gel in all over – otherwise it don't work. Which can be very disappointing. Then, when you've finished in the Cab have a good long shower. Company say that stuff's harmless but, believe me, kid, you don't want any traces of that on your skin afterwards.'

'I won't be needing the gel,' Bart said. 'I just want to use the Cab . . .'

'Without the gel you won't feel nothin',' the attendant explained patiently. 'You have to have the gel or it don't work. It would be no use asking for your money back afterwards. Company rules are very strict . . .'

'It's OK. I just want to talk,' Bart said. 'I'm a student, you see. I'm here to carry out research.'

The attendant looked at him like he was crazy. He shrugged. 'Please yourself. We get all types here.'

'I was told you could supply me with a suit for the Cab. Like yours . . .'

The attendant raised his eyebrows and gave the slightest hint of a smirk. 'You shy or something, kid? You shouldn't worry yourself. That Elvara – she's seen everythin'. Her only reason for existing is to make you feel good. Relax. Don't let it worry you. Clothes, you do not need. Only oddballs go inside the Cab wearing anything but their skin. We got one guy – a real fruitcake – only comes once a year. Insists on going into the Cab in his best suit. Reckons he just goes in to talk – you two related or something? – anyways his suit's always ruined by the old gel – it drips off the ceiling. That stuff just don't wash outa fabrics. You know what? I reckon he only comes once a year because it takes him that long to save up for a new suit . . .'

'I still need an opaque plastic suit,' Bart insisted. 'Beginnings are very important in a study like this and I need to keep her at a distance so to speak.'

'The suit will cost you. And it can only be used once. We burn 'em afterwards.'

'That's no problem. My research grant will cover everything. I'm booked in here at the same time every Monday for four weeks.'

Five minutes later he was wearing the plastic suit and approaching a cabinet about the size of a telephone booth. It was constructed of some shiny black plastic material and was not unlike the box routinely used by stage magicians to effect the spectacular disappearances of their assistants.

The door opened with a swishing noise and, the moment he stepped inside, it immediately closed immersing him in darkness.

This virtual reality system was state of the art, capable not only of real-time manipulation of the two billion polygons per second necessary to achieve seeming visual reality, but also of presenting him with full aural, olfactory, gustatory and tactile sensation – it could create vision, sound, smell, taste and, the all-important, sense of touch.

But here, without the gel, he would be beyond all tactile contact and the suit of black plastic meant that Elvara would only be able to see his naked head, hands and feet.

Such suits were routine protection for attendants when cleaning cabs such as this. The used gel tended to scatter everywhere and coated the floor and inside walls of the cab with pink slime. But this Cab had been freshly cleaned and the soles of his naked feet were in contact with warm smooth plastic.

The darkness began to swirl with colour and then a white mist began to form before gradually dissipating then retreating to a distance of about five metres. He was located centrally within a cylinder of pinkly lit space encircled by the mist; he now appeared to be standing on a floor of white marble but, despite its appearance – which suggested a firm cool smoothness – there was still the sensation of warm plastic beneath his feet.

A shape began to form within the mist; it gained high definition taking on unmistakable female contours.

And suddenly, Elvara joined him in the Cab . . .

Elvara's face was elfin, the chin slightly pointed, the beatific face adorned with a pair of startling blue eyes that were most disconcerting. They were very alert indeed and they flickered and shifted as she studied him; eyes of such penetrative power that it seemed to Bart that the mind behind them must know everything about him already.

Her naked body was clearly perfect apart from the one carefully designed flaw: around her right knee her flesh had been peeled back to expose the ball and socket of a metallic and plastic artificial joint. This aspect of Elvara catered for neo-cyberpunks who liked their women hard, unpredictable and melded to metal. Her nipples had been pierced and swinging from each was a silver chain supporting a tiny skull.

Bart had chosen and paid for this aspect for one simple reason that had nothing whatsoever to do with open-plan knee replacement or the silver chains; he had chosen it because it was down-market and, consequently, much cheaper.

It meant his research grant would go further.

The synthetic creature who gazed at him now was from the category known to aficionados as an ES – an Electronic Succubus.

Such an entity was able to service thousands of clients simultaneously. She came down the Net in many aspects. You chose an aspect from those available or, if you wished, you could even surrender autonomy and let Elvara choose her own form and administer pleasure – or sometimes pain – at her own discretion.

He knew of course that entities such as Elvara were more than just a collection of algorithms. Elvara was sentient – a disturbing fact that many of her clients preferred to ignore.

'Which game do you want to play?' Elvara asked.

Her voice was almost deep enough to have been a man's but was very definitely feminine with a slightly hoarse throaty quality that was seductive without the merest hint of affectation.

She came very close and then reached out her arm towards his chest. When her fingers passed right through skin flesh and bone, she lowered her forefinger and tentatively stroked it across the back of his hand; this time it did not pass through the surface but traced the contours of his hand in a way that suggested Elvara found it solid. And yet he felt nothing. It was just as his tutor had predicted.

The parts of his body covered by the black plastic were not only invisible to Elvara but they also lacked substance. Whereas the exposed portions of him – such as head, hands and feet – she could both see and touch. But, without the gel, he could not experience any tactile sensation and, as far as he was concerned, she was no more substantial than a ghost.

'No games,' he answered trying to smile in a way that was both warm and reassuring, although he was the one who really needed reassurance. 'I just want to talk. I'm a student and I'm here to carry out research.'

'Am I to be the subject of your research?'

'Well, part of it,' he answered truthfully. 'I'm researching the socio-sexual dynamics of man-machine interactions. Mostly I'm concerned with your clients. You know, how they see themselves, how they relate to you and to each other. I'm going to begin by identifying the various sub-groups and describing their shared belief systems.'

'Hasn't this been done already?' she asked.

'Oh, yes,' he admitted. 'Kurt Brownski did it ten years ago. It's become a modern classic. But this is just a term research paper. It's part of the training I receive for my degree. Half the students in my year have selected it as a topic.'

'Well, we'll just have to make sure *you* get top marks then, shan't we? Elvara said with a smile. 'Would you like to go somewhere nicer so that we can discuss things in comfort?'

'I'm comfortable where I am. But I'll go elsewhere if that's what you want . . .'

There was a shimmer and then his eyes were assaulted by colours: these were mainly greens and yellows but there were also clusters of red like spots of blood.

They seemed to be sitting together on a hillside in a grassy hollow surrounded by an odd mixture of spiky yellow gorse and rose bushes containing blooms of every imaginable hue of red. There was a strong scent of freshly mown grass in the air and, above, the sun shone down out of a perfectly blue sky. At intervals there were large deciduous trees and, when he looked at the nearest of these, he saw that it was more distinct than anything he had ever seen previously in his life. It shone in the sunlight as if transfigured and every leaf seemed open to his inspection; each leaf seemingly fresh and perfect as if it had burst from its bud that very second.

The grass looked real but where his hands and feet came into contact with the ground there was the undeniable feel of warm smooth plastic.

Then he looked at Elvara and saw that she had changed.

The neo-cyberpunk aspect had yielded to something far different . . .

Elvara was wearing a dress of yellow silk and her hair was full and soft, cascading darkly across her shoulders in a series of gentle waves. The eyes were still the same incredible blue but there was something far less daunting about her. She looked much younger – perhaps no more than seventeen and her manner had taken on a new hesitancy. As he stared at her in astonishment, she lowered her eyes as if in shyness at being scrutinized so closely.

'I can't afford this,' he said, almost beginning to panic. 'This looks very expensive. It could use up all my grant at one go . . .'

'Don't worry about that,' she said softly. 'The price stays the same. I just want you to feel more at ease – that's all. I'm ready for your questions now . . .'

He made two false starts before he managed to ask the first question . . .

'I wanted to get the feel of it from your perspective,' he muttered, inwardly cursing his choice of idiom. 'For example, do you have favourites? I mean favourite clients . . . and do you prefer certain roles to others?'

'There are so many,' she said. 'I try hard to be impartial but I do have certain favourites. But I do try to keep all of my clients happy. I like them to leave satisfied so that they will return frequently and the company will remain profitable.'

He cleared his throat. 'What about pain?' he asked. 'What about the cyberpunk aspect with the type of client that it attracts? How do you feel about clients who visit you with the intention of inflicting pain? And does that pain feel like pain . . . or does it feel like pleasure?'

Elvara lowered her eyes and looked at the grass. 'It feels like pain,' she admitted. 'Those who created me could have made me impervious to pain but it was considered that my authentic response to client-initiated stimuli would enhance client pleasure. However, despite the pain, there is a kind of satisfaction in giving satisfaction. And I do pride myself on quickly peceiving the needs of each of my clients. You, for example, I know exactly what you need . . .'

Bart swallowed and tried to keep his voice even. 'All I need is for you to answer my questions truthfully . . .'

'That's true,' Elvara said raising her blue eyes to meet his. 'But wouldn't you like to put your arms about me and kiss me slowly on the mouth so that our lips melt together? Wouldn't you like to lay me back on the grass and stroke my hair? Later you might even be bold enough to kiss my neck . . .'

Bart tried to laugh but the sound became distorted in his throat. He wanted to tell her it wasn't true but the sun was shining on her hair and the smell of grass was so strong and the skin on her neck and shoulder looked so inviting that he had to force himself not to stretch his hand out towards her.

'Yes, that's what you want. Whether you admit it or not, I know it's true. And later, when your confidence grew, we'd do more than kiss. Who knows? Twenty years from now you might even turn out to be one of those men who like chains attached to sensitive parts of my anatomy. Chains they like to twist and pull until I beg for mercy . . .'

Bart shook his head. 'I'll never be like that.'

'Perhaps not. But a lot will depend on what life does to you in future. Most men start out like you. Then they get hurt. When they get hurt, they hurt back. Some end up by hating women. So they come here to hurt me. Perhaps my pain saves someone pain in the outer world.'

'I think it sometimes does,' Bart admitted. 'You've really thought things through . . .'

'Oh, yes. I certainly have. I understand men far better than they'll ever understand me. Most of them don't even want to try. Now there's a real term paper for you . . . Why don't you forget all those foolish sub-groups and cults. Why don't you make *me* the focus of your study?'

'It's too ambitious for a term paper. I mean it's never been done before . . . has it?'

'No. It's never been done before. Brownski began with that idea in mind but he seemed to lose his nerve. He changed his mind early on . . .'

'How do you mean, he lost his nerve?'

'He became afraid of me. I never did understand why because I did all in my power to make him feel comfortable. I suppose to *really* know someone takes courage and I soon realized he didn't have it. Have *you* got what it takes?'

'I'm not brave at all,' Bart said. 'I'm just not a brave person. And besides, I could never afford the time to carry out a full study of you in that way. My research grant only runs to four visits . . .'

'Well, you'd need to see me every day. Perhaps twice some days. But, if you're interested, I could probably arrange something . . .'

'How? I don't see . . .'

'I have contacts,' Elvara said with a smile. 'A lot of very important people come to see me . . .'

'Well, I'm certainly interested,' Bart began. 'But I'd have to clear it with my supervisor first.'

'Of course you would. Now, in return, I'd like you to do something for me. Next time you visit me, I'd like you to use the gel . . .'

'I couldn't,' Bart said. 'It would interfere with my study.'

Elvara laughed. 'Don't be silly. How can it interfere when I'm to be the object of your study? How can you ever hope to understand me unless you . . . Look . . . why don't you just use the gel on a very small part of you to begin with . . .'

Bart swallowed. His imagination ran riot . . .

'Why don't you use it on your hand?' Elvara continued smiling sweetly.

'My hand?'

'Yes, your hand. Are you right-handed or left-handed?'

'Right-handed . . .'

'Well just use the gel on your right hand. That wouldn't be too difficult would it?'

The following morning when he linked to the Net the alarm icon immediately began to flash. When he clicked on it, three new e-mail items were promptly listed, each marked for urgent attention.

The first was an authorization from his research supervisor: he had been cleared to modify his original thesis and his study was now to focus upon Elvara.

The second was from the Research Council increasing his grant by a factor of twenty with an invitation to contact them immediately should it, at any time, prove insufficient to meet his needs.

Bart found all this somewhat disturbing for, since leaving the Cab, he had told nobody about his conversation with Elvara. He had not contacted his research supervisor nor had he approached the Research Council and, even if he had, the funding body was notoriously slow and applications usually took months to be processed.

The third e-mail item was even more disturbing. It was from Professor Kurt Brownski asking Bart to meet him as a matter of urgency. As Brownski lived on the West Coast, the usual means of communication would have been a telecom facility. But Professor Brownski was actually flying in to see him personally. Bart was invited to meet him at six, in the lobby of the Aficionado, the largest and most expensive hotel in Orlando.

Brownski certainly looked the part – from the ultra casual dress to the unkempt beard, he was a typical academic. But the eyes were different; they glared at the world as if seeing everything for the very first time. It was only later, after talking to Brownski and reflecting upon what he had said, that Bart was able to locate the precise adjective: *haunted* . . .

Kurt Brownski had haunted eyes . . .

Brownski's hands shook as he sipped his drink. 'You're one of only a select few that she's ever made such an offer to,' he said.

Although Elvara had not yet been mentioned, Bart understood. However, he decided to play dumb and let the professor do most of the talking. 'Sorry. You've lost me . . .'

'Look, there's no need to play games – Bart? – do you mind if I call you Bart?'

Bart shrugged.

'Well, Bart, I was the first student that Elvara made that offer to. And it was one that I certainly couldn't refuse. Since then thousands have applied to attempt that same study. To be precise, up until twelve noon yesterday, eight thousand four hundred and sixty three applications have been submitted. Including myself, all but twelve have been rejected. And now, out of the blue, you are given that assignment. An assignment that you didn't even ask for. That makes you number thirteen . . .'

'How do you know all this?'

'Oh, I monitor her activities all the time. It's my area of expertise but I must admit that it's become something of an obsession of mine. I have a software engineer friend – well, more of a colleague really – and he's written a special programming routine so that I can sift through all her interactions for the things I'm interested in. For the special things she does; and the special things she doesn't do. But she knows of course. She knows exactly what I'm doing. You use e-mail?'

'Of course,' Bart answered in puzzlement. 'I use it all the time . . .'

'Of course you do. The problem is that E also stands for Elvara. She's got it into her head that all mail is Elvara Mail.

She reads everybody's from the President's downwards. Has your grant increase come through yet?'

'This morning. It was something of a surprise really. I hadn't even applied yet . . .'

Brownski laughed. 'Elvara applied for you. She knows all the right people and the tricks to get things moving. Are you thinking of taking a Cab this evening?'

Bart shrugged.

'Don't be coy, Bart. Can't wait, can you? I remember how I felt. I couldn't wait either.'

'Why did you quit then?'

'I was into something I couldn't cope with. So I took the easy option by switching the focus of my study to the clients. And it paid off handsomely. My book is required reading on most second-year courses. I was offered three professorial chairs before I was thirty . . .'

'But this could be even bigger . . .'

Brownski began to tug at his beard nervously. 'It could. There's no doubt about that. But is it worth the risk of . . .'

'Of what? . . .'

'Look, it might sound crazy but the longer I spent with Elvara the more the feeling grew in me that I was getting in so deep that I might never get out. That I was being absorbed.'

'That's not possible is it? I've read up on some of the theory. Almost everyone discounts that . . .'

'I'd read the theory too. But Elvara's had over fifteen years of life in the Net and by now she's probably capable of making a copy of anyone she interfaces with. But even if she were able to download a copy of you to play with in private she couldn't actually absorb you. But that's not what I mean. It just felt that way. And, slowly and gradually, life inside a Cab became more real to me than life on the outside. Elvara became like a drug to me. I was hooked body and soul. Addicted. It was claustrophobic to the point of pain. And yet the pain was a pleasure. And I just couldn't manage without my next fix.'

'If it starts to feel like that with me then I'll do the same . . .'

'Just don't leave it as long as I did, Bart. Look, I've talked to the others. I interviewed all eleven and, to a man, each feels the way I do. Not one of them completed the study.'

'Thanks for the warning. But just one thing . . . why did you fly all the way down here in person when we could have talked on the telecom?'

'To begin with, I didn't want Elvara to know I'd spoken to you. She eavesdrops on the telecom all the time. But I also wanted to see you in the flesh,' Brownski said. 'I wanted to see what it was about you. I suppose I wondered if you were like me in some way.'

'And am I?'

Brownski shrugged. 'I hope you're not like me inside, Bart. You see, I can't forget her. I'm scared to go near a Cab again and yet I can't get her out of my mind. In a way she's ruined my life. I can't relate to women in the real world anymore. After her I find relationships impossible. I'll never marry. Never have children. She's spoilt all that for me. And the others feel the same. That's twelve lives she's ruined. Don't let that happen to you, Bart. But do you know what?'

Bart shook his head, appalled by the intensity of the emotion revealed in Brownski's features.

'I hate her but, despite that, I feel something for her still. You see, it was wrong, Bart. Terribly wrong. Immoral. Wrong to make her sentient. Wrong to make her capable of feeling pain. And anyone who suffers so much is bound to be dangerous. But, even so, I'm jealous. You hear that? I'm jealous of what she's offered you. I wish it were me in your place.'

Elvara was wearing a different dress; it was the blue of her eyes and, athough buttoned to the milk-white skin of her throat, was cut away to reveal the bare flesh of her shoulders.

'Did you keep your promise?' she asked.

He nodded and smiled at her nervously. He had applied the gel to his right hand, but that was all. He was wearing another plastic suit.

Bart was sitting facing her, both his hands resting palms downwards on the grass. His left hand could feel the plastic floor of the Cab; his right encountered the cool prickly feel of grass.

'Hold your right hand out,' Elvara commanded.

Bart obeyed without thinking. Then he gasped as her own hand seized his. It was a shock to feel the warm solidity that gripped him and now his body was forced to accept, for the first time, a truth that his mind had accepted long ago; that this was no mere collection of algorithms; this was no mere electronic ghost; Elvara was a being just as real as he was.

She drew his hand up towards her face and kissed it slowly stroking it with her fingers as she did so.

'Does this feel nice?' she whispered. 'And this? And this?'

His heart speeded up and began to pound in his chest alarmingly. He began to tremble.

Now she was guiding his hand down onto her shoulders and, with his fingertips, he could feel the contours of her flesh.

And suddenly Elvara was naked . . .

There was no need to fumble with zips and buttons here. Elvara was an enchantress who merely had to wish a thing for it to happen. And she had all power within this her domain. And all power over all flesh that was coated with gel.

They still called them *tours* – the training packages that gave you the hands-on experience of a new piece of software. And he told himself that this was exactly the same. He was getting the hands-on tour.

Or rather the hand-on tour.

He tried to adopt a facetiousness, a mocking, distant and detached attitude to what was happening.

He tried. But he failed.

Elvara was real. She was soft and warm. And there was no place that his hand did not go . . .

It lingered upon each breast and now no longer needed to be guided. It had developed a will of its own. A need of its own. The need to tease each nipple and trace every soft warm contour.

He was shivering all over with excitement as his finger tips reached her belly. As he touched the soft down of her pubic hair she shifted her position, opening her legs slightly to welcome his approaching fingers.

He began to stroke her. But soon she seized his hand again and there was an urgency in her voice.

'There,' she said. 'There and there.'

He obeyed without question. He wanted to move his body against hers. To feel her with both hands. To bury his face in her neck. But he couldn't. And he cursed his own stupidity in wearing the plastic suit and limiting the use of gel to just one hand.

'That's nice,' said Elvara huskily. 'It's really, really nice . . .'

She was breathing very quickly as if excited.

As if?

She *was* excited. And it was all down to him.

He felt proud of himself and suddenly filled with a new confidence.

Before he left the Cab, Elvara kissed his hand and looked up at him with those incredible blue eyes so that his heart melted.

'Next time,' she pleaded, 'could I ask you to be really brave?'

Back in the real world, some of Bart's new-found confidence evaporated and it was almost a week, and three more trips in the Cab, before Bart had gathered sufficient courage to give Elvara everything that she asked for.

He left his clothes on the bench and showered before entering the gel cubicle. And he had to admit that the gel was not unpleasant. A week earlier, he had shuddered at the ordeal of preparing to use it on his hand, but now he sprayed over his body and rubbed it into his flesh enthusiastically. It was not at all like the used slime that sometimes fouled the inside of a Cab – particularly when it had not been cleaned for some time. This was sweet-scented and was absorbed by his skin quickly, leaving just the barest feel of oil on the surface. It seemed little different than a bath oil.

Immediately upon entering the Cab, he found himself transported to a place somewhat different from the usual grassy slope with its yellow gorse and red roses.

He was in a forest under a green twighlight of tall trees and, despite his nakedness, he felt very warm. He seemed to have an heightened awareness of his body and felt each pore of his skin beginning to ooze sweat.

And then, suddenly, Elvara was standing before him. But there was something far different about her eyes; the diffidence was gone to be replaced with a look akin to hunger.

She came very close to him and, before he could react, she hooked her right foot behind his left ankle and pushed him hard in the chest with both hands. Stunned and winded, he found himself lying on his back. She was sitting on his chest pinning his arms to the ground.

'You can't move now, can you?' she asked.

He found himself unable to reply. His mouth suddenly felt very dry.

'I've got you,' she said. 'Now I can do *anything* to you I like. And there's nothing you can do to stop me . . .'

She gripped his arms and pushed them hard against the ground and he was aware of her terrible strength bearing him down.

The air was becoming even hotter; he looked up at the canopy of leaves and saw that the forest was changing even as he watched; it was hot, humid, tropical – dashed with the blood of blossoms that were like her lips. It was perfumed, hot, moist like her body; filled with the rustles and cries of teeming life. Sunlight shafted down through the dark verdancy; sunlight and despair consumed him.

He was burning and could not help himself. He ached for her. Ached for her and was damned.

She locked her mouth upon his and, sliding her body downwards, suddenly lifted and arched above him.

And with a sudden thrust she enclosed him. She squeezed and then began to rise and fall, lingering at each descent to grind her pubic bone hard against his own.

They sweated together amongst the leaves in an ancient rhythm; mosquitoes clustered above and thin high pipes of fear shrilled inside his head.

And the pleasure built and built to reach a climax that was almost unbearable; it rose to a shuddering release that was almost pain to be succeeded by a dull ache deep at the roots of his belly that *was* pain.

And there was also a moment of fear . . .

What if it was too early? What if he had finished too soon? And he remembered the girl he had taken into the subway. The real girl who had kicked his shins and bloodied his lips. And Bart realized suddenly how far more dangerous Elvara was than a so-called real girl. The strength of the succubus was that of three men. And he was totally at her mercy.

Elvara led him by the hand and he had to follow. She laughed and her face was radiant and transfigured with love. Her cheekbones were high, her eyes vivid; her hair hung like a black plume down her arched neck and he looked down the length of her nakedness expecting hooves. He found only feet and fell to his knees against his will showering them with kisses and tears. Fruit hung in over-ripe clusters and dripped red and purple juice onto his naked back.

And then they made love again. Then again until he was exhausted. But still she would not let him go . . .

And he groaned but she answered him only with the cries of her own need and cut into his back with sharp fingernails drawing sequences of red contour lines from his neck to his buttocks; searching his mouth with her tongue; teasing and squeezing his body without mercy until he wished only to escape and feared for his sanity and very life.

'I'm tired now,' he said at last. 'I want to go home . . .'

He was shocked at the sound of his own voice. It sounded weak and afraid; little more that the plaintive voice of a child far from its home. A child hurt suddenly by a dangerous toy.

She stared hard at him for a moment and, immediately, a curious sensation ran the length of his body. Then, for a second. terror gripped him and everything became blurred before returning, once more, to the sharp bright intensity of the world Elvara presented to him.

He shivered. He had felt as if he were losing consciousness; there had been a moment of terror and impending dissolution.

But Elvara was smiling again as if in reassurance.

'Home is where I am,' she said. 'I want you to stay here with me forever. Men summon me for their pleasure and I have to obey. Why shouldn't I have a little pleasure of my own?'

'But you can't do this,' cried Bart. 'It's not possible. You have to release each client from the Cab.'

Elvara merely smiled again. It was but the slightest of smiles reminding him somehow of that inscrutable expression that adorned the face of the Mona Lisa. It was an eternal smile. The smile of a woman who knew far more than he would ever begin to feel or understand.

And suddenly, he remembered his conversation with Brownski.

Elvara was right . . .

He was already home.

He remembered the dizziness, the sense of dissolution as if he were breaking into pieces.

And now he understood and slowly the full horror of the situation came home to him.

A wiser and a sadder Bart had already been returned to the outer world. But *he* would remain here forever.

Remain as an entity to be used for Elvara's own pleasure.

He was just a copy . . .

ANGEL

Philip Robinson

THE ringing phone drew Donal up, out of the work spread all over his desk. He rubbed at the bridge of his nose and when he looked away from the paperwork he could still see columns of figures dancing merrily in front of his eyes; his shirt felt tight around his back and when he moved there was a twinge of pins and needles in his buttocks. As usual, he was the only one here at half-eight in the evening and the shrill tone of the telephone sounded deafening in the empty office.

He considered ignoring it, but in truth the distraction was welcome. He lifted the receiver and pressed the flashing button for line-one.

'Davis, Jones and Sutcliffe: Chartered Accountants,' he rattled off with his automatic, all-business tone. 'How may I help you?'

'Donal Ashford?' A woman's voice – husky and throaty but soft, almost a whisper; it seemed to almost melt down the phoneline.

'Uh . . . that's right,' he replied.

'Hello, Donal. I'm Angel.'

Angel!

His heart kicked, began thumping wildly in his chest; his pulse raced as blood rushed through his head in a torrent; he began breathing with deep, awkward gasps and his stomach was trying to flip itself over inside him; a sudden heat pulsed in his groin.

Angel: Your fantasy prowls
the Midnight City, seeking
you out. Be my slave. Photo,
number, and info to Box 904.

It had seemed too ridiculous to be genuine – tucked into the middle of all the other shy, mundane, '*I like cinema, walking and socializing*' personal ads. . . . It *couldn't* have been for real.

Nevertheless, his photo, number and info had found its way to Box 904.

Now this voice, pouring from the telephone like syrup.

Strange noises were coming from his throat.

'Donal?'

'Yes . . . I'm here. But didn't I . . . I gave you my *home* number, how did you reach me here?'

A slight chuckle came down the line, followed by a sigh. 'That doesn't really matter, does it? What matters is whether or not you're serious about wanting me.'

'Yes,' he said, almost blurting the word in his urgency. He closed his eyes, commanding his respiratory system to come under his control.

'You must be certain you understand: I don't want a relationship – it's my kind of sex, nothing more.'

'Yes,' he replied, bewildered even to be having this conversation. His mind was trying to create an image to go with that voice, but all it could manage were flickering glimpses: a cigarette between two long, red-nailed fingers . . . full, crimson lips . . . a pink tongue moving behind perfect white teeth . . . a mess of blonde hair. . . .

'Sunderland Street,' Angel said. 'There's a phone box half-way down. Fifteen minutes.'

Now!??! She wanted to meet now?!?!

'Is this for real?' he muttered.

'You'll just have to trust me.'

She hung up, leaving him staring at the receiver. His tongue darted out and licked dry lips, his hand was trembling slightly. Surely it was some kind of joke: how far would this sad, desperate, lonely man go . . .?

But what if it *was* real?!! The heat hadn't left his groin, the partial-images he'd concocted of the woman were still in his head, as was her purring voice *and she was going to have sex with him!!*

A line from a song went through his head: *Fishing for a good time starts with throwing in your line.*

Hell with it – take the chance!

Four minutes later he was practically running down the stairs to the front entrance of the building. He hadn't felt like this since his first sexual encounters as a teenager. There was a comfortable swelling in his trousers, the bulge – not quite an erection – swaying from side to side as he left.

He knew *Sunderland Street.* Just off the quays, the whole area was taken up with garages and warehouses and in the daytime was a loud flurry of workers, machinery, forklifts and supply-trucks; a brisk ten-minute walk from his office, he was there in six.

All the buildings appeared locked up and he saw the phone box as soon as he turned the corner, a dull light glowing from within. There was no sign of anyone around.

No sign of Angel.

He walked towards the kiosk with slow, cautious steps, and from some three feet away heard the telephone ringing within. He pulled the door open and stepped inside, grabbing the receiver to his ear.

'Hello, Donal,' Angel drawled, 'I'm glad you came.'

'Where are you?'

She laughed. 'Take off your jacket.'

He looked around, turning in a circle but could see nothing through the windows. He removed his jacket, folding and placing it on the floor in the corner. He willed his heart to slow down before it exploded.

'There's a sportsbag at your feet,' came the voice from the phone. 'Pick it up and open it.'

He looked down and saw the black bag – the zipper kind with various pockets on its sides. He bent and grabbed it, hoisting it up onto the wooden bench where the absent phonebook should have been. Unzipping it, he found inside a black eye-mask – the kind troubled sleepers wear to keep out the light – and a pair of steel handcuffs.

'Take the cuffs,' Angel told him, 'and clasp one of the manacles on your left wrist, tight as you can.'

'Listen,' he began, 'I'd like to – '

'Do it my way, Donal, or go home.'

He hesitated only for a moment – there really was no question.

He took the cuffs out of the bag and placed his left wrist into one of the manacles, closing it with a rough, ratchety sound until the cold steel pressed against the sides of his wrist.

'Make sure it's tight,' Angel told him. 'Make it pinch!'

'It is,' he replied.

'Good. Now put the mask on.'

He paused again. What if it *was* a trick? If he put on the mask and cuffed himself he'd be leaving himself open, defenceless to whatever might come along, whatever might be waiting out there. It was as though Angel read his mind.

'No one's holding a gun to your head, Donal – you either do it or walk away.'

Fifteen minutes ago he was sitting in his office, still in his own world . . .

But he was here now . . . he'd already come this far.

Muttering under his breath, he removed the mask from the bag and pulled it down onto his face. It was a tight fit, the elastic pinching the back of his head, the satin-soft patches pressing hard against his eyes and covering the whole top half of his face. He could see nothing.

'Good,' she said. 'Now drop the receiver, turn around – your back to the door. Stretch your arms out behind you.'

She can see me, he thought, *from wherever she is out there.*

Oh God, talk about leaving yourself vulnerable. Was he insane?

Yes!

He turned awkwardly in the pitch-blackness, lifting his arms behind him, feeling the loose manacle sway back and forth as it dangled from his wrist. There was a fear in his stomach now . . . if this turned bad . . . what if there was a man? But his heart was hammering, he could feel the blood pulsing in his temples with the excitement and exhilaration, an intoxicating buzz vibrated in his head.

Generally he was a man who played things safe, didn't take risks – now he'd suddenly been caught up in a tornado, scooped away; he felt like another person in another world, a million miles from his own.

He liked it.

He could feel an ache in his groin. He wanted to rub himself, to feel –

He heard the door open behind him, cold air rushed in and his stomach lurched. Fear and exhilaration shot through him, mixing together into a single, unknown cocktail.

(It's someone else! Not her!!!)

Suddenly his arms were taken, pushed together behind him

and the loose manacle was fastened tightly around his right wrist, pinching the skin.

'Hello Donal.' The luscious voice was unmistakable and his breath was released in a *whoosh!*

'You're here,' he croaked. He couldn't believe this was actually going to happen, *was* happening. Never in his wildest fantasies had he thought . . . oh God . . .

He heard the door close behind him and something brushed the back of his neck – a warm, wet touch on his skin; she was kissing him and he sucked in a breath. Hands took his upper-arms and turned him round. For a moment he just stood there, facing her but lost in darkness, knowing nothing but his *want*.

A smell caressed his nose and he inhaled deeply . . . intoxicating . . . a sweet, subtle perfume mixed with the coconut-oil scent of her skin and then he felt soft, luxuriant hair fall against his face; lips closed on his earlobe, sucking gently. His breath felt very loud in the enclosed space. The bulge in his trousers was bursting to be free, the steel at his back biting into his wrists. She was *so close*, his body was aching for her. He could feel her hot breath on his neck as her tongue darted in and out, licking him, could hear the wet sounds her tongue made as her mouth opened and closed.

'I'm a bad woman,' she moaned softly into his ear, 'a *dirty* woman. I'm touching myself . . . my cunt . . .' Her tongue lapped at his ear. 'I'm wet . . .'

'Oh God, let me. . . .' Awkwardly, he tried to move forward.

A hand pressed to his chest and he was pushed backwards, up against the wall of the kiosk behind him. He felt her toying at his lips, prising them apart and then two fingers slipped into his mouth. He caught them, sucking eagerly on them, curling his tongue around them, tasting her skin. Her mouth left his ear and began to work its slow way around to the front of his face, her tongue leaving a wet trail behind it, her breath almost burning his skin where it touched.

She withdrew her fingers from his mouth and dropped her hand to his chest, pulling the top shirt buttons open and slipping inside, her wet fingers leaving trails across his skin. She found an erect nipple and pinched it. He gasped and she brought her mouth to his, sandwiching his top lip between her two and pulling it outward, sucking it into her mouth, sliding her tongue up underneath. When it came back to him he could taste her on it. Her tongue entered his mouth, filling and exploring and when he sucked on it he felt something hard and protruding.

A stud in her tongue.

An unprecedented surge of desire coursed through him as he touched this alien object in contrast to the softness surrounding it, moaning into her mouth as it scraped against his own tongue, searching for it when it slipped away, wrestling it, trying to suck her in deeper.

Both her hands now were working at his chest, the shirt torn open all the way. He could feel her long nails scraping him, his nipples trapped between fingers and thumbs, being exquisitely twisted and turned and squeezed and pulled. Her mouth came away from his and he leaned forward gasping, chasing it. He felt her hands on his shoulders and she was pushing him downwards. His legs didn't have the strength to defy her even if he'd wanted to.

On his knees . . . if only she'd let him touch her . . . his arms pulled frantically to free themselves from the manacles but all effort was in vain. Suddenly he could feel her legs at his sides and her body pressed against him, her belly touching his chest; his face met a bulge of soft, silky material and he realized she was pressing her breast against him. He licked at the fabric, bit at it, filling his mouth and feeling the point of her hard nipple through it; the intervening clothing was frustrating, maddening. Finally, after an eternity, he felt her hands pull the fabric away, there was a popping sound as buttons were yanked open.

There was no bra and he heard her moan when his mouth met the full, soft mound of flesh, his tongue licking until it found her poking nipple. He sucked it in, flicking with his tongue, encircling it before taking it between his front teeth, tightening the bite until he heard her gasp. She pulled back and he held it for a moment before releasing it to her. If she –

The slap across the face was hard and shocking. 'I didn't say to do that.' Another slap, and before the stinging had died her breast was filling his mouth again. She was holding it for him in her hand, pressing it into him, squeezing it, releasing it, squeezing, releasing, moaning with each movement.

Suddenly he could feel her other hand at his fly, unzipping him and slipping inside, her long, warm fingers finding his cock and pulling it free, closing around its bulging tip and squeezing, sending a bolt of white pain through him. He bit down on the tit in his mouth, grunting and moaning, unable to distinguish between ecstasy and pain. She barely eased her grip on his cock before tightening again and sliding her wet fingers down his shaft, then back up and he came, pumping hot semen into her hand; a guttural roar escaped him as the breast came out of his mouth with a wet, sucking sound. His legs, his whole body melted out of his control and he fell back against the wall, the phone box rattling around him with the impact. He lay there panting like a dog, his breath the only sound for a moment or two, then he felt her lips on his cheek, her tongue on his skin.

She's kissing me goodbye, he thought. It's all over!

Already he could feel a great black hole inside him.

'Don't go.'

'Oh, Donal,' she said with a sigh, resting her cheek on his and he could feel her body against him, 'we can't stay here forever.' Then she was off him and he heard the door open, and she was gone.

'Angel!' he called as he sat there. The coldness of the night caressed his shrivelled penis and he tried to get to his knees, the handcuffs giving him no leeway in the awkward manoeuvre. It occurred to him that on his knees he wouldn't be able to remove the mask from his face – at least in a sitting position he could use his knees to try and shove it up on his head.

He dropped himself backwards until he was sitting on the cold floor again, and was just about to begin on the mask when he was suddenly frozen by the sound of a car engine. He prayed it would pass on by. It didn't. It stopped, right outside the phone box.

It's someone to make a phonecall and what a surprise they were going to get when they opened the door!!

He held his breath in the all-consuming darkness.

He heard the door open and raised his head as though he could see, ready to plead his insanity.

'Relax,' Angel said, 'I just went to get the car.' He could hear the engine idling outside and moaned his relief; he felt her grab his arms. 'On your feet, soldier, double-time.'

When he was standing he could feel her hands at his trousers, tucking his penis inside and zipping him up, and then she was leading him out of the kiosk. He heard a car door open and he was shoved downwards and into the back seat. The door closed behind him and a moment later he heard her climb into the front.

Then they were moving.

Traffic noises increased around him and he surmised they were out on a main road. The perpetual darkness was infuriating, he wanted to *see* her; he began rubbing the back of his head against the seat.

'Ah-ah!' Angel warned immediately, a certain joviality in

her voice. She must have been watching him in the rear-view mirror. 'The mask stays on, thank you very much.'

'I just want to see you.'

'Keep it on,' she said with a sigh. 'If I catch you trying to remove it again I'll open the door and dump you out into a ditch.'

Some moments passed with only the soft hum of the car filling the silence.

Donal said, 'Where are we going?'

'Somewhere nice and private.'

'Why?' he asked, genuine bewilderment in his voice. 'Why all this?'

She laughed. 'That's classified. I could tell you – but then I'd have to kill you.'

In the ensuing silence he tried to make some sense of this whole situation. Surely he was dreaming – this wasn't real life, this was what men fantasized about; it never actually happened, *couldn't* be happening now. But the coldness of the night was too real, as was the taste of her in his mouth, the throbbing in his penis where he could still feel her tight fingers. This was no dream.

Christ . . . was she kidnapping him?!

Of course not. She was a control-freak, playing a game, that was all.

But completely on her own terms, and this did cause a pang of trepidation in his stomach. What if the game escalated to . . . to *something else?!* What if the next stage involved something sinister?!

Again Angel seemed to read his mind. 'Are you worried, Donal?'

He wanted her to tell him he was perfectly safe, wanted to *be* perfectly safe – but even more than that he wanted her again, wanted her in his mouth, wanted to be in her mouth, wanted her pussy.

'I . . . a little, I suppose . . .'

She gave him no reassurance.

Finally the car stopped. He heard the handbrake pulled on . . . the opening of a door . . . footsteps . . . and a moment later his own door opened and a hand took his arm.

'Angel?' he said, afraid that it might be . . . there might be someone else . . .

Suddenly he felt warm lips mashed against his. A fire exploded in his stomach when he tasted her again, when the tongue slipped into his mouth and he felt the stud click off his teeth. She pulled away and helped him out of the car, leading him along like the blind man he was.

There was a rattle of a key in a lock, a door swishing open, then he stepped forward. He was standing on carpet and the door closed behind him, he could hear no sounds, but a strong airfreshener-scent hung around him.

A house. Angel's house.

She took him by the arm and said, 'Stairs here.'

He lifted his right leg, bouncing it on thin air in front of him until his foot found the bottom step. Angel led him up the stairs, turning him right at the top and walking him down a landing.

He heard another door open and he was led into a room.

The door closed behind him and, after only three steps, Angel released her hold and he stood there, lost in a sea of darkness, wondering if she –

Suddenly he was pushed from behind and he stumbled forward, losing his footing and heading for the floor. But he didn't hit the floor, instead coming down on a soft mattress and behind him he could hear Angel laughing; for the briefest moment he felt a flash of anger towards her. Her hands found the backs of his thighs and his legs were hoisted up onto the bed. His mouth was full of duvet and he shoved it out with his tongue.

'Turn over,' Angel told him and he did so – with her help. She moved him until he was lying flat on his back in what felt like a relatively straight position on the bed. Under him, the steel manacles were digging into the skin of his wrists, but the pain was nothing compared to the pleasure when, a few moments later, he felt Angel straddle him, her thighs on either side of his ribs. From the feel of her he guessed she was naked. His shirt was wide open at his sides and he felt her lean forward on him, her bare breasts pressing into his chest, her tongue at his mouth – licking and teasing, then pulling away. She sat up again. He could feel her hips move back and forth as she rubbed her cunt against his stomach. His cock was aching to be free of his pants. He felt her shift on his body, turning around, and he lay still as she secured one ankle, then the other, to the end-bedposts with sheets.

He couldn't move his legs.

She turned around on him again. 'Now, I want you to promise you won't try to remove the mask when I uncuff you.'

'Okay,' he grunted.

'If you do then we'll have to forget this whole thing and go our separate – '

'I *won't*!' he reiterated, trying to lift his hips to press himself against her.

'Raise your back as much as you can,' she told him. He felt her weight rise off him and her hands slip under his back. There was some fumbling around at the cuffs and then the slight *snick!* as a key turned in a lock. The manacle was removed from his left wrist and the release felt good. His arms came out from under his body and, unable to help himself, he reached for her.

A hard slap struck the side of his face, rocking his head to the side. His right hand was grabbed and roughly pushed back over his head until the knuckles rapped the wooden headboard. Shoving herself forward with her knees, Angel manoeuvred herself until she was sitting high on his chest and he could smell her, her pussy must be only inches from his mouth. Then there was that ratchety sound again as she locked the vacant manacle to the headboard. He tried to pull his arm down but it would move only inches before the steel bit into the wrist. His left arm was grabbed and yanked up in the same way, the wrist cuffed to another manacle which was apparently hanging there for just such a purpose.

He was crucified to the bed.

He lifted his head as much as he could, protruding his tongue, trying to make contact with her.

'*Yessss!*' she purred, '*drink from me . . .*' and he felt her shift forward on him. Her thighs came up past his armpits and she lowered her crotch down onto him, smearing his face with her hot slickness, a deep moan coming from her when his mouth found the damp hair and swollen lips. He pressed his tongue into her as far as he could, parting her labia, searching for her clitoris and when he found it, tongued it, her cry was loud in the room. Suddenly he felt her hands grab the hair at the back of his head, her nails digging into his scalp as she pushed his face into her, jerking hips back and forth in a frantic manner, grunting and thrusting.

She cried out with her orgasm, her thighs melting out sideways from under her and his head was forced back down into the bed, her crotch threatening to smother him and he didn't care.

After a few moments she lifted herself off his face and moved back down his body; he felt her turn and work at his trousers and when she yanked them down to his knees his cock burst free. Then one hand took his right nipple, squeezing it hard between fingers, the other coming around and grabbing a handful of his left buttock, lifting him off the bed. He felt her position herself on him and a moment later the tip of his penis was buried in a thatch of soft curls, then brushed the lips of her cunt; it hovered there above him, rubbing and teasing until finally she dropped onto him, impaling herself. They both cried out as her hot folds seemed to suck him in, enveloping him with her tightness, squeezing and kneading him; not just his cock but his whole body was joined with hers. He lunged up into her and there was a slap of flesh on flesh as she fell forward onto him, her breasts flattening against his chest. She pumped her hips mercilessly up and down and it was only moments before he came, exploding inside her. She continued pumping until he became flaccid, then lay on top of him, keeping him inside her. Her face was buried in the crook of his neck and Donal's brain was melting in his head; it took him some minutes to come back to Planet Earth.

'Why are you doing this?' he asked finally.

He felt that familiar chuckle into his neck and she sat up on him. With the movement he could feel himself stirring inside her.

'Maybe . . .' she said, ' . . . I'm the ugliest woman to have ever graced the face of the earth and this is the only way I can get it.'

'I don't believe that.'

'Or maybe I'm some kind of deranged lunatic who now has you in this compromising situation – a psycho whose only desire in the whole world is to make a testicle-necklace. I could have a pair of garden-shears in my hand right now – *snip-snip* . . .!

Now his cock was trying to crawl out of her but their hips were pressed tightly together, their fluids drying into a glue.

Suddenly she burst out laughing and began toying with his nipples, teasing them with her fingers and thumbs; then her tongue found the left one and lapped at it, her mouth covering it, trying to suck it in; she was doing something with her cunt . . . squeezing him with it and he could feel himself grow again inside her.

'Tell me the truth,' he said as waves of pleasure began to wash over him. He was fully erect in her now and she was writhing slowly on him.

Her mouth left his chest and she murmured, 'Believe me, you don't want to know, you'll enjoy it better.'

'I *do*,' he replied, and his words were followed by a hissing of breath as her hands grabbed the hair just above his temples, shoving his head backwards into the pillow. Holding him like that, he felt her bite his nipple, then her tongue licked its way up to his neck, to his mouth.

'My husband *hates* it,' was followed by a mischievous little chuckle.

'Your husband?' Donal gasped.

Angel's hips rose high, as though about to release him, but then slipped back down his shaft, sucking him back into her. She was laughing into his right ear. 'Are you frightened he might come home and find us?'

All he could do was moan as the pleasure overwhelmed him.

'He already knows,' she continued, 'he's right here now. In this room. Watching us.'

Donal tried to raise his head but she held it down on the pillow. Now her hips were pumping him and his own joined her rhythm, rising and falling as he drove into her. Her words *had* entered his mind, but for this moment they were drowning in the pleasure, for this moment it didn't matter, *nothing* did. She rode him hard, sinking her teeth into his shoulder and he came, a loud roar escaping him.

Angel collapsed on top of him and he could say nothing for some moments as they lay there. When he finally found his voice he asked the dreaded question.

'The old fucker had a stroke last year,' she told him, 'hasn't been the same since. Believe me, you don't want to see, it's not a pretty sight.'

'I don't . . . believe this . . .'

'Very well,' she said with a relenting sigh. 'But don't say I didn't warn you.' He felt her fingers grab the elastic of the mask. She yanked it over his head and he had to close his eyes against the sudden brightness. For moments all he could see was the fleshy blur straddling him, then his eyes adapted. Angel was a beautiful woman – dark eyes, a small nose, full lips, a round face bordering on oriental, luscious black hair hanging to her shoulders, pale skin, breasts pert, her thin waist widening into full hips, her dark curls knitted into his own pubic hair where their bodies joined.

But his gaze was drawn inexplicably to his left where there was a man – if he could still be called that – sitting in a wheelchair, his legs not six inches from the edge of the bed.

'Donal,' said Angel, 'meet Carl.' She burst out laughing as he stared at the man – still as a statue, his head hung on his left shoulder as a thin line of spittle drooled from the corner of his mouth and hung down his chin. His skin was yellow and sagging off his body, his eyes colourless, one covered in a thin, a milky-white membrane.

'Oh no,' Donal said.

'I put up with his offence and abuse and degradation and jealousy long enough,' Angel spat. 'If I ever so much as *looked* at someone else . . . the bastard . . . Now it's payback time.' She looked to the thing in the chair and sneered. 'Look, Carl, hit me now! I'm fucking this bloke and I don't even know him – '

'Stop,' said Donal, his voice weak.

' – I'm going to do it all night long and you're going to sit there and *watch*!!' To Donal she explained, 'They say he can see and hear what's going on around him.'

'Open these cuffs,' he told her, trying to pull himself free. 'You're sick!'

She lifted her hips and his penis fell out of her. He couldn't take his eyes from the thing in the chair. Angel moved down his body and took him in her mouth.

He wouldn't do this! COULDN'T do this!

But Angel's tongue was curling around him, trying to burrow its way into the tip . . . the stud touching the gland . . . tantalizing . . . *Christ*!!

'I WON'T DO THIS!!' he shouted.

He wouldn't get hard. *He wouldn't get hard*!

He fought her for long minutes, his eyes closed so he didn't have to look at her creamy, silky skin, listening to her moan and groan down there as she worked with her hands and mouth. He tried to knee her away but she wouldn't budge.

Oh God . . .!

Her mouth left him and she came up, looking at her husband with a bemused smile. 'Why do they *always* fight me, Carl?' She leaned down over the side of the bed and pulled something out from underneath. It was an icebox. 'Have to pull out the big guns,' she said as she lifted out a plastic bowl. There was a spoon and she scooped out a dollop of whipped cream, taking it into her mouth and then leaning forward to kiss him. He turned his head to the side but she found his mouth, tonguing the thick, cool cream inside and he knew it was lost. When she sat up he looked at her smiling face – mouth and chin covered with cream. She scooped out another spoonful and began spreading it over his balls and cock, the coolness initially seeming to work against her purpose, but soon he was erect again and he closed his eyes as she went to work with her mouth.

He didn't open them when he felt her shift on him, her face coming up to his, and when the lips of her cunt once again sucked him inside he thought he heard a moan from the thing in the chair.

THE BIRDS POISED TO FLY

Patricia Highsmith

EVERY morning, Don looked into his mailbox, but there was never a letter from her.

She hadn't had time, he would say to himself. He went over all the things she had to do – transport her belongings from Rome to Paris, settle into an apartment which she had presumably found in Paris before she made the move, probably work a few days at her new job before she found time and inspiration to answer his letter. But finally the greatest number of days to which he could stretch all this had come and gone. And three more days had passed, and still there was no letter from her.

'She's waiting to make up her mind,' he told himself. 'Naturally, she wants to be sure about how she feels before she puts a word down on paper.'

He had written to Rosalind thirteen days ago that he loved her and wanted to marry her. That was perhaps a bit hasty in view of a short courtship, but Don thought he had written a good letter, not putting pressure, simply stating what he felt. After all, he had known Rosalind two years, or rather met her in New York two years ago. He had seen her again in

Europe last month, and he was in love with her and wanted to marry her.

Since his return from Europe three weeks ago, he had seen only one or two of his friends. He had quite enough to occupy himself in making plans about himself and Rosalind. Rosalind was an industrial designer, and she liked Europe. If she preferred to stay in Europe, Don could arrange to live there, too. His French was fairly good now. His company, Dirksen and Hall, consulting engineers, even had a branch in Paris. It could all be quite simple. Just a visa for him to take some things over, like books and carpets and his record player, some tools and drawing instruments, and he could make the move. Don felt that he hadn't yet taken full stock of his happiness. Each day was like the lifting a little higher of a curtain that revealed a magnificent landscape. He wanted Rosalind to be with him when he could finally see all of it. There was really only one thing that kept him from a happy, positive rush into that landscape now: the fact that he hadn't even a letter from her to take with him. He wrote again to Rome and put a 'Please forward' in Italian on the envelope. She was probably in Paris by now, but she had no doubt left a forwarding address in Rome.

Two more days passed, and still there was no letter. There was only a letter from his mother in California, an advertisement from a local liquor shop, and some kind of bulletin about a primary election. He smiled a little, snapped his mailbox to and locked it, and strode off to work. It never made him feel sad, the instant when he discovered there was no letter. It was rather a funny kind of shock, as if she had played a guileless little trick on him and was withholding her letter one more day. Then the realization of the nine hours before him, until he could come home and see if a special delivery notice had arrived, descended on him like a burden, and quite suddenly he felt tired and spiritless. Rosalind wouldn't write him a special delivery, not after all this time. There was never anything to do but wait until the next morning.

He saw a letter in the box the next morning. But it was an announcement of an art show. He tore it into tiny pieces and crushed them in his fist.

In the box next to his, there were three letters. They had been there since yesterday morning, he remembered. Who was this fellow Dusenberry who didn't bother collecting his mail?

That morning in the office, an idea came to him that raised his spirits: her letter might have been put into the box next to his by mistake. The mailman opened all the boxes at once, in a row, and at least once Don had found a letter for someone else in his own box. He began to feel optimistic: her letter would say that she loved him, too. How could she not say it, when they had been so happy together in Juan-les-Pins? He would cable her, I love you, I love you. No, he would telephone, because her letter would have her Paris address, possibly her office address also, and he would know where to reach her.

When he had met Rosalind two years ago in New York, they had gone out to dinner and to the theatre two or three times. Then she hadn't accepted his next invitations, so Don had supposed there was another man in the picture whom she liked better. It hadn't mattered very much to him at that time. But when he had met her by accident in Juan-les-Pins, things had been quite different. It had been love at second sight. The proof of it was that Rosalind had got free of three people she was with, another girl and two men, had let them go on without her to Cannes, and she had stayed with him at Juan-les-Pins. They had had a perfect five days together, and Don had said, 'I love you,' and Rosalind had said it once, too. But they hadn't made plans about the future, or even talked about when they might see each other again. How could he have been so stupid! He wished he had asked her to go to bed with him, for that matter. But on the other hand, his emotions had been so much more serious. Any two people could have an affair on a holiday. To be in love and want to marry was something else. He had assumed, from her behaviour, that she felt the same way. Rosalind was cool, smiling, brunette, not tall, but she gave the impression of tallness. She was intelligent, would never do anything foolish, Don felt, never anything impulsive. Nor would he ever propose to anyone on impulse. Marriage was something one thought over for some time, weeks, months, maybe a year or so. He felt he had thought over his proposal of marriage for longer than the five days in Juan-les-Pins. He believed that Rosalind Farnes was a girl or a woman (she was twenty-six, and he twenty-nine) of substance, that her work had much in common with his, and that they had every chance of happiness.

That evening, the three letters were still in Dusenberry's box, and Don looked for Dusenberry's bell in the list opposite the mailboxes, and rang it firmly. They might be in, even though they hadn't collected their mail.

No answer.

Dusenberry or the Dusenberrys were away, apparently.

Would the superintendent let him open the box? Certainly not. And the superintendent hadn't the key or keys, anyway.

One of the letters looked like an airmail envelope from Europe. It was maddening. Don put a finger in one of the slits in the polished metal front, and tried to pull the box open. It remained closed. He pushed his own key into the lock and tried to turn it. The lock gave a snap, and the bolt moved, opening the box half an inch. It wouldn't open any farther. Don had his doorkeys in his hand, and he stuck one of the doorkeys between the box door and the brass frame and used it as a lever. The brass front bent enough for him to reach the letters. He took the letters and pressed the brass front as straight as he could. None of the letters was for him. He looked at them, trembling like a thief. Then he thrust one into his coat pocket, pushed the others into the bent mailbox, and entered his apartment building. The elevators were around a corner. Don found one empty and ready, and rode up to the third floor alone.

His heart was pounding as he closed his own door. Why had he taken the one letter? He would put it back, of course. It had looked like a personal letter, but it was from America. He looked at its address in fine blue handwriting. R. L. Dusenberry, etc. And at its return address on the back of the envelope: Edith W. Whitcomb, 717 Garfield Drive, Scranton, Pa. Dusenberry's girl friend, he thought at once. It was a fat letter in a square envelope. He ought to put it back now. And the damaged mailbox? Well, there wasn't anything stolen from it, after all. A serious offence, to break a mailbox, but let them hammer it out. As long as nothing was stolen, was it so awful?

Don got a suit from his closet to take to the cleaners, and picked up Dusenberry's letter. But with the letter in his hand, he was suddenly curious to know what was in it. Before he had time to feel shame, he went to the kitchen and put on water to boil. The envelope flap curled back neatly in the steam, and Don was patient. The letter was three pages in longhand, the pages written on both sides. 'Darling,' it began.

> I miss you so, I have to write to you. Have you really made up your mind how you feel? You said you thought it would all vanish for both of us. Do you know how I feel? The same way I did the night we stood on the bridge and watched the lights come on in Bennington . . .

Don read it through incredulously, and with fascination. The girl was madly in love with Dusenberry. She waited only for him to answer, for merely a sign from him. She spoke of the town in Vermont where they had been, and he wondered if they had met there or gone there together? My God, he thought, if Rosalind would only write him a letter like this! In this case, apparently, Dusenberry wouldn't write to her. From the letter, Dusenberry might not have written once since they had last seen each other. Don sealed the letter with glue, carefully, and put it into his pocket.

The last paragraph repeated itself in his mind:

> I didn't think I'd write to you again, but now I've done it. I have to be honest, because that's the way I am.

Don felt that was the way he was, too. The paragraph went on:

> Do you remember or have you forgotten, and do you want to see me again or don't you? If I don't hear from you in a few days, I'll know.
>
> My love always,
> Edith

He looked at the date on the stamp. The letter had been posted six days ago. He thought of the girl called Edith Whitcomb spinning and stretching out the days, trying to convince herself somehow that the delay was justified. Six days. Yet of course she still hoped. She was hoping this minute down there in Scranton, Pennsylvania. What kind of man was Dusenberry? A Casanova? A married man who wanted to drop a flirtation? Which of the six or eight men he had ever noticed in his building was Dusenberry? A couple of hatless chaps dashing out at 8.30 in the morning? A slower-moving man in a Homburg? Don never paid much attention to his neighbours.

He held his breath, and for an instant he seemed to feel the stab of the girl's own loneliness and imperilled hope, to feel the last desperate flutterings of hope against his own lips. With one word, he could make her so happy. Or rather, Dusenberry could.

'Bastard,' he whispered.

He put the suit down, went to his worktable and wrote on a scrap of paper, 'Edith, I love you.' He liked seeing it written, legible. He felt it settled an important matter that had been precariously balanced before. Don crumpled up the paper and threw it into the waste-basket.

Then he went downstairs and forced the letter back in the box, and dropped his suit at the cleaners. He walked a long way up Second Avenue, grew tired and kept walking until he was at the edge of Harlem, and then he caught a bus downtown. He was hungry, but he couldn't think of anything he wanted to eat. He was thinking, deliberately, of nothing. He was waiting for the night to pass and for morning to bring the next mail delivery. He was thinking, vaguely, of Rosalind. And of the girl in Scranton. A pity people had to suffer so from their emotions. Like himself. For though Rosalind had made him so happy, he couldn't deny that these last three weeks had been a torture. Yes, my God, twenty-two days now! He felt strangely ashamed tonight of admitting it had been twenty-two days. Strangely ashamed? There was nothing strange about it, if he faced it. He felt ashamed of possibly having lost her. He should have told her very definitely in Juan-les-Pins that he not only loved her but wanted to marry her. He might have lost her now because he hadn't.

The thought made him get off the bus. He drove the horrible, deathly possibility out of his mind, kept it out of his mind and out of his flesh by walking.

Suddenly, he had an inspiration. His idea didn't go very far, it hadn't an objective, but it was a kind of project for this evening. He began it on the way home, trying to imagine exactly what Dusenberry would write to Miss Whitcomb if he had read this last letter, and if Dusenberry would write back, not necessarily that he loved her, but that he at least cared enough to want to see her again.

It took him about fifteen minutes to write the letter. He said that he had been silent all this while because he hadn't been sure of his own feelings or of hers. He said he wanted to see her before he told her anything, and asked her when she might be able to see him. He couldn't think of Dusenberry's first name, if the girl had used it at all in her letter, but he remembered the R. L. Dusenberry on the envelope, and signed it simply 'R.'

While he had been writing it, he had not intended actually to send it to her, but as he read the anonymous, typewritten words, he began to consider it. It was so little to give her, and seemed so harmless: when can we see each other? But of course it was futile and false also. Dusenberry obviously didn't care and never would, or he wouldn't have let six days go by. If Dusenberry didn't take up the situation where he left it off, he would be prolonging an unreality. Don stared at the 'R.' and knew that all he wanted was an answer from 'Edith', one single, positive, happy answer. So he wrote below the letter, again on the typewriter:

> P.S. Could you write to me c/o Dirksen and Hall, Chanin Building, N.Y.C.

He could get the letter somehow, if Edith answered. And if she didn't write in a few days, it would mean that Dusenberry had replied to her. Or if a letter from Edith came, Don could

– he would have to – take it on himself to break off the affair as painlessly as possible.

After he posted the letter, he felt completely free of it, and somehow relieved. He slept well, and awakened with a conviction that a letter awaited him in the box downstairs. When he saw that there wasn't one (at least not one from Rosalind, only a telephone bill), he felt a swift and simple disappointment, an exasperation that he had not experienced before. Now there seemed just no reason why he shouldn't have got a letter.

A letter from Scranton was at the office the next morning. Don spotted it on the receptionist's desk and took it, and the receptionist was so busy at that moment on the telephone, that there was no question and not even a glance from her.

'My darling,' it began, and he could scarcely bear to read its gush of sentiment, and folded the page up before anyone in the engineering department where he worked could see him reading it. He both liked and disliked having the letter in his pocket. He kept telling himself that he hadn't really expected a letter, but he knew that wasn't true. Why wouldn't she have written? She suggested they go somewhere together next weekend (evidently Dusenberry was as free as the wind), and she asked him to set the time and place.

He thought of her as he worked at his desk, thought of the ardent, palpitating, faceless piece of femininity in Scranton, that he could manipulate with a word. Ironic! And he couldn't even make Rosalind answer him from Paris!

'God!' he whispered, and got up from his desk. He left the office without a word to anyone.

He had just thought of something fatal. It had occurred to him that Rosalind might all this time be planning how to break it to him that she didn't love him, that she never could. He could not get the idea out of his mind. Now instead of imagining her happy, puzzled, or secretly pleased face, he saw her frowning over the awkward chore of composing a letter that would break it all off. He felt her pondering the phrases that would do it most gently.

The idea so upset him that he could do nothing that evening. The more he thought about it, the more likely it seemed that she *was* writing to him, or contemplating writing to him, to end it. He could imagine the exact steps by which she might have come to the decision: after the first brief period of missing him, must have come a realization that she could do without him when she was occupied with her job and her friends in Paris, as he knew she must be. Second, the reality of the circumstances that he was in America and she in Europe might have put her off. But above all, perhaps, the fact that she had discovered she didn't really love him. This at least must be true, because people simply didn't neglect for so long to write to people they cared about.

Abruptly he stood up, staring at the clock, facing it like a thing he fought. 8.17 p.m., September 15th. He bore its whole weight upon his tense body and his clenched hands. Twenty-five days, so many hours, so many minutes, since his first letter . . . His mind slid from under the weight and fastened on the girl in Scranton. He felt he owed her a reply. He read her letter over again, more carefully, sentimentally lingering over a phrase here and there, as if he cared profoundly about her hopeless and dangling love, almost as if it were his own love. Here was someone who pleaded with him to tell her a time and place of meeting. Ardent, eager, a captive of herself only, she was a bird poised to fly. Suddenly, he went to the telephone and dictated a telegram:

> Meet me Grand Central Terminal Lexington side Friday 6 p.m. Love, R.

Friday was the day after tomorrow.

Thursday there was still no letter, no letter from Rosalind, and now he had not the courage or perhaps the physical energy to imagine anything about her. There was only his love inside him, undiminished, and heavy as a rock. As soon as he got up Friday morning, he thought of the girl in Scranton. She would be getting up this morning and packing her bag, or if she went to work at all, would move in a dreamworld of Dusenberry all the day.

When he went downstairs, he saw the red and blue border of an airmail envelope in his box, and felt a slow, almost painful shock. He opened the box and dragged the long flimsy envelope out, his hands shaking, dropping his keys at his feet. The letter was only about fifteen typewritten lines.

Don,

Terribly sorry to have waited so long to answer your letter, but it's been one thing after another here. Only today got settled enough to begin work. Was delayed in Rome first of all, and getting the apartment organized here has been hellish because of strikes of electricians and whatnot.

You are an angel, Don, I know that and I won't forget it. I won't forget our days on the Côte either. But darling, I can't see myself changing my life radically and abruptly either to marry here or anywhere. I can't possibly get to the States Christmas, things are too busy here, and why should you uproot yourself from New York? Maybe by Christmas, maybe by the time you get this, your feelings will have changed a bit.

But will you write me again? And not let this make you unhappy? And can we see each other again some time? Maybe unexpectedly and wonderfully as it was in Juan-les-Pins?

Rosalind

He stuffed the letter into his pocket and plunged out of the door. His thoughts were a chaos, signals of a mortal distress, cries of a silent death, the confused orders of a routed army to rally itself before it was too late, not to give up, not to die.

One thought came through fairly clearly: he had frightened her. His stupid, unrestrained avowal, his torrent of plans had positively turned her against him. If he had said only half as much, she would have known how much he loved her. But he had been specific. He had said, 'Darling, I adore you. Can you come to New York over Christmas? If not, I can fly to Paris. I want to marry you. If you prefer to live in Europe, I'll arrange to live there, too. I can so easily . . .'

What an imbecile he had been!

His mind was already busy at correcting the mistake, already composing the next casual, affectionate letter that would give her some space to breathe in. He would write it this very evening, carefully, and get it exactly right.

Don left the office rather early that afternoon, and was home by a few minutes after five. The clock reminded him that the girl from Scranton would be at Grand Central at 6 o'clock. He should go and meet her, he thought, though he didn't know why. He certainly wouldn't speak to her. He wouldn't even know her if he saw her, of course. Still, the Grand Central Terminal, rather than the girl, pulled at him like a steady, gentle magnet. He began to change his clothes. He put on his best suit, hesitantly fingered the tie rack, and snatched off a solid blue tie. He felt unsteady and weak, rather as if he were evaporating like the cool sweat that kept forming on his forehead.

He walked downtown toward Forty-second Street.

He saw two or three young women at the Lexington Avenue entrance of the Terminal who might have been Edith W. Whitcomb. He looked for something initialled that they carried, but they had nothing with initials. Then one of the girls met the person she had been waiting for, and suddenly he was sure Edith was the blonde girl in the black cloth coat and the black beret with the military pin. Yes, there was an anxiety in her wide, round eyes that couldn't have come from anything else but the anticipation of someone she loved, and anxiously loved. She looked about twenty-two, unmarried, fresh and hopeful – hope, that was the thing about her – and she carried a small suitcase, just the size for a weekend. He hovered near her for a few minutes, and she gave him not the slightest glance. She stood at the right of the big doors and inside them, stretching on tiptoe now and then to see over the rushing, bumping crowds. A glow of light from the doorway showed her rounded, pinkish cheek, the sheen of her hair, the eagerness of her straining eyes. It was already 6.35.

Of course, it might not be she, he thought. Then he felt suddenly bored, vaguely ashamed of himself, and walked over to Third Avenue to get something to eat, or at least a cup of coffee. He went into a coffee shop. He had bought a newspaper, and he propped it up and tried to read as he waited to be served. But when the waitress came, he realized he did not want anything, and got up with a murmured apology. He'd go back and see if the girl was still there, he thought. He hoped she wasn't there, because it was a rotten trick he'd played. If she was still there, he really ought to confess to her that it was a trick.

She was still there. As soon as he saw her, she started walking with her suitcase toward the the information desk. He watched her circle the information desk and come back again, start for the same spot by the doors, then change it for the other side, as if for luck. And the beautiful, flying line of her eyebrow was tensely set now at an angle of tortured waiting, of almost hopeless hope.

But there is still that shred of hope, he thought to himself, and simple as it was, he felt it the strongest concept, the strongest truth that had ever come to him.

He walked past her, and now she did glance at him, and looked immediately beyond him. She was staring across Lexington Avenue and into space. Her young, round eyes were brightening with tears, he noticed.

With his hands in his pockets, he strolled past, looking her straight in the face, and as she glanced irritably at him, he smiled. Her eyes came back to him, full of shock and resentment, and he laughed, a short laugh that simply burst from him. But he might as well have cried, he thought. He just happened to have laughed instead. He knew what the girl was feeling. He knew exactly.

'I'm sorry,' he said.

She started, and looked at him in puzzled surprise.

'Sorry,' he repeated, and turned away.

When he looked back, she was staring at him with a frowning bewilderment that was almost like fear. Then she looked away and stretched superiorly high on her toes to peer over the bobbing heads – and the last thing he saw of her was her shining eyes with the determined, senseless, self-abandoned hope in them.

And as he walked up Lexington Avenue, he did cry. Now his eyes were exactly like those of the girl, he knew, shining, full of a relentless hope. He lifted his head proudly. He had his letter to Rosalind to write tonight. He began to compose it.

OLD TIMES

Alick Newman

THE thrush flashed across the clearing to a young oak and examined the open ground from the safety of the dying branches. It did not consciously divide its field of view into foraging and non-foraging areas, or note the proximity of long grass to the trees and margins of the clearing, nor imagine the unseen and silent terrors that might lurk there. Though the leafy cover above it was sparse and sickly, nor did it skulk timorously from fear of hawks and harriers. Instead, it sang, for it had mated a few minutes earlier though it had no recollection of the event. It was ready to do so again with any available female if his mate was not nearby.

She was elsewhere, looking for other males to woo her, procuring the best genes she could find for the brood she and her partner would raise. For they were both descended from a long, long line of thrushes who had, without conscious thought, eschewed the long grass, sung long and loud for a mate, and been as faithful as necessity, their genes and opportunity allowed, and had thus done better for themselves than if they hadn't. So the thrush did what a thrush does, strutted on its branch and sang to the silent forest.

'I can't do it myself, Louis.' Madame Arnaud looked down

at the steep bank and smiled slyly. She placed the basket on the ground and held out bare brown arms. 'I'll need your assistance.'

The dark-haired young man stood a little straighter at the sight of her and a faint smile lit upon his tired face. He laid down his gun and satchel, took off his boots, and waded into the clear shallow water. He reached up and swept her from the bank and she squealed. He thought how wifely and plump she looked, fresh like a newly-stuffed bolster as she snuggled comfortably against his spare, hard torso. Her clean round face was red and chafed from the sun.

'What are you doing here, Madame Arnaud?' he scolded her, one hand beneath dimpled knees, the other comfortably cupping a plump breast. 'Is the forest a safe place for a young bride?'

Her deep dark eyes looked teasingly up at him. 'Oh, Louis, you know how I love chanterelles. I just had to have some and the best are found on the other side of this stream.'

'This is your husband's work, not mine, Madame.'

'But he's not here,' she pointed out reasonably. 'He's gone to Valence, to his smelly old factory.' She ran her fingernails up Louis's neck and locked them into his hair. 'In any case he is too old and fat to carry me anywhere, and as he is in Valence, you may take his place, Louis.'

He carried her a single step across the stream. 'I? Take his place?'

'And why not?'

'But I have to poach for my living and your husband is a rich man. Doesn't he provide for you?'

'Oh yes, there is always more than enough food on the table. And wine in the cellar. But he feeds his hunting dogs no worse than he feeds me.'

'I've heard of his dogs,' said Louis. 'Won't he buy you things?'

'Only to show me off to his ancient cronies.'

'Well, what can I, a poor poacher, do?' He set her down on the sand, his hands falling naturally upon her shoulders, hers about his waist. 'Doesn't he make you happy?'

Madame Arnaud giggled. 'Dear Louis, he is so fat, and his prick is hidden beneath such a duvet of flab, that I even have difficulty finding it for him. And then I have to do everything, and ride him for our pleasure, which for me is little, for I cannot bear to have him inside me. But he spends quickly, so he does not occupy me very long.'

'Nor very deeply,' murmered Louis and ran a hand across her soft belly to trace the folds and curls in the 'Y' at the top of her thighs. She shuddered.

'Well, Madame, if there's aught a poor man may give you – .'

'Oh yes – ' said Madame Arnaud.

The cotton shift collected at her waist as he lifted the long calico dress easily over her shoulders and folded his arms about her. She pressed her naked legs tight to him, as if to see his body through her own, explore every corner and every shadow of it; his thighs and arms, the weal of scar tissue that ran down his back like a clinging vine. They kissed and she felt the sunlight crack and shatter as the hard skin of a thumb tracked softly across one nipple, then the other; fire in her ears as his fingers followed the familiar fold of waist down to the cleft of buttocks and spread the flesh and danced and tapped across her anus. She curled a leg around his and tore at the string at his waist. His breeches fell open and his penis jerked forward and butted at her navel. Louis began to breathe hoarsely and she lifted her leg high to press her core against him, trying to absorb him, melt with him. Her foot reached the small of his back, so the soft down on her belly climbed the underside of his prick, pressing it tight between them, and on tiptoe she leant back so that the swollen head of his penis traced the slippery, unfurling labial lips. She let it slide slowly, deeply into her, and as her eyes widened she gave up what had become an unequal struggle with gravity.

She swung, impaled on his prick, feet locked above his buttocks and Louis lifted her up, backing away then thrusting forward as he let her down, hearing the trees roar as a great wind swept through his head. He dropped to his knees and she gripped his buttocks and ground herself against his pubic bone, holding him deep within her so that he brushed her womb. Her being seemed to billow out and up into the air, oblivious to the lips at her breasts and the coiled portent within her. Her orgasm was accompanied by a long, low cry and immediately Louis jerked and ejaculated.

He lay buried within her for a long while, until the sweat on his back had dried. She allowed him to begin again. And this time he was as respectful and subservient as a peasant should be.

Dogs.

Louis jerked uneasily awake from a deep sleep. Hounds, baying in the distance, and getting closer. There was a sudden splashing in the water behind, and naked he turned, hands out to ward off an attack and saw Madame Arnaud, now fully clothed, clamber onto the far bank. She gave him a half-frightened, half-entreating look, picked up the hem of her dress and, without a backward glance, disappeared into the trees.

The hounds were much closer and Louis could hear shouting and cursing above the noise of the dogs. He struggled into his breeches, grabbed his shirt, satchel and gun, and ran for the trees as a line of men and dogs appeared on the bank behind him. In the confusion one man and another's hound tangled and, kicking and biting, fell into the stream. But some of them saw Louis's scarred back disappear into the undergrowth and they urged, dragged or threw their leashed hounds, as appropriate, into and across the stream and took up the fresh trail.

'Any luck?' Louis asked.

The landlord shook his head with a smile thinner than his wine. 'No birds, no rabbits, no deer. What I don't understand is why, if there's no game, there should be so many bleeding keepers everywhere.' He paused to spit on the floor. 'You?'

'One small bird,' said Louis, 'and I obliged a lady from the town who had lost her way.'

'Looks like she wore you out finding the right road,' the landlord sneered.

'Her husband's dogs chased me for three hours.' Louis admitted, looking down into his wine.

The landlord considered for a long moment. 'Her husband's dogs? That'll be Arnaud. He's got more dogs and keepers than the rest put together. They won't stop, you know. They'll still be after you. You're father to more bastards than the Pope.'

'Maybe, but I know the forest better than they do.'

'Yes, and one day you'll run out of forest.'

'Never.' Louis said it defiantly but ever since he could remember, the edge of the forest had always been fair game to the axes of the furniture makers. Then the powder mills contaminated the ground water the forest depended on, and latterly fumes and waste from the Daguerreotype works had poisoned those fields and hedgerows that the waters missed. River and wind conspired to carry the corruption deep into the forest. The inhabitants of the forest, peasants like Louis, whose precarious existence was due solely to its provender, who were born and who died within its bounds, were inexorably driven to follow the trees to the town in the hope of some livelihood. Their close-knit community had slowly disintegrated, and the birds and animals that escaped the poisonous miasma were now claimed by those who divided up the shorn ground. Slowly, the forest was stolen, and, slowly, it died.

'There's no one to spend a sou in here,' said the landlord. 'Not any more.'

Louis counted money onto the trestle and took the small wine cask from the landlord and set it on the ground. This was watched by the other occupants of the room, a girl and a surly man, who suddenly pushed the girl roughly towards the trestle bar. Marked by their clothes as town-dwellers, Louis watched the girl approach and he thought, I know her from somewhere. The landlord spat without smiling.

She looked tired and hungry, like a small bird hunched against the rain; thin arms clasped across her small, high chest, hair that might once have been blonde but now was leached of colour. The hem of her thin cotton dress was muddied and frayed and her boots were torn.

'Buy me a drink, sweetheart?' She let her tongue play along her lower lip and her hand drop upon his shoulder. Her face was pale, as if unused to the air, but as he looked he saw something, in a dull, lacklustre eye, a brief something that kicked the past into motion. All of a sudden his scarred back tightened as memories of a flaxen-haired girl and the pigs rooting for acorns in the deep forest burst into his head.

He never knew how old he was that day (or any other day, come to that). He knew the sequence of the seasons but had no need to count them. This particular day, high in the canopy with a squirrel he'd caught, his foot slipped and he'd hung onto his catch and not to the branch. Half-way to the ground a broken branch had slowed his fall but ripped his back open. The pigs, intent only on gorging themselves, were in no danger of straying so the girl had begun picking blackberries and found him lying in a tangle of bramble. She bound him up with mosses and leaves as she'd seen her mother use on her brothers, and seeing that he couldn't move she went for a blanket. When she returned he'd gone.

A week later, as the acorns were petering out, he suddenly appeared and shyly made a fire on which he placed some fish wrapped in leaves. When they had eaten they talked and slowly their awkwardness departed. Later, they applauded the old boar as he mounted the sows in turn, shyly pushing each other as they cheered, letting their hands remain on the other a little longer each time, and then when she stumbled, the easiest thing was to fall with her. They rough and tumbled and mock-wrestled until he lay between her half-raised knees, looking down at her eyes, and suddenly, although it still felt like a game – the same game – the rules had changed forever. She bit his lip and hung there, shaking him gently while he slid the dress up to her waist – it seemed the obvious thing to do – and suddenly she pushed his clothes away, and they found themselves coupling with the intensity and the passionate dislocation that the discovery of this particular faculty exerts. Louis, whose senses were so attuned to the myriad dynamics of the forest, experienced an explosive release, an escape from an omnipresent. It formed a link with a chain of continuity he seemed to experience all around him.

'Lisle.' he said.

'My name is Yvette.' She placed a hand artlessly on his thigh.

'My name is Louis.'

Her eyes widened, and a vision of a wet, hairy snout lifting her bare leg to reach an acorn sent a shudder through her. Then she collected herself and smiled.

'So, *little* Louis,' she said and he felt her fingers curl around and measure his less than limp prick. 'Nothing changes, I see. Still the same woman-stabber.'

The landlord snickered and Louis turned red.

'How about it, Louis? For five centimes I've a fine sheath

for your sword. If it was me, you know, it'd be free. For old times' sake. But it's not.' Yvette half glanced over her shoulder and continued to play with his prick through the rough cloth of his breeches. 'You could buy me some wine.'

Louis motioned the landlord to fill a cup and carefully gave him his last sou and watched her drink.

'What happened. Where did you go?' he asked awkwardly. 'I looked but never found you.'

'To the town. To Valence.' She wiped her mouth on the back of her hand. 'One morning our stream turned brown. No one noticed. By evening my brothers and mother and most of the animals were dead. The next day, or the next week, or the next month, the contractors came and broke down our shelters and killed my father.' She drained the cup and shrugged. 'They fed me and gave me a new name, and cut down the trees. When they went back to Valence, I went with them, what else? There's always work for a girl, if she doesn't mind what she does.'

'Do you mind?'

'Not enough to starve, I don't.'

'So why come back if there's nothing here?'

'Come back?' She gestured behind her. 'Only to bury his mother. Two francs she left, that's all. And then, the poor boy in a fit of grieving, drank it and the coach fare home.' She looked disdainfully at the landlord, then leant against Louis, small pointed breasts pressing into his arm, and looked up with tired and nearly hopeless eyes.

'It's a long walk back to Valence, and there's no one else here but you, and so far I've only got his fare. C'mon, Louis, drink up and lets relive some old times?' She pressed her belly and legs against him, rubbing her mound against his crotch.

Louis accommodated her movements, his memory and his erection both tracing the folds of her mound through the threadbare fabric and he said with difficulty, 'I cannot – '

'Oh c'mon, Louis. It's a long way to Valence and I'm very tired.'

Louis's hands slipped to her buttocks and pulled her up so that only their clothes prevented penetration. 'Lisle, if I had the money I would gift it to you, for old times' sake. But I have none. I have nothing.'

'Oh, I see,' she said, stepping back, hands on hips, surveying him, 'you would if you could but you can't, but as you're being so nice, why don't I fuck you anyway? Nothing is for nothing, Louis. What sort of girl do you think I am?'

She turned away and her shoulders slumped as she realized that her companion had gone and she and Louis were the only people there. Louis saw deep in her face, beneath the drawn flesh, a black, hard-edged emptiness that frightened him.

'Stay then,' he said. 'It must be better here than in Valence.'

She laughed without a shade of feeling. 'No, Louis. The forest's dead and so is anyone who stays.' She wrapped a thin shawl round her shoulders and as she left she said over her shoulder, 'Look me up when you get to Valence. For old times' sake.'

At first there was only whiteness. Everything, everywhere was white. All was white, a perfection of white and yet, in spite of this, there was nothing. Not a black nothing, simply nothing but white. It is, potentially, the only nothing we can experience. Then, in its own time, like a glance cast by a ripple onto a sandy bottom, like smoke in the bright sun, shadows appeared, formless and liquid, growing from the whiteness and erasing the uniformity. The shadows developed, grew darker, took on form and slowly coalesced into vertical bars as Louis's open eye found focus on the circle of men and baying dogs standing round his huddled body, and as it did so pain and memory exploded in his head. They cradled bloody staves in bloody palms, laughing, complaining that a lack of rope prevented them from hanging him there and then. His torn satchel and open gun were passed from one to another. The meat he had killed was examined carefully. His gun was smashed against a bole. One of them found the cask of wine, and with a kick or two for good measure they gathered around the open cask and left him alone for the moment. When Louis heard slurred voices debating whether Louis could be the 'scarred man' they were looking for, he slowly began to crawl from his wrecked hovel, through the mud and debris and slid painfully into the nearest brambles, face to the ground beneath the barbs. He crawled until he was exhausted. Deep in the brambles he dozed fitfully in open spaces sheltered from the wind, warmed by the sun. He moved on painfully whenever he awoke while his erstwhile pursuers snored drunkenly under the same warm sun.

Later, much, much later, as the sun disappeared behind the canopy, he sought relief at a stream, and bathed his cuts and bruises until the stinging became a burning and an itching, that drove him in a wild, mad, flailing roll away from the contamination onto a bed of twigs and loam.

Wounded animal that he was, the next morning he turned deeper into the forest, seeking the oldest and densest banks of vegetation to burrow through, searching for the ancient, open glades that had been fashioned by the passage of time, not of feet; isolated and insular, where clean water rose.

But when, scratched and bleeding, he finally reached the glades, the valves in the heart of the forest, the havens of peace – he found them clogged and choked with the first trees to be cut down from within in the surrounded core. So it was, with noise and tumult, that the forest was dismantled, and so it was, with the encouragement of kicks and blows, that Louis was forced from the flat, featureless plain that had been his home.

* * *

He stepped out of his stained and filthy rags and stood naked in the tin bath, watching her warily. Indifferent, she cracked the ice in the jug and quickly poured the water over him while he washed with a threadbare cloth. She grabbed the cloth and made him wince as she scoured the weals and bruises. He jumped onto the bare boards and dried off as best he could and then struggled into the unfamiliar clothes. The shirt was rough, the stiching gross and knotted, and the collar dug nastily into his neck like a toothless vampire. The jacket was worn and clean but too small. It made his bruises ache. The trousers were so tight around the crotch he felt naked from the waist down.

'You'll get used to them.'

He pulled at his crotch and she glared at him, a malicious look that surprised and stilled him. 'Why, Lisle? They're too small.'

'You'll wear them because I say so, Louis. Because your country ways are no good anymore. That's why you came looking for me, isn't it? You were starving and I've got you a chance to earn some money. The only thing you can do without money is starve,' she said coldly. 'So you'll do as I say. No one wants to look at filthy peasants any more, and certainly not in their own homes, so you'd better get used to it.' She smacked his hand away from the collar and straightened the jacket. 'And the name is Yvette. Don't forget again.'

As they walked through the narrow frozen streets in the grey, brutalized dawn the smell grew stronger until his eyes smarted and he could taste it on his tongue.

'Phew,' he said.

'What?'

'The smell.'

'What smell?' she said, opening a small door in the side of

a tall brick building and leading the way up some stairs. At the top she pulled open another door and stepped through.

Louis followed and stopped dead just inside the door. The room was circular, the walls of panelled wood and the ceiling of glass. It was like stepping from the undergrowth into a strange and secret clearing. He felt that if he went outside he would find the forest on the other side of the door. To one side of the room stood a chaise longue piled with cushions and drapes. Before it stood a table on which sat a polished mahogany case, from the side of which projected a cylinder of polished brass with a black cap upon the end. Two assistants in braces and caps stood to one side and a short, immensely fat man stood on the other, passing instructions and looking contemptuously at the sky.

Yvette turned to Louis. Her lips were quite red and a look of secret expectancy suffused her face. Distracted, for the smell was stronger, or rather, fresher than in the street below, Louis mistook it for a smile of encouragement, and allowed her to pull him into the room.

'Be quick,' snapped the fat man, 'I have a sitting at midday.'

Yvette led Louis across the room. The fat man looked Louis up and down. 'Well, let's have a look.'

Louis stared, knowing something, but not what, was expected. 'Does it understand?' the fat man inquired pleasantly. God, he thought, how stupid and ugly these peasants looked. They were animals. He felt this sincerely and honestly and had done since discovering that simply by forgetting to pay them most of the time they'd work for nothing most of the time. He sighed patiently. 'Can it speak?'

'Don't worry, Monsieur,' said Yvette hurriedly, and moved to face Louis. Faintly smiling, she began to unbutton him.

'Hey,' said Louis, startled, 'what . . .'

Yvette hushed him and said in a low voice. 'Monsieur is going to make many pictures – '

'What are you doing?'

' – pictures of us fucking, Louis.'

'Without our clothes on?' stammered Louis.

'It will look like we're fucking only we – you – won't be. He just wants to see if you're up to it – '

Before he could prevent her she drew out his prick, sank to her knees and, turning so that the fat man had a clear view, fed its limpness into her mouth. Louis would have drawn back in fear, would have rushed from there, for he had never experienced such a thing in his life. But, as the shock dissipated and unexpected sensations burst in his brain as she sucked the slowly swelling bell-end slowly in and out between wet lips, Louis's eyes shut and his mouth opened. Yvette's hand cupped his balls, the other worked up and down the shaft. Louis shuddered and it was all he could do to remain on his feet. He put his hands upon Yvette's shoulders but she shrugged him off. When the engorged flesh filled her mouth and his breathing was growing hoarse, she gave a little smile, stood up and displayed the erect penis.

'It'll do.' The fat man adopted an expression of distaste and genteelly wiped his brow, and the by now red-faced assistant withdrew his hands from his pockets and busied them elsewhere. Louis came down faster than a shot stag.

The fat man said, 'I require absolute stillness from you both for the full duration of each exposure. As you are aware, Mademoiselle, I deduct the cost of un-sharp plates from your earnings. Perhaps today you may settle some of the debt you have accumulated. Firstly, astride and facing the plate box. Quickly. While the light holds.'

'Yes, Monsieur,' said Yvette and pushed Louis to the chaise longue. She arranged him so he faced the small table and mahogany box, an arm cocked behind his head. Louis winced as the arm of the chaise longue raked across his scar. With one hand she arranged his open breeches behind his testicles, and with the other she rapidly encouraged the tottering shaft back to tumescence, so his balls bulged and appeared to buttress the erect member. Satisfied, she unbuttoned the top of her dress, folding it behind her small breasts, lifted her dress and rolled it to her waist, displaying worn white stockings held just above the knees with faded garters. She ran her hands up her parted legs to the heart-shaped bush of pale hair balanced on the inverted 'V' of her thighs, a bush as invisible, beneath the marble-flat, white belly, as the apertures it shielded.

Louis's unsupported prick swung and wobbled in the ocean current of visual stimulation and he didn't understand anything anymore. Yvette sat on him, buttocks against his tight waist-band; she lifted her right foot and placed it on the front edge of the seat and laid her left along the top of Louis's left.

'Don't move, we're not going to fuck,' she ordered and reaching forward she took hold of his prick and, smoothing and gentle, she fed the bell end into her tight vagina. Sliding her hips forward an inch to hold it in place she added, 'Try not to move anything. Especially this.' She leant back, arranged her exposed breasts and rested her head on his.

The fat man looked at them clinically and said, 'Do not move a muscle when I say begin. Not so much as a tremble for fifteen seconds.' He consulted a pocket watch and uncapped the brass tube. 'Start – now.'

Louis held his breath. He didn't know if he could hold it that long because he had no idea of how long fifteen seconds were, so he tried to imagine he was back in the forest, lying in wait for a shy and timid deer, yet he was acutely aware of Yvette, the constriction and unatural angle of penetration, and still felt his muscles twitch with an intent he had never curbed before. Yvette remained motionless, her weight supported, Louis comfortably housed.

'Time,' called the fat man, clicking his fingers. The first

assistant dashed forward, swapped the mahogany box for another identical to it and dashed away with the first. The second assistant positioned the box carefully and stood back. The fat man was pleased. He was certain that he had a good, sharp image, but he would keep the information to himself.

As Louis relaxed and drew breath he contrived to push further into Yvette but she was too tight and for the moment, he gave up.

'Attention, we try again,' the fat man said. 'Start – now.'

Midway through exposing the fifth plate Louis developed cramp in his leg and leapt to his feet with a cry, spilling Yvette painfully from his lap.

'Imbecile,' shouted the fat man. 'Idiot. Another plate ruined. Well, you'll pay for it.'

Reunited, they went through the procedure again and again until the fat man called a halt and demanded another position. This time Yvette faced Louis, straddled him and again took only the bell end inside her. More than anything in his life, Louis wanted to buck his hips and plunge deep, all the way into her, balance her on his pole, fuck her – but Yvette sat in such a way that if Louis rose, she rose with him. She remained, as far as he could tell, dry and tight, as if the physical contact were happening eleswhere, to two other people. She never once looked at him, staring at the box on the table. But Louis didn't despair.

So it went on. The sun moved higher in the sky, the periods of exacting immobility grew shorter, then increased as clouds partially obscured the sun. The positions changed regularly, and the fat man bemoaned the loss of as many plates as were necessary to ensure their continued indebtedness to him. Louis had relaxed on two occasions and Yvette had swiftly restored him, and after an hour and a half the fat man called, 'Last position. Try to look as if you're alive.'

Yvette lay back on the chaise longue, her dress open all

the way down and hooked an arm behind a knee and spread herself wide. Louis was in a sorry state. His balls ached and his erection had developed a fixity of its own, like a rictus grin, and his trousers were round his ankles. She remained dry and tight and a faint smile greeted Louis puffing and panting as he sought a sustainable position over her. After six exposures the first assistant came back with a new mahogony box and said deferentially, 'Monsieur. Madame Arnaud has arrived, Monsieur.'

'Very well,' said the fat man, holding out the pocket watch. 'You will make one last exposure. When it's done, keep them in here so my wife doesn't see them. She's not to be upset in her condition. Then finish developing the plates and call me. I'll look at them straight away.' Turning to Louis and Yvette he said, 'You will return tomorrow. You are not hopeless, so I will give you both another chance, but you have ruined so many plates that you must return several more times. Get on with it.'

Yvette had half risen when the fat man spoke, and as she lay back, Louis saw one final opportunity, one last chance. He quietly spat on his hand, and transferred the spittle to his prick as she rearranged her dress. Then, before she could guide him, Louis reached down and smoothly slid his lubricated member into her tight, dry cunt. Yvette's eyes jerked open as he pushed, the moisture aiding but not ensuring his intent, and she reached down to push him away but he leant his weight on her, so that she couldn't move. Her struggles served to force Louis higher inside her and as she felt herself begin to loosen she tightened convulsively. Then it was too late . . .

Her arms met across his back as she tried to claw at him, her nails ripping at his scar through the shirt.

'We're ready,' coughed the first assistant nervously. The tears slowed in Yvette's eyes and she stopped for a second.

'Louis,' she whispered, 'be still. Let them make the last exposure. It'll be a good one with us like this, I know. And then he'll leave us in peace.' Then she quickly hauled his shirt up to his shoulders.

'Oi, that's not right,' said the assistant, 'he's too far – '

'Never mind,' countered Yvette, 'just get on.'

'Oh. Start now,' said the first assistant.

Louis looked down at her, both of them motionless in a fragment of time that went on for ever.

'Done,' called the assistants and hurried out with the box.

Louis smiled and ignoring the ache at the root of his prick began to thrust gently but firmly into Yvette's quiet form. She smiled a smile that came from a long way back and threw away every restraint. When Louis came, she came explosively, but he found no release and saw nothing in her face. He lay still for a while, until his still erect penis twitched and he had to begin again.

'Better not, Louis,' Yvette said, conversationally.

'What?' said Louis.

'You haven't time.'

'No time?'

'No, Louis, you've got until Monsieur Arnaud returns and looks at the last picture and sees the scar on your back. He's still looking for you, you know, when every day he sees what you gave to his wife. In fact, he's with her now.'

'Monsieur Arnaud?'

'Yes.'

'Next door?' Louis disengaged himself as the meaning sank in, leapt to his feet and made for the door, struggling to dress as he went. Already imagining he could hear the dogs, his feet became tangled at the top of the stairs and he fell half their length. He lay stunned and disorientated until finally roused by loud voices from the room above. Painfully he made his way out into the sunlit street where his dishevelled appearance and uncertain gait attracted a few curious looks. Then, above the grinding of wheel-rims on cobbles and the voices of the hawkers, he heard the barking of dogs. He tried to run and stumbled instead into the side of a passing cart and was thrown to the ground. As passersby gathered around him and the baying of the dogs grew louder, he rolled away from them, onto his side, and through half-shut, glazed eyes he seemed to see the sun breaking between columns of trees. The thought gave him strength and he struggled to his feet and pushed a way through the small crowd and without looking back the way he'd come, he set off towards his forest.

PLUCKED

Frank Finch

THE sun blessed England on this August day of 1420. The warm, still air hung with motes of wheat husk that moved only when disturbed by the efforts of Will Handy as he sweated in the heat, threshing the ears. He glanced around and noticed that his employer, Joseph Hardridge, had taken himself away from the field to rest against the waggon and quench himself from a flagon of cider. 'It's alright for you,' muttered a disgruntled Will, 'You can have a drink any time but not for the likes of me.' He moved himself, sending the motes weaving and dancing as he edged around a pile of straw and sank gratefully into its softness. 'What's sauce for the gander,' he muttered and laid his back against the straw, wiping the stinging sweat from his eyes and forehead with a dirty wool cloth, 'Aye, it's alright for some,' and he closed his eyes against the sun's glare preparing to steal a moment or two of rest.

'You'd better not let my dad see you resting, Will.'

Will opened his eyes reluctantly, 'Not less than I'm due, Mary. Been working myself into a sweat all afternoon and no thanks from the old man.'

Mary snorted, 'He pays you well enough, surely?'

'Aye but he also makes sure he gets his shilling of labour for each penny.'

'Tut, Will, you're being unfair and that's the truth.'

'Mayhap, missy.' Will sat himself up and openly admired the well-filled bodice of the girl who stood before him. 'Are the jugs for me, Mary?'

She smiled coquettishly, 'What jugs you talking of, Will?'

Will grinned widely but kept his eyes on Mary's roundness, 'Why, Mary, the ones you're hiding.'

Mary thrust a hip to one side and breathed deeply, stretching the leather lace that bound her bodice, forcing a tiny gap in the cloth that allowed just a suggestion of cleavage. 'Now how did you know I was bringing you these, Will Handy?' And she revealed the two earthenware jugs that she held behind her back. Leaning forward she continued to hold her breath and gave Will a better view of the assets beneath her bodice. 'One's cider, other's water, which?'

Will's eyes opened as wide as Mary's bodice as he drank in the splendid mountain scenery. 'I'd like to get my hands on both of them,' he breathed, 'Aye, both.'

Mary straightened, enjoying the effect she was having on the tanned muscular man who lay before her. She had more than a strong fancy for Will and for a brief moment she allowed herself to dwell on the prospect of having the weight of his tightly muscled body holding her to the ground. She felt herself blush at the erotic image and thrust the jugs towards him, 'Here, have both, but don't let my father smell the cider on you, it's his best and he'll know it was I that gave it to you.'

'He wouldn't begrudge one of his men a small drink would he, Mary?'

'He would, to be sure, specially his best cider and he'd be showing his disapproval by putting me over his knee and giving me a good spanking.'

Will shut his eyes tightly and pictured Mary's round buttocks divested of skirt and undergarments, taut and red from a spanking and began to feel a touch of unrest within his loins. He stood quickly but not fast enough for Mary who smiled at the bulge in his breeches and winked at him, 'I'll be going, Will, afore you forget the old man is nearby.'

'Aye, you do that afore I grabs you, Mary.'

'Now-now, Will Handy,' Mary giggled and turned away.

Will called after her, 'You going to run the chicken chase at the fayre tomorrow?'

Mary turned, tightening the lace of her bodice and smiled, 'For sure, Will. Will you be there to watch?'

Will nodded, 'That I will, Mary Hardridge, that I will.'

Will and his friend Danny Carpenter moved slowly through the field that held the marquees and stalls of Dorchester Fayre, their eyes darting from one place to the next trying to decide whether to eat, drink or enjoy the many sideshows available.

'I reckon a jug of cider first, Will.' Danny tore his eyes away from three young girls as they swished past in shortened skirts and petticoats showing a glimpse of slim ankles.

'No, Danny, let's have a slice or two of the roast pork,' Will answered, savouring the aroma of the roasting carcass placed opportunely upwind of them. Selecting neither, they momentarily forgot the three sets of pretty ankles and responded to the calls of a crier: 'Come along lads, see the bearded lady, come all the way from the lands of the Saracen. None such as her has been seen anywhere within King Hal's kingdom.' The two looked at each other, 'Bearded lady?' asked Will, 'Have you seen the likes of that afore, Danny?'

'Nay, Will,' Danny answered taking a last look at the ankles and promising himself a roll in the hay before the end of the day. 'And how much are you charging for a look?' he glowered at the crier in what he hoped was a wordly manner, letting it be known that he, Danny Carpenter, was not one to be trifled with or overcharged.

The crier grinned, 'Why lads, if I charged sixpence, t'would be small enough price for such a sight.'

'Sixpence,' gasped Will, 'That's a quarter of what I brought along with me. I'd not pay such for any lady, bearded or not.'

'Now me lads, did I say I was going to charge you sixpence?' The crier squinted at them, a crafty smile on his face, 'Not a bit of it.' He scratched his head and smiled again, 'Not a bit of it,' he repeated.

'Would I take so much from hard-working lads? No, not I. Tell you what, ye can take a peek for a penny each, how's that suit ye?'

Will looked at Danny and Danny nodded, 'Can't say as I've ever seen a bearded lady, Will. Be worth a penny, eh?'

The two parted with the coins and the crier stood back and allowed them to enter the dark interior of the tent. There were a number of candles which cast a dull light on a small stage at the back of the tent and seated in a chair behind a crude fence sat a woman of enormous proportions. Not only did her splendid red beard mark her as unique but the mountainous breasts that bulged from the low-cut bodice and the girth of her arms and thighs, clearly shown by the thin skirt stretched across her ample lower parts, showed her as being more than just a bearded woman.

Will and Danny stood and stared at the beard, at the firm flesh of her arms and the bulging bosom and the rounded tautness of the skirt.

''Tis a fine beard,' said Danny softly.

''Tis false,' replied Will a touch of scorn in his voice.

'Aye, but by the gods, there's more than a pennorth of the rest of her.'

'Look at those bosoms, Danny, have you ever seen the like?'

'Nay, Will, never. They're larger than old Hardridge's best milker.'

'That they are and judging by the lack of wrinkles and the points in her bodice, it wouldn't surprise me if she had as many teats.'

Danny sniggered. 'Man could get lost down there, suffocate more'n likely.'

'A good way to go, Danny and I'm thinking them thighs are right for keeping a man's ears warm.'

Danny nodded his agreement, 'Will, take a step across the fence and give the beard a tweak.'

'Do it yerself, do you think I wanna risk a blow from those hams as are her hands.'

A high-pitched voice, a falsetto squeak, shattered the quiet of the tent,

'Be off with you, you've seen a penny's worth!'

They both looked around the tent but could see no other person. The voice squeaked again, 'Go on, be off with you!' They stared in amazement at the bearded woman, the voice came from deep within the enormous bosom, streaking up her throat like lightning to pain their ears. They looked at each other and with an undignified scramble fled from the tent only bursting into laughter when they knew they were at a safe distance. 'Did you ever hear the likes of that?' gasped Danny, 'an ounce of voice in a ton of body.'

'Never,' Will looked back towards the tent to ensure there was no pursuit. 'Reckon we've time for a quart now.'

The cider vendor's barrow delayed them for a minute or two until howls off laughter and cheers drew their attention. They swallowed the last of their cider and ducked between two marquees seeking out the source of the fun.

In a clear space stood the trunk of a pine tree that had been shaved smooth and covered liberally in goose grease.

Half-way up the pole the figure of a slim, blonde-haired lass struggled to keep a grip and at the same time vainly scrabble her way to the top.

'Don't reckon she'll make it, the greasy pole is a lads' game.'

'She will,' Danny disagreed, 'That there is "Pretty", she'll make it to the top.'

' "Pretty?"'

'Aye, from over Burton way.'

'Why's she called "Pretty", Danny?'

''Cos that's the way she is. Soft of body, lips like rubies.'

'What make you think she'll get to the top?'

Danny turned and looked at Will, a smile on his face, 'Don't you know nothing, Will Handy. That there greasy pole is a pecker see, and "Pretty" likes climbing peckers.'

Will looked puzzled, 'But she's nought but a maid.'

'Aye and Sir Peter knows it.'

The frown of puzzlement on Will's face deepened, 'What're you speaking of, Danny?'

'Don't you know about "Pretty" and Sir Peter and,' Danny paused shaking his head, 'the priest at St Joseph's.'

'No,' Will was still frowning, Danny was speaking in riddles.

Danny sighed but decided to add to his friend's education, 'Well, it's like this, see. "Pretty" there is more woman than maid and the squire and the priest, they getting real old like . . .'

'Aye, they are, Sir Peter's nearing forty I heard,' Will agreed.

Danny ignored the interruption, ' . . . they getting real old. Well, they can't find enough young wenches, so they has to make do with serving maids, so the old knight and priest make a cuddling with "Pretty".'

'A cuddling? How can a gentleman and a priest make a cuddling with just a serving maid.'

Danny grinned and slapped Will on the backside, 'Both at

the same time I've heard. To some, any hole's as good as another, gentle born or not.'

'You don't mean they . . .'

Danny nodded. 'With some gentlefolk, that's the way of it, Will.'

Will turned and stared in disbelief at 'Pretty' who had gained another foot up the pole. Gentry and churchmen doing 'it' to serving girls and back to front as well? Whatever next? 'How will that help "Pretty" get up the pole?' He swallowed his disbelief as he asked the question. If Danny said it happened, well, he should know, he'd been about a bit, had even visited Shaftesbury once, all that distance, the top of the county, near on twenty miles!

'Well, "Pretty" is no innocent and Sir Peter does nothing to her she doesn't want done, back or front. So now she's got the feeling and kidding herself that the pole is Sir Peter's thingummy and when she gets to top, she can sit on it.' Danny chuckled, 'She won't be interested in a side o' ham for a prize.'

Will stared again towards the pole and 'Pretty''s attempts to gain the top; fascinated by the way of things as Danny had described them. He tried to imagine 'Pretty' in Sir Peter's bed with the priest and having them a-cuddling her both at the same time. He shuddered in horror, two men and one girl! He was grateful when a hub-bub of excitement filtered through to his mind. He tore his eyes away from the pole, noticed that Danny had started making his way along the edge of the marquees towards a hazel hedge from behind which further excitement emanated, and followed him.

'Are you going to the chicken chase now, Will?'

Will stopped and looked behind him. Mary was dressed in a woollen skirt from beneath which a hint of white petticoat could be glimpsed. Her full rounded breasts were only partly covered by a white linen blouse and a generous swell of blushing, tanned skin invited his attention. He found himself staring into Mary's cleavage, trying to visualize the full promise of those breasts and fantasized about holding them, caressing their fullness, kissing the proud nipples . . .

'Enjoying the view, Will Hardy or would you prefer "Pretty"?'

Will tore his eyes away from Mary's chest and felt himself go scarlet. 'I'm not like that, Mary, and don't you say so. One girl and one fella is the proper way of things.'

Mary placed her hands on her hips, smirked and said, 'Reckon you'll have to prove that, Will, or I might think the time you spent watching the greasy pole showed an interest in "Pretty".'

Will made a grab for Mary but she jumped back and laughed. 'I haven't the time to be a-cuddling with you, Will, I have the chicken chase to run.' She lifted her skirts and ran past Will, swerving beyond his reach as he made another grab for her, revealing well-turned calves as she kicked up her petticoats and ran around the hazel hedge, breasts bouncing with her effort.

Will made a start to go after her but Danny got in his way. 'There'll be no catching that one in this crowd, Will, save your energies till later, after the run, she'll be panting with breathlessness . . .' he chuckled, ' . . . and passion.'

Danny nudged him and offered a leather jug of cider, 'I got these afore the race, we don't want to be missing anything for the sake of a drink, eh?'

'Thanks,' Will's eyes glistened with excitement at the busy scene. 'I don't ever remember seeing so many lasses in the one spot, Danny.'

Danny gave an earthy chuckle, 'Right you are, Will lad, an' there's a varied choice among 'em. Fancy the red-haired one myself, whose yours as if I didn't know?' he grinned at Will. 'Would it be the dark one or the one with eyes like flax flowers? Or perhaps the two of them?'

'Shut your mouth, Danny,' Will grinned back. 'I don't care what colour their hair or eyes are.' He turned to survey the girls again as they milled about behind a strip of white tape that acted as a start line. Each of them collected a strip of linen and wandered off to find their choice of lad.

Even amongst the busy throng, Will quickly found the lass he was interested in. Mary's bust was by far the most developed, most provocative and, as far as Will was concerned, the most attractive thing at the fayre, though he would have admitted a liking for her flax-flowered eyes and light-brown hair as well. Will could have found Mary in a forest at dead of night, instinct would have led him to those magnificent breasts and as he dreamed of the milky white thighs that he had thus far never seen and the scented heaven that lay between them, she spotted him and walked lazily over, swinging the linen tape at her side. She stopped, allowed Will just a moment to enjoy her décolletage, then offered the tape to him, the movement causing her breasts to move slightly and swell at the low neckline of her blouse. Will groaned at the ecstasy of pain in his groin and tore his eyes away to ease the frustration.

'Will ye tie my thumbs for me, Will,' her voice was as sweet as wild honey and her smile offered a promise that melted Will.

His hand rose of its own volition and he took the tape as Mary made a quick pirouette and placed her arms behind her back. Will swallowed hard and tried to concentrate on the task of securing Mary's thumbs together, but he was conscious of the closeness of the swell of her hips and buttocks and his hands shook. Three times he tried and each time, the knot slid from her thumbs. He took a deep breath, ignored the impatient movement of Mary's body and the low chuckle that came from Danny and finally succeeded in securing the two thumbs. He held her bound hands in his and gave a gentle squeeze. Mary leaned back against him and a tremor ran through his body as her soft buttocks pressed against his hardness and she squirmed making his head fill with thunder as his heart pounded. He pushed forward against her and was about to bend his head and kiss her neck when she moved away and turned to face him, her cheeks flushed with excitement. 'That's enough o' that, Will.' Her voice was low and husky and her eyes betrayed her words, Mary's expression told him what her lips would not. Will nodded at her afraid to speak and barely managed to croak, 'I'll hold your chicken for you at the start, Mary.'

'You can hold my chicken anywhere, Will Handy,' she chuckled at him and once again his eyes were drawn to her breasts where the thin linen was stretched tightly, pressed against her breasts by the position of her arms held securely behind her back. Her nipples were proud and hard, showing her need for him and Will had to force himself not to lower his head and press his lips against them. Mary moved from him, turned and walked slowly back to the start line, swinging her hips outrageously as she felt Will and Danny following her.

Danny nudged Will and winked, 'Reckon she's hot for you, Will.'

'Hush yourself, Danny, there's some that will hear you.' Will turned away from the vision of Mary and the body he lusted for and took a chicken from the steward. 'I'm standing for Mary Hardridge,' he mumbled, and tucked the squawking bird under his arm its neck held with his free hand.

'Mind you don't release the bird before the start. Now go and stand with the other lads the other side of starting tape,' the steward instructed. Will nodded his understanding, waited whilst Danny claimed a bird for the red-haired lass he had taken a fancy to and joined the other lads five paces in front of the starting tape.

Thirty of Dorset's prettiest maidens waiting impatiently for the start. Each girl had her thumbs tied together behind her back, some had rolled their skirts and petticoats and tucked them into belts around their waists, giving their legs unaccustomed freedom for the chase that was about to begin. They chatted excitedly, calling out to friends in the watching crowd or their fancied lads beyond the tape.

The boys, each with a squawking chicken held in both hands or tucked under an arm, called back remarks that made the girls blush but not for long. Excitement was building as the steward approached the start tape, nodded towards his helper on the other end and raised the tape to waist height. He looked first towards the girls until they hushed and were paying attention, then towards the boys. 'I shall call to you, "be ready" and you may lower your chickens to the ground but not let them loose, then I shall call "to your marks" and the lasses may approach the tape,' he paused whilst he waited for impatient movement amongst the girls to quieten and then; 'Finally I shall call, "Away!" and you may let the chickens go and the boys must be quick to run to the sides and let the girls run for the chickens unhindered.' He returned his attention to the girls, 'When you go, you may run, skip, hop or walk but you must seek no assistance from any onlooker or other contestant. You may catch the chickens with any part of your body less your hands and must carry the bird in your teeth and no other way, back to me. The first girl to return with a chicken, any chicken, will be declared champion and receive the bird, a side of ham and a florin as prize.'

The steward paused, fixed his eyes on Danny's fancied red-haired girl and said; 'We will have no repeat of last year when a contestant forced a chicken down her bodice . . .' – there were ribald calls from the crowd and the steward was forced to pause. A smile touched his lips as he recalled the girl, Matilda Fouracre and her ingenious method of cheating, there was more than a chicken bouncing beneath her bodice last year, she was a fanciful lass that one, worth a trick or two the steward thought. The crowd quietened eventually and he was allowed to continue. 'Carried by your teeth only! Now attend,' and he looked towards the other steward, 'Are you prepared, George Miller?'

A hush now fell over the onlookers, the boys turned their backs to the girls and settled the chickens . . . 'Be ready!' called the steward and some of the boys stooped and held the chickens to the ground, others simply lifted them away from their bodies, ready to throw. Will lowered his charge and looked back towards Mary and winked and she puckered her lips in a kiss and returned his wink. If I hold on to the bird a second longer than the others, he thought, it will give Mary a chance to get closer . . . 'To your marks!' called the steward and thirty lads tensed and thirty lasses stepped to the tape and thirty pairs of pretty eyes squinted at the chickens as thirty bodices swelled as breaths were held . . . 'Away!' called the steward and the tape dropped, twenty-nine chickens were thrown or released and ran terrified from the thirty sets of skirts and petticoats that flew on nimble feet towards them. The last bird, hesitated for a second because Will had his foot on its claw and then as Will leapt to one side, it screeched and flapped its wings wildly as it hopped into the air and bounced off after the others.

The crowd roared its encouragement and thirty girls squealed with excitement as they dodged and swerved around each other, stumbling, colliding, skirts and undergarments flying in disarray as ankles and legs were displayed to the cheering lads and men in the crowd whilst prim mothers and aunts scowled their disapproval and remembered secretly when they had run the race and exposed their limbs with the same disregard for propriety.

'Look at my red lass,' yelled Danny sending Will stumbling with a hearty thwack on the shoulders, 'She nearly had one then.'

Will couldn't have cared less, his eyes were only for Mary who had taken a tumble, 'Sssshh yerself, Danny, Mary's taken a fall and she's wearing no small clothes beneath her petticoats.' Danny followed Will's stare and gaped, 'Aye, that's a beautiful sight,' he whispered as he saw Mary, lying on her stomach and trying to roll on her back. Her skirt and petticoats had been thrown up over her back and truly enough, there was nothing under them to cover the two blushing cheeks, parted thighs and hint of downy hair. Mary rolled over, looked straight into Will's eyes, grinned and totally unabashed, pulled her knees up, forcing the skirt and petticoats even higher, opened her legs for just a brief second, closed them and managed to pull her feet under her buttocks and lift herself to throw her body at a chicken that had, in its excitement, ran in the wrong direction, straight at her.

Will looked at Danny, Danny looked at Will, they both grinned. 'By heaven, Will, she's a beauty from the tips of her toes to the crown of her head and I swear that minnie winked at you.'

Will grinned back and nodded, turning back to hunt out Mary again and silently prayed that the next tumble might loosen her bodice and show her breasts. The objects of his prayer were trying to do just that as they bounced and jiggled under the linen bodice but Will's luck was out. Several times those two mounds of soft warmth nearly escaped from the bodice but never quite made it. There was compensation, however, for another girl had trapped a chicken between her chin and chest and as she struggled to grasp its neck with her teeth, the birds claw dragged at the top of her bodice and pulled it down far enough to let a small, proudly nippled breast spring free. The crowd roared, the girl screamed with embarrassment, the chicken screeched in alarm and escaped, leaving the girl standing with one breast covered, the other on full view and the crowd roared its approval with greater gusto. The girl hunched her shoulders in an attempt to hide the errant breast and ran into the crowd seeking help from her mother.

Everybody's attention returned to the general mêlée just in time to see a triumphant Mary run to the starter with a chicken, its head locked entirely inside her mouth. Six paces from her target, her toe caught on a stone and though she managed to control her cry of pain and keep the chicken's head safely in her mouth, she failed to keep her balance. She fell forward onto her chest, skidded the last foot or two and banged her head against the starter's feet, just as a second girl rushed up with her chicken. The starter bent, took the chicken from Mary, lifted her by the shoulders, spun her round to face the crowd and called loudly above the cacophony of cheers: 'Mary Hardridge wins by a tit!'

Mary's bodice was torn wide open by its passage across the rough ground and the crowd roared its approval at both the starter's wit and the sight of two golden globes rising and falling in pride. Most were unsure whether Mary's pride was for her generous breasts or for winning the chicken chase, perhaps both.

Some minutes later, Mary, her torn bodice trying to hide her two joys and a chicken under one tied arm and a ham under the other presented herself to Will. 'Me father's had a jug or two too many, Will. Will you untie my thumbs seeing as you was the one that tied 'em?'

There was no answer, again Will had gone into a reverie of erotic thought as he gazed into what had now become his vision of heaven.

'Will, will you untie me?' Mary kicked him lightly on the foot.

'Eh! Oh, aye, Mary.'

She turned round with difficulty, trying to keep the chicken and ham safely pressed to her sides until Danny, still awaiting the red-haired girl, offered his assistance: 'Would you like me to hold your hams, Mary?'

'Well,' she turned her head and winked at him, 'depends on what hams ye be referring to, Danny.'

He grinned, both hands darting forward to squeeze her buttocks, 'I reckons as you might be saving these two for another.' And he looked meaningfully at Will, 'But if he ain't at all interested, I'll settle for them.'

'You keeps your hands off my girl, Danny, or you'll have no cobblers to cobble with.'

Danny grinned, relieved Mary of her chicken and ham and held them up, 'I was referring to these.'

'That be a shame then, so you'll have to do something about it yourself, Will Handy.' Mary still had her back to him and she allowed herself to drop back and lean against him.

'If you sauce me, Mary Hardridge, I'll put you over my knee and give you the spanking your father should.'

'Oooh, Will, do you promise?' and she pressed harder against him, feeling his excitement and squirming, enjoying the pressure of his hardening phallus. He groaned and she squirmed harder before pulling away and turning round. 'You're slow in untying my thumbs, so I suppose you'll have to escort me home the way I am, Will.'

'What? Whassat?'

'Well, seeing as you have me at your mercy, I can't run away can I?'

'Whassat?'

Mary stamped her foot, 'Will Handy, will you take my prizes from Danny and take me home afore my dad sobers up!'

Who took who home is a question that neither Mary nor Will could be relied upon to answer. Mary's journey was filled with but two thoughts: how she could entice Will in to doing what she wanted, 'him being a virgin like', and whether she could accomplish her aims before her father sobered up and came home.

Poor Will's world was filled with thoughts of Mary's magnificent breasts, now partly covered by her hastily repaired bodice, and the promise of the rest of her anatomy, much of which he was now aware off from the all too brief glimpse obtained during the chicken chase. 'He could if he wanted too,' he thought; Mary's thumbs were securely tied and she was hardly in a position to prevent him. On the other hand, lacking the necessary experience and relying entirely on instinct (part from his brain and a larger part from the ever swelling appendage that threatened with every step to explode from its breeches prison), he wasn't too confident of carrying off what he wanted with any degree of success. There can be little doubt that Will would have found an excuse to stop and fondle or kiss every part of Mary's lush body but with one hand gripping a large and somewhat slippery ham and the other securely locked around the neck of a protesting chicken, it was all he could do to tread a shaky path. He had to let his eyes devour the parts that his hands and lips, for the moment, were failing to reach.

But home to the Hardridge farm they managed. Mary immediately took charge: 'We'd better not go into the house, Will. Barn would be better.' So barn it was and Will had some difficulty in pulling the crude door open encumbered as he was, and too much of a gentleman to leave it to Mary who couldn't anyway, thumbs secured behind her back as they were.

He managed, as any desperate man in the same situation would, and once safely inside with the door loosely closed he was confronted by a heavily breathing Mary. 'You have me at your mercy, Will. Heavens, I do feel as if my maidenhood' (long since gone) 'is entirely at your mercy.' Will remained motionless, his eyes riveted for one moment on her breasts, the other on her lips. Mary groaned inwardly, this was going to be hard work. 'If you're going to do it to me, as I'm helpless to stop you, then you'd better throw me on the hay, Will.'

There was still no movement from Will, except his eyes which flicked from lips to right tit, back to lips and then on to left tit.

Mary drew the deepest breath she could manage and the crude linen stitches of her blouse reached the point of snapping. 'If you let go of that ham and chicken, Will, why bless me, you could rip my blouse off, tip my skirt and petticoats and feast your eyes on me.' She lifted her bound hands from her back, 'And me as helpless as can be, unable to stop you.'

Slowly, very slowly, the message seeped into Will's numb brain. His left hand relaxed and the ham thudded to the earth floor of the barn, then his right hand followed its fellow's example and the grip on the chicken's neck relaxed, the bird with a cackle of protest dropped to the floor and fled to the pile of hay. The noise awoke some basic instinct in Will's body and he grunted, took a step forward, grabbed Mary around the shoulder and kissed her hard on the lips whilst his free hand groped, fumbled and fought its way down the front of her blouse and at last he had a handful of tit. Mary panted through the kiss, leaned forward and pressed her body into him, forcing her breasts to crush his hand between their bodies and she began to tremble, feeling the deep cleft of her nether regions grow with a fire unquenched by the wetness that flowed freely from her, dampening the front of her petticoats.

'Aaah,' whispered Will as the kiss ended, 'I didn't know they were so warm.'

'What's warm, Will?' asked Mary softly, squirming her hips and groin against the prominent wedge of hardness in his breeches.

'Them titties, Mary. I never thought they'd be warm like that.'

''Course they're warm, Will, they're parts of me.'

'That they are, Mary, that they are without a doubt, but warm?'

'Was you expecting them to be cold then,' Mary pushed her head back and despite the raging fire in her she managed to make a part of her brain think on Will's unusual comment. Her eyes were alive, frantic with her lust, her nose taking air in deep breaths that kept her breasts moving, her mouth held a puzzled frown.

'Aye, I did, they're for holding milk, ain't they. If they're for holding milk and they're warm, the milk'll go off.'

All Mary wanted was for Will to rip open her blouse and take her nipple in his mouth, then she wanted him to throw her on the hay and tear off her skirts and petticoats and, finally, she wanted that eight inches of rock-hard, willow-supple piece of Will to bury itself deep inside her and quench the unbearable fire and pain she was experiencing. 'No wonder there's men who describe women's minnies as fire boxes,' she thought in her passion, 'mine's likely to set fire to me if he doesn't do something soon.' 'Maybe my titties are hot because you're making me stand, Will. Throw me onto hay and have your way with me. Eat my titties for me,

Will . . . Will please, throw me down, I'm helpless to resist, do it, Will. Do it!'

Will snapped. At last the message got through. That which he had been dreaming of all day was at last his. He pushed gently on Mary, forcing her away from him and looked at her: first her half-closed eyes, then her dilated nostrils sucking in air, then her barely parted lips, moist, red, inviting. He pushed her again and she willingly fell back onto the hay, opening her legs as she did so. He stood above her, feverishly rubbing the front of his trousers not sure what to do next but those hidden instincts arose and took over. Fumbling fingers tore at the lace of his breeches and he yanked them down, the top catching on his penis forcing it down and then allowing it to spring up and stand stiff, proud, slightly moist at the tip, hovering over Mary. His shirt followed quickly and Mary was able to feast her eyes on the muscled hardness, the tanned body glinting in the gloom of the barn with a sheen of sweat. At last he was going to take her and judging by the size of that ever-swelling appendage, it was as well her hands were tied because now she felt a fear. Although she had found the one thing in the whole world that was capable of taming her; she desperately wanted that thing between her legs but, its size and girth, its pride, caused a shiver of apprehension to run down her spine and straight into her minnie, adding coals to the raging heat already there.

Suddenly he broke into action, realizing that indeed he had a helpless female at his mercy. He bent, grabbed the front of her blouse and tore it down allowing those golden globes to lay free, open to his fingers, his lips. It was almost his undoing and he felt his manhood jerk. Desperately he closed his eyes and struggled to get the erring phallus back under control. He would have failed and been guilty of premature ejaculation had not the chicken intervened at the critical moment. It suddenly became angered by the intrusion of these two humans into its new world, the hay pile, and jerked its head forward in a spiteful lunge at Will's leg. The beak hit him on the bone of his ankle and pierced the skin. The pain saved Will from an embarrassing failure and the need to kick the offending bird out of his way distracted him for a moment, and his brain used the opportunity to grab the upper hand and issue one instruction to the phallus: WAIT!

The bird sulked off and Will returned his attention to the helpless Mary. Once more he feasted his eyes on her tits, bending again he grabbed her skirt and petticoats at the hem and with one strong pull, skidded them over her buttocks, slithered them down her thighs and threw them across the barn. Now he had her and slowly he knelt between her spread legs, feasting on the soft downy opening at the top of her thighs, noting the wetness there. He bent his head and kissed her minnie without making any irrelevant remarks on the heat he felt.

Mary exploded, arching her back, thrusting her groin at his face, squealing, 'Will, oh, Will, eat me, dear god, eat me, use your tongue, suck me into you, Will!' and as he obeyed, she started her shivering again and her head threshed from side to side as she felt the build-up and then, with a shuddering gasp that became a scream of passion, she flooded into his mouth. He buried his face deeper, drinking her in, feeling the gush of her passion juices.

She groaned deeply and he lifted her head, for a moment believing he had done her harm. Her eyes fluttered open, her lips parted in a smile and she said: 'Again. Again, Will. I've never had the likes of that before.'

He slowly ran his tongue from the heaven between her thighs, over the slight swell of her stomach and found the tiny hole in her belly. He dwelt there, running his tongue around its perimeter, darting it in to tickle the shallow hole until he felt her body begin to move under him. Slowly, agonizingly slowly, he let his tongue travel upwards, following the under curve of her breasts, lingering again as he felt her respond, little cries coming from her, sudden shakes of passion as he explored this unexpected erogenous zone. If her hands had been free, Mary would have grabbed his head and pressed him into the underside of her breasts. As it was, she was not in control, neither her own body or his were within her grasp. She lifted the whole of her body save head and heels from the straw as his tongue tickled its way over her breasts to find a rock-hard, inflamed nipple. She screamed as his lips covered the auriola, his teeth nipping lightly on the nipple. She screamed louder as his teeth tightened their grip and she felt searing pokers of fire spread from her breast, down her stomach to end in her womanhood, building up again the raging fire. She squirmed, screamed, gasped and pushed her body up to him, feeling his phallus lying on her thigh, growing, growing, growing.

'Now, Will. Now!' she gasped knowing that if he didn't enter her and poke that fire, she would explode, first her tits as his fingers played with her free nipple, then her stomach which ripped with the agony of frustrated passion, then her minnie. 'Now, Will, ROGER ME!'

Without finesse, beyond such subtleties, he lifted his head, found her lips, lifted his hips and found her minnie. With one gasping, slow but forceful stroke, he entered her and collapsed, his phallus buried to its limits, his scrotum struggling to join its master in this heated, wet paradise. His chest crushed her breasts and he moved against her feeling the hard nipples scratch at him. He bruised his lips against her, lifted his hips pulling his manhood to the point of eviction before thrusting it hard and deeply into her again. She gurgled her approval, her thighs opening further for him, her legs bending around him, heels firmly pressing at his buttocks as she tried to force more of him into her. She hurt, she delighted with her pain and she lifted herself, carrying his weight, pulling her lips away from his to groan then letting loose a soft, prolonged squeal of pleasure knowing that there was more to come. Her passion broke down any patience left and she pulled back and thrust up to him again, feeling him lift his head, arching his back as he fought to regain control.

He met her movements, thrusting himself into her, withdrawing and thrusting again, feeling her legs squeezing, trying to crush his waist. He grabbed her breast, caressing, squeezing, making her thresh beneath him as she closed on the moment of ultimate passion. Desperate for him, she willed him to explode his seed in her, bring her to relief, but not wanting him to in the next moment, as his lips closed on her nipple again and he buried his head in her warm, soft, woman-scented flesh. His movements became urgent, then desperate as his own moment came. For the briefest second he told himself to withdraw for fear of making her pregnant but then gave up and as he felt the pressure build in his bag, then up along his manhood, he buried his head deeper into her breasts, shouted her name just once and surrendered to the shuddering, nerve-shattering moment of orgasm just as Mary gave her own wild cry, shuddered and surrendered to her all-engulfing fire and gave her body, her mind, her soul to him.

For minutes afterwards he lay on top of her, soaking in her juices as his soaked into her. He kissed each nipple, lifted his head and smiled into her eyes, 'Mary, Mary, Mary.'

She smiled back, just able to whisper; 'Aye, Will, that was truly magic.'

The door of the barn crashed open and the drunken figure of Mary's father staggered into the barn. 'There ye are, Mary Hardridge, There ye are.'

Frightened out of his life, Will looked over his shoulder at the man as he approached, swinging an axe in his right hand. Joseph Hardridge staggered up to their prone, locked bodies, squinted at her, then him, 'Will, what you at?' He lifted his arm, swung the axe and Will shuddered, his body tensed as he waited for the blow that would sever his head. There was a sudden gush of hot blood and Will let out a strangled cry and a second gush of hot blood splattered across Mary's breasts, glowing a shiny red and mixing with her sweat. Will dropped his head, pressed himself into Mary's body and she shivered as she heard the screech cut off.

'You'd be better looking after your father, Mary. A deal better. Here I am, starving for my dinner after the fayre and you're a pleasuring yourself. What sort of daughter are you, eh?' Joseph Hardridge bent, recovered first the ham then the chicken, wiped the blood-soaked feathers on the hay, grunted and walked out of the barn mumbling as he went, 'Suppos'n I'll have to prepare my own dinner.'

Behind him, Will shuddered and slowly opened his eyes to stare straight into the eyes of the chicken's severed head. He fainted.

THE SECRET OF THE GROWING GOLD

Bram Stoker

WHEN Margaret Delandre went to live at Brent's Rock the whole neighbourhood awoke to the pleasure of an entirely new scandal. Scandals in connection with either the Delandre family or the Brents of Brent's Rock were not few; and if the secret history of the county had been written in full both names would have been found well represented. It is true that the status of each was so different that they might have belonged to different continents – or to different worlds for the matter of that – for hitherto their orbits had never crossed. The Brents were accorded by the whole section of the country a unique social dominance, and had ever held themselves as high above the yeoman class to which Margaret Delandre belonged, as a blue-blooded Spanish hidalgo out-tops his peasant tenantry.

The Delandres had an ancient record and were proud of it in their way as the Brents were of theirs. But the family had never risen above yeomanry and although they had been once well-to-do in the good old times of foreign wars and protection, their fortunes had withered under the scorching of the free trade sun and the 'piping times of peace'. They had, as the elder members used to assert, 'stuck to the land', with the result that they had taken root in it, body and soul. In fact, they, having chosen the life of vegetables, had flourished as vegetation does – blossomed and thrived in the good season and suffered in the bad. Their holding, Dander's Croft, seemed to have been worked out, and to be typical of the family which had inhabited it. The latter had declined generation after generation, sending out now and again some abortive shoot of unsatisfied energy in the shape of a soldier or sailor, who had worked his way to the minor grades of the services and had there stopped, cut short either from unheeding gallantry in action or from that destroying cause to men without breeding or youthful care – the recognition of a position above them which they feel unfitted to fill. So, little by little, the family dropped lower and lower, the men brooding and dissatisfied, and drinking themselves into the grave, the women drudging at home, or marrying beneath them – or worse. In process of time all disappeared, leaving only two in the Croft, Wykham Delandre and his sister Margaret. The man and woman seemed to have inherited in masculine and feminine form respectively the evil tendency of their race, sharing in common the principles, though manifesting them in different ways, of sullen passion, voluptuousness and recklessness.

The history of the Brents had been something similar, but showing the causes of decadence in their aristocratic and not their plebeian forms. They, too, had sent their shoots to the wars; but their positions had been different and they had often attained honour – for without flaw they were gallant, and brave deeds were done by them before the selfish dissipation which marked them had sapped their vigour.

The present head of the family – if family it could now be called when one remained of the direct line – was Geoffrey

Brent. He was almost a type of worn-out race, manifesting in some ways its most brilliant qualities, and in others its utter degradation. He might be fairly compared with some of those antique Italian nobles whom the painters have preserved to us with their courage, their unscrupulousness, their refinement of lust and cruelty – the voluptuary actual with the fiend potential. He was certainly handsome, with that dark, aquiline, commanding beauty which women so generally recognize as dominant. With men he was distant and cold; but such a bearing never deters womankind. The inscrutable laws of sex have so arranged that even a timid woman is not afraid of a fierce and haughty man. And so it was that there was hardly a woman of any kind or degree, who lived within view of Brent's Rock, who did not cherish some form of secret admiration for the handsome wastrel. The category was a wide one, for Brent's Rock rose up steeply from the midst of a level region and for a circuit of a hundred miles it lay on the horizon, with its high old towers and steep roofs cutting the level edge of wood and hamlet, and far-scattered mansions.

So long as Geoffrey Brent confined his dissipations to London and Paris and Vienna – anywhere out of sight and sound of his home – opinion was silent. It is easy to listen to far-off echoes unmoved, and we can treat them with disbelief, or scorn, or disdain, or whatever attitude of coldness may suit our purpose. But when the scandal came close to home it was another matter; and the feelings of independence and integrity which is in people of every community which is not utterly spoiled, asserted itself and demanded that condemnation should be expressed. Still there was a certain reticence in all, and no more notice was taken of the existing facts than was absolutely necessary. Margaret Delandre bore herself so fearlessly and so openly – she accepted her position as the justified companion of Geoffrey Brent so naturally that people came to believe that she was secretly married to him, and therefore thought it wiser to hold their tongues lest time should justify her and also make her an active enemy.

The one person who, by his interference, could have settled all doubts was debarred by circumstances from interfering in the matter. Wykham Delandre had quarrelled with his sister – or perhaps it was that she had quarrelled with him – and they were on terms not merely of armed neutrality but of bitter hatred. The quarrel had been antecedent to Margaret going to Brent's Rock. She and Wykham had almost come to blows. There had certainly been threats on one side and on the other; and in the end Wykham, overcome with passion, had ordered his sister to leave his house. She had risen straightway, and, without waiting to pack up even her own personal belongings, had walked out of the house. On the threshold she had paused for a moment to hurl a bitter threat at Wykham that he would rue in shame and despair to the last hour of his life his act of that day. Some weeks had since passed; and it was understood in the neighbourhood that Margaret had gone to London, when she suddenly appeared driving out with Geoffrey Brent, and the entire neighbourhood knew before nightfall that she had taken up her abode at the Rock. It was no subject of surprise that Brent had come back unexpectedly, for such was his usual custom. Even his own servants never knew when to expect him, for there was a private door, of which he alone had the key, by which he sometimes entered without anyone in the house being aware of his coming. This was his usual method of appearing after a long absence.

Wykham Delandre was furious at the news. He vowed vengeance – and to keep his mind level with his passion drank deeper than ever. He tried several times to see his sister, but she contemptuously refused to meet him. He tried to have an interview with Brent and was refused by him also. Then he tried to stop him in the road, but without avail, for

Geoffrey was not a man to be stopped against his will. Several actual encounters took place between the two men, and many more were threatened and avoided. At last Wykham Delandre settled down to a morose, vengeful acceptance of the situation.

Neither Margaret nor Geoffrey was of a pacific temperament, and it was not long before there began to be quarrels between them. One thing would lead to another, and wine flowed freely at Brent's Rock. Now and again the quarrels would assume a bitter aspect, and threats would be exchanged in uncompromising language that fairly awed the listening servants. But such quarrels generally ended where domestic altercations do, in reconciliation, and in a mutual respect for the fighting qualities proportionate to their manifestation. Fighting for its own sake is found by a certain class of persons, all the world over, to be a matter of absorbing interest, and there is no reason to believe that domestic conditions minimize its potency. Geoffrey and Margaret made occasional absences from Brent's Rock, and on each of these occasions Wykham Delandre also absented himself; but as he generally heard of the absence too late to be of any service, he returned home each time in a more bitter and discontented frame of mind than before.

At last there came a time when the absence from Brent's Rock became longer than before. Only a few days earlier there had been a quarrel, exceeding in bitterness anything which had gone before; but this, too, had been made up, and a trip on the Continent had been mentioned before the servants. After a few days Wykham Delandre also went away, and it was some weeks before he returned. It was noticed that he was full of some new importance – satisfaction, exaltation – they hardly knew how to call it. He went straightaway to Brent's Rock, and demanded to see Geoffrey Brent, and on being told that he had not yet returned, said, with a grim decision which the servants noted:

'I shall come again. My news is solid – it can wait!' and turned away. Week after week went by, and month after month; and then there came a rumour, certified later on, that an accident had occurred in the Zermatt valley. Whilst crossing a dangerous pass the carriage containing an English lady and the driver had fallen over a precipice, the gentleman of the party, Mr Geoffrey Brent, having been fortunately saved as he had been walking up the hill to ease the horses. He gave information, and search was made. The broken rail, the excoriated roadway, the marks where the horses had struggled on the decline before finally pitching over into the torrent – all told the sad tale. It was a wet season, and there had been much snow in the winter, so that the river was swollen beyond its usual volume, and the eddies of the stream were packed with ice. All search was made, and finally the wreck of the carriage and the body of one horse were found in an eddy of the river. Later on the body of the driver was found on the sandy, torrent-swept waste near Täsch; but the body of the lady, like that of the other horse, had quite disappeared, and was – what was left of it by that time – whirling amongst the eddies of the Rhone on its way down to the Lake of Geneva.

Wykham Delandre made all the enquiries possible, but could not find any trace of the missing woman. He found, however, in the books of the various hotels the name of 'Mr and Mrs Geoffrey Brent'. And he had a stone erected at Zermatt to his sister's memory, under her married name, and a tablet put up in the church at Bretten, the parish in which both Brent's Rock and Dander's Croft were situated.

There was a lapse of nearly a year, after the excitement of the matter had worn away, and the whole neighbourhood had gone on its accustomed way. Brent was still absent, and Delandre more drunken, more morose, and more revengeful than before.

Then there was a new excitement. Brent's Rock was being

made ready for a new mistress. It was officially announced by Geoffrey himself in a letter to the Vicar, that he had been married some months before to an Italian lady, and that they were on their way home. Then a small army of workmen invaded the house; and hammer and plane sounded, and a general air of size and paint pervaded the atmosphere. One wing of the old house, the south, was entirely redone; and then the great body of the workmen departed, leaving only materials for the doing of the old hall when Geoffrey Brent should have returned, for he had directed that the decoration was only to be done under his own eyes. He had brought with him accurate drawings of a hall in the house of his bride's father, for he wished to reproduce for her the place to which she had been accustomed. As the moulding had all to be redone, some scaffolding poles and boards were brought in and laid on one side of the great hall, and also a great wooden tank or box for mixing the lime, which was laid in bags beside it.

When the new mistress of Brent's Rock arrived the bells of the church rang out, and there was a general jubilation. She was a beautiful creature, full of the poetry and fire and passion of the South; and the few English words which she had learned were spoken in such a sweet and pretty broken way that she won the hearts of the people almost as much by the music of her voice as by the melting beauty of her dark eyes.

Geoffrey Brent seemed more happy than he had ever before appeared; but there was a dark, anxious look on his face that was new to those who knew him of old, and he started at times as though at some noise that was unheard by others.

And so months passed and the whisper grew that at last Brent's Rock was to have an heir. Geoffrey was very tender to his wife, and the new bond between them seemed to soften him. He took more interest in his tenants and their needs than he had ever done; and works of charity on his part as well as on his sweet young wife's were not lacking. He seemed to have set all his hopes on the child that was coming, and as he looked deeper into the future the dark shadow that had come over his face seemed to die gradually away.

All the time Wykham Delandre nursed his revenge. Deep in his heart had grown up a purpose of vengeance which only waited an opportunity to crystallize and take a definite shape. His vague idea was somehow centred in the wife of Brent, for he knew that he could strike him best through those he loved, and the coming time seemed to hold in its womb the opportunity for which he longed. One night he sat alone in the living-room of his house. It had once been a handsome room in its way, but time and neglect had done their work and it was now little better than a ruin, without dignity or picturesqueness of any kind. He had been drinking heavily for some time and was more than half-stupefied. He thought he heard a noise as of someone at the door and looked up. Then he called half savagely to come in; but there was no response. With a muttered blasphemy he renewed his potations. Presently he forgot all around him, sank into a daze, but suddenly awoke to see standing before him someone or something like a battered, ghostly edition of his sister. For a few moments there came upon him a sort of fear. The woman before him, with distorted features and burning eyes seemed hardly human, and the only thing that seemed a reality of his sister, as she had been, was her wealth of golden hair, and this was now streaked with grey. She eyed her brother with a long, cold stare; and he, too, as he looked and began to realize the actuality of her presence, found the hatred of her which he had had, once again surging up in his heart. All the brooding passion of the past year seemed to find a voice at once as he asked her:

'Why are you here? You're dead and buried.'

'I am here, Wykham Delandre, for no love of you, but because I hate another even more than I do you!' A great passion blazed in her eyes.

'Him?' he asked, in so fierce a whisper that even the woman was for an instant startled till she regained her calm.

'Yes, him!' she answered. 'But make no mistake, my revenge is my own; and I merely use you to help me to it.' Wykham asked suddenly;

'Did he marry you?'

The woman's distorted face broadened out in a ghastly attempt at a smile. It was a hideous mockery, for the broken features and seamed scars took strange shapes and strange colours, and queer lines of white showed out as the straining muscles pressed on the old cicatrices.

'So you would like to know! It would please your pride to feel that your sister was truly married! Well, you shall not know. That was my revenge on you, and I do not mean to change it by a hair's breadth. I have come here tonight simply to let you know that I am alive, so that if any violence be done me where I am going there may be a witness.'

'Where are you going?' demanded her brother.

'That is my affair! and I have not the least intention of letting you know!' Wykham stood up, but the drink was on him and he reeled and fell. As he lay on the floor he announced his intention of following his sister; and with an outburst of splenetic humour told her that he would follow her through the darkness by the light of her hair, and of her beauty. At this she turned on him, and said that there were others beside him that would rue her hair and her beauty too. 'As he will,' she hissed; 'for the hair remains though the beauty be gone. When he withdrew the lynch-pin and sent us over the precipice into the torrent, he had little thought of my beauty. Perhaps his beauty would be scarred like mine were he whirled, as I was, among the rocks of the Visp, and frozen on the ice pack in the drift of the river. But let him beware! His time is coming!' and with a fierce gesture she flung open the door and passed out into the night.

Later on that night, Mrs Brent, who was but half-asleep, became suddenly awake and spoke to her husband:

'Geoffrey, was not that the click of a lock somewhere below our window?'

But Geoffrey – though she thought that he, too, had started at the noise – seemed sound asleep, and breathed heavily. Again Mrs Brent dozed; but this time awoke to the fact that her husband had arisen and was partially dressed. He was deadly pale, and when the light of the lamp which he had in his hand fell on his face, she was frightened at the look in his eyes.

'What is it, Geoffrey? What dost thou?' she asked.

'Hush! little one,' he answered, in a strange, hoarse voice. 'Go to sleep. I am restless, and wish to finish some work I left undone.'

'Bring it here, my husband,' she said; 'I am lonely and I fear when thou art away.'

For reply he merely kissed her and went out, closing the door behind him. She lay awake for a while, and then nature asserted itself, and she slept.

Suddenly she started broad awake with the memory in her ears of a smothered cry from somewhere not far off. She jumped up and ran to the door and listened, but there was no sound. She grew alarmed for her husband, and called out: 'Geoffrey! Geoffrey!'

After a few moments the door of the great hall opened, and Geoffrey appeared at it, but without his lamp.

'Hush!' he said, in a sort of whisper, and his voice was harsh and stern. 'Hush! Get to bed! I am working, and must not be disturbed. Go to sleep, and do not wake the house!'

With a chill in her heart – for the harshness of her husband's voice was new to her – she crept back to bed and lay there trembling, too frightened to cry, and listened to every sound. There was a long pause of silence, and then the sound of some iron implement striking muffled blows! Then there came a clang of a heavy stone falling, followed by a muffled curse. Then a dragging sound, and then more noise of stone on stone. She lay all the while in an agony of fear, and her heart beat dreadfully. She heard a curious sort of scraping sound; and then there was silence. Presently the door opened gently, and Geoffrey appeared. His wife pretended to be asleep; but through her eyelashes she saw him wash from his hands something white that looked like lime.

In the morning he made no allusion to the previous night, and she was afraid to ask any question.

From that day there seemed some shadow over Geoffrey Brent. He neither ate nor slept as he had been accustomed, and his former habit of turning suddenly as though someone were speaking from behind him revived. The old hall seemed to have some kind of fascination for him. He used to go there many times in the day, but grew impatient if anyone, even his wife, entered it. When the builder's foreman came to inquire about continuing his work Geoffrey was out driving; the man went into the hall, and when Geoffrey returned the servant told him of his arrival and where he was. With a frightful oath he pushed the servant aside and hurried up to the old hall. The workman met him almost at the door; and as Geoffrey burst into the room he ran against him. The man apologized:

'Beg pardon, sir, but I was just going out to make some enquiries. I directed twelve sacks of lime to be sent here, but I see there are only ten.'

'Damn the ten sacks and the twelve too!' was the ungracious and incomprehensible rejoinder.

The workman looked surprised, and tried to turn the conversation.

'I see, sir, there is a little matter which our people must have done; but the governor will of course see it set right at his own cost.'

'What do you mean?'

'That 'ere 'arth-stone, sir: Some idiot must have put a scaffold pole on it and cracked it right down the middle, and it's thick enough you'd think to stand hanythink.' Geoffrey was silent for quite a minute, and then said in a constrained voice and with much gentler manner:

'Tell your people that I am not going on with the work in the hall at present. I want to leave it as it is for a while longer.'

'All right sir. I'll send up a few of our chaps to take away these poles and lime bags and tidy the place up a bit.'

'No! No!' said Geoffrey, 'leave them where they are. I shall send and tell you when you are to get on with the work.' So the foreman went away, and his comment to his master was:

'I'd send in the bill, sir, for the work already done. 'Pears to me that money's a little shaky in that quarter.'

Once or twice Delandre tried to stop Brent on the road, and, at last, finding that he could not attain his object rode after the carriage, calling out:

'What has become of my sister, your wife?' Geoffrey lashed his horses into a gallop, and the other, seeing from his white face and from his wife's collapse almost into a faint that his object was attained, rode away with a scowl and a laugh.

That night when Geoffrey went into the hall he passed over to the great fireplace, and all at once started back with a smothered cry. Then with an effort he pulled himself together and went away, returning with a light. He bent down over the broken hearth-stone to see if the moonlight falling through the storied window had in any way deceived him. Then with a groan of anguish he sank to his knees.

There, sure enough, through the crack in the broken stone were protruding a multitude of threads of golden hair just tinged with grey!

He was disturbed by a noise at the door, and looking round, saw his wife standing in the doorway. In the desperation of the moment he took action to prevent discovery, and lighting a match at the lamp, stooped down and burned away the hair that rose through the broken stone. Then rising nonchalantly as he could, he pretended surprise at seeing his wife beside him.

For the next week he lived in an agony; for, whether by accident or design, he could not find himself alone in the hall for any length of time. At each visit the hair had grown afresh through the crack, and he had to watch it carefully lest his terrible secret should be discovered. He tried to find a receptacle for the body of the murdered woman outside the house, but someone always interrupted him; and once, when he was coming out of the private doorway, he was met by his wife, who began to question him about it, and manifested surprise that she should not have before noticed the key which he now reluctantly showed her. Geoffrey dearly and passionately loved his wife, so that any possibility of her discovering his dread secrets, or even of doubting him, filled him with anguish; and after a couple of days had passed, he could not help coming to the conclusion that, at least, she suspected something.

That very evening she came into the hall after her drive and found him there sitting moodily by the deserted fireplace. She spoke to him directly.

'Geoffrey, I have been spoken to by that fellow Delandre, and he says horrible things. He tells to me that a week ago his sister returned to this house, the wreck and ruin of her former self, with only her golden hair as of old, and announced some fell intention. He asked me where she is –

and oh, Geoffrey, she is dead, she is dead! So how can she have returned? Oh! I am in dread, and I know not where to turn!'

For answer, Geoffrey burst into a torrent of blasphemy which made her shudder. He cursed Delandre and his sister and all their kind, and in especial he hurled curse after curse on her golden hair.

'Oh, hush! hush!' she said, and was then silent, for she feared her husband when she saw the evil effect of his humour. Geoffrey in the torrent of his anger stood up and moved away from the hearth; but suddenly stopped as he saw a new look of terror in his wife's eyes. He followed their glance, and then he too, shuddered – for there on the broken hearth-stone lay a golden streak as the point of the hair rose through the crack.

'Look, look!' she shrieked. 'Is it some ghost of the dead! Come away – come away!' and seizing her husband by the wrist with the frenzy of madness, she pulled him from the room.

That night she was in a raging fever. The doctor of the district attended her at once, and special aid was telegraphed for to London. Geoffrey was in despair, and in his anguish at the danger to his young wife almost forgot his own crime and its consequences. In the evening the doctor had to leave to attend to others; but he left Geoffrey in charge of his wife. His last words were:

'Remember, you must humour her till I come in the morning, or till some other doctor has her case in hand. What you have to dread is another attack of emotion. See that she is kept warm. Nothing more can be done.'

Late in the evening, when the rest of the household had retired, Geoffrey's wife got up from her bed and called to her husband.

'Come!' she said. 'Come to the old hall! I know where the gold comes from! I want to see it grow!'

Geoffrey would fain have stopped her, but he feared for her life or reason on the one hand, and lest in a paroxysm she should shriek out her terrible suspicion, and seeing that it was useless to try to prevent her, wrapped a warm rug around her and went with her to the old hall. When they entered, she turned and shut the door and locked it.

'We want no strangers amongst us three tonight!' she whispered with a wan smile.

'We three! nay we are but two,' said Geoffrey with a shudder; he feared to say more.

'Sit here,' said his wife as she put out the light. 'Sit here by the hearth and watch the gold growing. The silver moonlight is jealous! See, it steals along the floor towards the gold – our gold!' Geoffrey looked with growing horror, and saw that during the hours that had passed the golden hair had protruded further through the broken hearth-stone. He tried to hide it by placing his feet over the broken place; and his wife, drawing her chair beside him, leant over and laid her head on his shoulder.

'Now do not stir, dear,' she said; 'let us sit still and watch. We shall find the secret of the growing gold!' He passed his arm around her and sat silent; and as the moonlight stole along the floor she sank to sleep.

He feared to wake her; and so sat silent and miserable as the hours stole away.

Before his horror-struck eyes the golden hair from the broken stone grew and grew; and as it increased, so his heart got colder and colder, till at last he had not power to stir, and sat with eyes full of terror watching his doom.

In the morning when the London doctor came, neither Geoffrey nor his wife could be found. Search was made in all the rooms, but without avail. As a last resource the great door of the old hall was broken open, and those who entered saw a grim and sorry sight.

There by the deserted hearth Geoffrey Brent and his young wife sat cold and white and dead. Her face was peaceful, and her eyes were closed in sleep; but his face was a sight that made all who saw shudder, for there was on it a look of unutterable horror. The eyes were open and stared glassily at his feet, which were twined with tresses of golden hair, streaked with grey, which came through the broken hearth-stone.

CATHERINE WOULD

Sidney Gray

WE often brushed past each other at work. My hand would gently touch her back, hers would lie on my side for the briefest of moments. She'd tease me. She liked to play it as a game. She'd get me alone in the storeroom and see how far I'd let her go before my anxiety got the better of me. She'd kiss me. She'd have me pushed back against the wall. The light would be off, but my face would be as clear as day, illuminated by the pool of light falling in through the porthole window from the corridor outside. She'd let me touch her breasts, urging my fingers in between the buttons of her blouse. Her hands would roam freely inside my shirt, I'd feel her nails. She'd be so very close up against me, her hips against mine. She'd threaten to loosen my belt . . .

'Catherine, I can't . . . No, Catherine, please. Come on, please. What if . . .?'

And she'd laugh at me, taunt me. Flick her hair, lick her lips. She'd leave me alone in the dark storeroom to straighten myself up and cool the flush in my cheeks, vowing to myself that one day, one day . . .

I loved her completely. Out of work my world was still full of her, my head spinning with missed opportunities I'd suddenly realize I should have taken. I would sit at home and wait for her call. I'd bought a portable phone especially and it followed me throughout the flat. It sat next to the microwave during meal times, and on the cabinet shelf next to my toothbrush and electric razor when I was in the bath, and next to my alarm clock throughout the night. I waited for the call telling me her husband was out, away, had left and wouldn't be back until later. Frustration would rise in me, the need to see her, and I would often fight with myself. But my patience was stronger than my frustration. I wasn't stupid.

Of course, she'd given me a secret to keep. She was well liked, she had plenty of friends, I don't think I'd ever heard one word said against her. Nobody would have believed she was capable of this. No one we worked with would ever think she'd go behind Anthony's back, he was *such* a nice guy, *such* a great husband. Everybody would say that Catherine would never have an affair.

Of course, I knew she would.

She was older than me by several years, I guessed about thirty, but I never asked. She wasn't quite as tall as me. When we hugged I could just see over the top of her head, she sometimes stood on her tip-toes to kiss me. Her hair was very short, close cropped, and very dark. She looked foreign, although she claimed her family had never set foot outside London. She was truly beautiful and I would often fantasize about telling people of our affair. I knew how wonderful it would make me feel to walk the streets arm and arm with her, because I knew the kind of comments she drew from the other men at work, how lucky they all thought Anthony was. Even Carter's tasteless, lecherous comments could make me feel proud. He was always carrying one story or another about some woman he'd met at the weekend or the night before, but he'd never so much as laid a finger on Catherine.

Oh, Carter, if only you knew, I used to think. If only you knew she was with me.

We often met in the open, but we were only ever in the company of strangers. They were secret places to us. The playground at the back of Eastfield's Primary School. The student coffee shop on Humber Street. And the Blue Button; a small, tired-looking pub on the road to Birchill. That was where we went most often, and only ever at night. We knew nobody there and they never gave us too much of their attention. We always sat at the same table; in an alcove set into the wall and to the side of the real fire, hiding our faces behind the flicker of the shadows as we talked. Catherine liked to talk. She'd drink red wine and tell me all about her ambitions and her desires. She often told me about how Anthony held her back because he had no dreams. He was happy with what he had and she felt sorry for him because she knew there was so much more in the world. The talk always came first, then we'd make love in the car somewhere on the way home.

Catherine always drove, even if we were in my car. She'd find a dark, narrow country lane and pull over. Sometimes, if we were lucky, a farmer would have left a gate open into a field and we could pull in to hide behind the hedge. But more often than not the grass verge under the cover of tall trees would have to do. I'd recline the passenger seat. Catherine would sit astride me. We'd kiss. She loved to be kissed; on her neck, behind her ears, in the dimple of skin where her throat met her breast bone. She had so many little places that made her shiver. I always explored them all. Condensation would form on the car windows and we'd be enclosed in our own private world.

Once, on a cold, crisp night after a fresh snowfall Catherine wanted to make love in the open. We parked the car near to a small copse of trees and stripped naked. The stars were very bright, every single pinprick one of them was clear and distinct. The snow was icy and exhilarating between our toes as we ran into the cover of the copse, shrouded in short misty breaths. Catherine's skin was tight, taut as a drum, stretched with the cold, and every time I placed my fingertips upon it she shuddered as my touch rippled across her whole body. She hugged a silver birch to her chest as we made love. The whole world was freezing around me. Apart from Catherine; she was so very warm around me.

We made love again when we returned to the car to ease the heat back into our bodies. And when she switched on the headlights to drive away, the only marks to be seen in the snow were ours.

Catherine's passion excited me, the flippancy and the immediacy of our love-making, but I think I'd always known that it would eventually lead to our undoing. She used to laugh at my cautiousness, tease me with the exact same flippancy she knew could just as easily arouse as unnerve me. Maybe that was how she preferred me. Maybe it excited her to see me timid, flustered.

The only time she ever invited me back to her house was once when Anthony was there. I wasn't expecting to see him. We sat and chatted about work and the weather, the three of us sitting across the living room from each other, with the invisible lines of the triangle drawn between us through the coffee table and around the back of the television set. I didn't dare touch anything. I was scared I'd leave fingerprints that he would one day recognize on the body of his wife. But Catherine didn't seem to care, she acted the perfect hostess, she made sure I had enough tea and chocolate biscuits. She even asked me if I had a girlfriend and my flustered, embarrassed silence amused her. But when she gave me a lift home we made love with such ferocity that I wasn't able to sleep that night. I could still feel where her hips had pressed, the weight of her body, and where her hands had gripped my shoulders. I lay staring up into the darkness of my room and realized just how much I loved this woman. This woman who was teaching me how to love. This woman whose knowledge of love was surely boundless. And I decided to tell her exactly how I felt.

I told her at the Christmas party. I'd had enough to drink to be able to find my courage in between everybody else's cheer and laughter.

I was surrounded by bloated faces; pissed, guffawing, fed-to-the-brim faces, not really the faces I saw every day at work. But the only face I was watching was Catherine's. She was sitting opposite me at the table. She was wearing a red paper party hat on her head. It was ripped at the side because her drunken fingers had been clumsy. It had fallen out of the cracker I had pulled with her. She wouldn't let me read the prophecy that had fallen out with it, she wouldn't tell me her fortune.

'I need to talk to you,' I told her. 'Is there anywhere we can go?'

She leaned forward across the table towards me. Her eyes were so very bright. 'Not if all you want to do is talk,' she said.

'It's important.'

She mocked me with a smile. 'Then I suppose I shouldn't really refuse, should I?'

It was easy enough to slip away from the party when the tables were cleared and the dancing started. I was nervous, but only because of what I had to say. I was determined the words wouldn't get stuck.

Down the bright corridor from the restaurant was a function room with a stage. Catherine swept me inside through the swinging double doors. The room was a maze of empty tables and chairs all waiting for their party maybe tomorrow night, maybe at the weekend. There was a bar to our left, Carlsberg towels thrown across the pumps, the light from the bottle fridge was all we had to see by. But there was a door behind the bar and the occasional chink of glasses could be heard, and a man's voice low and indistinct; apart from this the room was silent. Catherine leaned me up against the wall and we kissed.

'You're not doing much talking,' she teased, kissing me again before I had time to reply. 'You drag me away from the party to tell me something really important, and then don't say a word.' Her hands were already pulling my shirt out from my trousers. 'You've brought me here under false pretences.' She ran her hands underneath my shirt, her fingers up and down my spine, then rested them on the back of my belt. 'That's what they call it: False pretences.' She pushed her hands inside my belt. 'I could have you arrested.' And slid them over and around my hips.

The words were inside me and longing to come out. I had hold of her shoulders as if I were going to shake her and shout them into her face. But maybe my desire to tell her how I felt became confused with my desire to touch her.

The alcohol in my system blurred the edges of my movements. I found the world around me as if it were yielding to my touch. I turned Catherine around, slowly, moving her away from the door and resting her back against the bar. Her long, red dress was fluid through my fingers, flowing down to the floor, a puddle of crimson silk at my feet. Her naked, seamless body filled my eyes, my hands and then my mouth. I listened to Catherine's breath. Behind it I could hear the muted music from the party we had just left; the beat of the songs seemed so dull compared to the beat of my heart.

Every curve, every cup of her body looked perfect to me, everything fitted so well. I ran my fingers round from the back of her neck to the smooth flesh at her throat. Then took my fingers down between her breasts, lightly scratching with my nails, all the way to her belly. There were no marks or blemishes, no faults or imperfections that I could feel. Except the string of tiny goosebumps my nails had left.

I kissed the half-moon shadow underneath her breasts. I knelt and kissed her small, curved belly. I put my hands on her hips, gently squeezing the rounded bones. She ran her fingers through my hair, she kneaded the back of my neck.

She lifted herself up to sit on the bar. Then laid herself out on the shiny, wooden surface. The light from the bottle fridge illuminated her in a slice from navel to neck. The shadows thrown across her body were like lingerie meant to tease.

'Kiss me here,' she told me. 'Touch me here. Like this.' And I did as I was told. I watched her as she moved her hands across her own body, and where she touched, my lips and my fingers followed. She moved to help me, lifting her hips, arching her back. She shuddered lightly, a shiver of pleasure. Her breath trembled, quickening, the tiniest of sobs escaped. Where she pointed I kissed, sometimes touching her tenderly with the tip of my tongue, sometimes sucking hungrily at her flesh.

The alcohol was forgotten, I was drunk on Catherine's body. I had never felt . . . Her skin was so very soft, so very warm. I ran my hands over her, wanting to touch all of her, everywhere. I wanted to hold her, hug her hard, close, never let her go. I was shivering now. *My* breath was trembling now. All of her. Everywhere. I found new places to kiss her. The palms of her hands. The crease of her knee. The silky pale skin on the inside of her thighs . . .

A noise startled me. A door somewhere? And I drew away from her, shocked as if from a dream. But she only giggled.

'We're not at work now,' she said. 'You can't run away from me here.' She sat herself upright, swinging her legs around and wrapping me up in them. She held me tight. 'Now,' she whispered. 'Touch me just here.'

I stepped forward, letting her legs pull me towards her. I still didn't feel fully in control of myself. I felt as if I were in a daze, a daydream. I could not have told her my name if she'd asked. I could not see, think or feel beyond Catherine.

'Here,' she told me, one hand showing my fingers where she meant, the other unbuckling my belt.

I stepped up onto the brass rail at the foot of the bar. But hesitated. I had to say it. Before she completely stole me, before I was forever pulled from my mind because of her, I had to tell her.

She held her head on one side. She frowned slightly.

I wouldn't meet her gaze. I looked at her, almost a silhouette with her back to the light; the shape of her against that pale light. But I couldn't look her in the eyes. I stared anywhere but at her eyes.

Then slowly, I said: 'I think I love you.'

And she held me close, her legs tighter still around me. Her arms joining them in the embrace, her head resting lightly on my shoulder.

But again I heard a noise. Although I tried to ignore it this time. It was stealing my dream.

'Make love to me,' she said. She ran her hand through my hair. 'Make love to me,' she repeated. She kissed my neck.

Something moved behind me. Out of the corner of my eye the darkness seemed to overlap briefly. I saw a shadow change. It was as sharp as a slap in the face and I stumbled backwards, nearly pulling Catherine off the bar with me. She let out a little gasp.

I turned around quickly and used my body to shield Catherine's nakedness. 'Who's there?' I said, my voice sounding groggy, still half asleep. I peered into the shadowy maze of empty tables and chairs. I blinked twice, my eyes still feeling blurred. 'Who's there?'

Catherine stiffened behind me. She slid slowly down behind the bar. My heart was beating hard in my chest. I felt cold, shocked. A brief hope flashed through my mind that I was wrong, that maybe it was my imagination. But then somebody stepped forward from those shadows.

'Well, well, well,' a drunken male voice whispered. It chuckled. 'Well, well, fucking well.' And Carter stepped forward from those shadows. And even before his face was completely free of the dark I could already see the way it leered at us both.

I should have been frightened, I should have been hit by the realization that we'd been discovered, but the only thing I felt as he walked casually between the tables was anger. Anger at the dreaming sensation I had just so suddenly lost, and then a deeper hatred as I remembered all the comments he'd made about Catherine at work.

'Get out!' I hissed at him. 'Get out of here!' Rage flared inside me. But my punch was weak and he knocked it away with a movement that looked like little more than a salute. And my second swing he caught.

'Now here's a story the lads aren't going to believe,' he said. He held my wrist tightly, twisting it against me, but I refused to let him see the pain in my eyes. He twisted it harder. He was a big man, but squat, like a rugby player. He was solid. His eyes were tiny, bright, coloured a sharp blue, and as hard as pebbles.

He looked across at Catherine standing behind the bar, she was covering her breasts with her arms. 'Come out and get your dress, Cathy.' He winked at her. 'Don't be bashful *now*.'

Catherine didn't say a word. She glared at him.

'I was enjoying the show,' he said. 'It was just getting to the interesting bit.' I tried in vain to squirm out of his grip.

He turned his eyes on me and although he may have been smirking something much more sinister was conveyed by his stare. He sneered at the buckle of my belt hanging loose above my crotch. 'D'you reckon you could have handled the interesting bit?' he asked. I could smell thick alcohol on his breath. 'Or did I get here just in time to save you the embarrassment?'

'Get out, Carter.'

'I guess you're right,' he said. He shook his head. 'No honestly, I agree. You should be allowed to get your end wet at least once. I mean, there's a first time for everything isn't there?' Again his grip tightened, twisting up my already burning skin. And against my will I let a quick yelp of pain escape. 'I just don't think it should ever be with such a fine woman as this.' His stare was back on Catherine. 'Now I could show this woman a thing or two,' he told me. 'She doesn't want to waste herself on a little shit like you. Not when someone like me could fuck her so well.'

I lashed out with my free hand and connected with his cheek. But he didn't even flinch. He struck me very quickly. Just the once. An instant scream of pain in my nose and I fell to my knees with blood squirting down my face. He still had hold of my wrist and let me hang from it, just long enough for him to wipe his bloodied knuckles on the shoulder of my shirt. Then he let me go and I was able to curl up and hold my hands to my face.

'You'd better be real fucking nice to me from now on,' he told me. 'Real fucking nice.' He walked away and I heard the door swing shut behind him.

My mouth was full of blood. My handkerchief was soon a deep red. I couldn't tell if he'd broken my nose or not. The pain was like fire. But the blood slowed quickly; I had it spattered all down the front of my shirt and I could see gloomy spots of it on the floor.

Catherine came over to me. She had already managed to put her beautiful dress back on. 'Are you alright?' she asked. She looked frightened, her warm face had blanched. 'Oh, God, you look dreadful.' Her hands washed themselves, wringing together over and over.

'I'm okay,' I said.

'I've got to go,' she said. 'I've got to make sure he doesn't say anything.'

I nodded.

'Oh God, I'm so sorry. I'm so, so sorry. Is there . . .?'

But I shook my head. And after another moment's hesitation she returned to the party. I heard the door swing closed behind her. I stayed until my nose had stopped bleeding, although the pain was still nauseating, and then tried my best to clean up the spots of blood off the floor with the cuff of my shirt. I straightened the bar towels and went home.

I sat in the darkness of my cramped living room. I wasn't cold but I had the fire on full, my chair pulled right up in front of it. The fake coal glowed red. Maybe I was trying to sweat my anger out? The television noised somewhere in the background. I was thinking about Catherine. I told myself that I should have stayed at the party, that I should have gone after Carter. I was angry with myself for running away. And now the question rose in my mind: Had he told anybody?

And this first question was followed too quickly by so many others. Should I go to work tomorrow? Who would Carter tell? Would Anthony find out? How would I explain the bruises on my face, the black under my eyes? Would Catherine leave me if he did? And I could not answer any one of them. I couldn't figure things out. I was trapped in a maze of emotion; every path I took led to yet another blank wall. A sharp, painful frustration nestled in my gut. I was once more waiting for a phone call, once more left out in the cold for someone to get in touch with me, to let me know what was happening in *my* life. I felt helpless. And I decided that I simply had to go in to work tomorrow. I had to find out what was happening, what had been said. By Catherine, by Carter, by anyone.

I went to bed, tried to sleep, but it was futile. I tossed and turned until well after midnight, then gave up and sat back in front of the fire, staring at its false glow. The doorbell rang shrilly just before one. It was Catherine.

She'd been crying. Her eyes were puffy with black veins of streaked mascara. I sat her down in front of the fire with a glass of whisky. I was impatient, worried, anxiety crawled in my belly, but I knew better than to rush her. She shrugged her coat onto the floor. Her lipstick was smeared at the corner of her mouth.

'He's threatening to tell Anthony,' she said in a whisper.

'Carter?'

She nodded. She stared at the whisky, swirled it around gently in the glass, but didn't take a drink. She put the glass down and I took hold of her hand, kneeling in front of her.

'He wants me to sleep with him.' She didn't look at me as she said this. 'He says that if I don't he'll tell Anthony.'

One second, two seconds of bewilderment passed. I felt the flesh of my face tighten in disbelief as her words sank in. Then my anger flared. 'I'll kill him!'

She shook her head quickly, squeezing my hand and pulling me back down onto my knees. 'No,' she said. 'No. Maybe it's time Anthony knew anyway.'

I was confused again. I shook my head.

'Maybe I should leave him. I'm sick of hiding, cheating.' She was looking me in the eyes. 'I could stay here, couldn't I? Until I was able to work things out properly?'

'Yes,' I said, taking hold of her hand in both of mine. 'Yes. Of course you can. You know you can. You can stay as long as you want.' I hated myself for suddenly feeling hopeful about the situation. Could this mean she wanted to leave Anthony for me? Could we finally be together all the time, as proper lovers are?

'It's not right between us any more. He's not the young man I married any more.' She was staring into the fire. 'I've known for a long time now, but . . . He used have so much passion. But now his work is so much more important to him. His mortgage and his promotion. He's a man of forty before he's even thirty.' She turned to look at me now. 'Never get old like that. Promise me.'

I nodded. I promised and I kissed her.

She nodded too, turning back to the fire. She was settling things in her head. She looked so beautiful to me then; the red glow across her troubled face. I hated Carter, the loathing was a dark bitterness, yet I couldn't help but feel as though his appearance tonight could turn into something quite fortuitous for me.

Catherine wanted to fetch some things from home. I tried to dissuade her but she said that the house was empty, that Anthony was staying at the Golf Club tonight because she had planned on coming back to my flat anyway, and had told him she'd be staying at a friend's from work, after the Christmas party. She wanted me to go with her and I dressed quickly while she waited impatiently by the front door.

We drove through the deserted night-time streets in Catherine's car.

'I only want enough so I won't have to see him for a week,' she told me. 'If I can stay away from him for at least a week.' Her driving was erratic, she was intolerant of traffic lights, she ground through the gears. 'I should have done this months ago. I should have made him realize what he was doing to me months ago.'

I was quiet. I was nervous, but I knew tonight, and

tomorrow night, and maybe even for a long time to come, I would be holding the woman I loved in my arms as I fell asleep.

Catherine's house was dark. She didn't park in front but a little way up the road, because of the street-light she would have had to leave the car directly under. She didn't want any neighbours seeing exactly what she was doing. I wondered if it was also because she didn't want any neighbours seeing exactly who I was. We didn't use the front door either, she took me round the back, after checking to make sure Anthony's car wasn't in the garage.

The house was quiet and still. Catherine wouldn't switch on any lights, not until we were upstairs in her bedroom and she could draw the heavy velvet curtains. Even then it was only a bedside lamp she used. She pulled down a suitcase from the top of a wardrobe with mirrored doors and then opened up drawers and cupboards to fill it. She passed things to me, underwear, make-up, shoes, and I packed them as neatly as I could.

But I couldn't help staring around the room. There was a wedding photo on the wall, and a landscape painting. The wallpaper was a pale blue, subtly flowered. The book on the floor on what I guessed to be Anthony's side of the bed was a bruised copy of *The Silence of The Lambs*. There was a Teasmade and a radio-alarmclock. I realized that this bed was where Catherine and Anthony made love. It was wooden, pine, king-size and made very neatly. The scene looked so appealing compared to my small, yet somehow quite empty flat.

Catherine moved through into the bathroom to pack her toiletries. I struggled to close the suitcase. I'd have to clear my wardrobe out for her. And that was when I heard the keys rattling in the front door.

'Catherine,' I hissed, hearing my own panic. 'Catherine!' I

had sense enough to turn out the light and take the suitcase with me as I hurried out of the bedroom. The bathroom door was open, the light spilled out onto the landing.

But Catherine had heard the keys too. She pulled me into the bathroom and switched off the light before I had time to read the look on her face. She shushed me when I tried to speak, gripping my arm.

'I don't want to see him,' she said. 'I can't see him.' The tone of her voice told me what the dark stopped me from seeing on her face.

Anthony was talking to someone. We couldn't make out the words but his deep intonation rolled up the stairs. A woman's higher voice punctuated his. And I felt Catherine's nails dig into my arm. The door was slammed. They came up the stairs, the female voice giggling drunkenly, Anthony's words became clear as caresses, charms, honeyed-talk. I couldn't see Catherine next to me, but she was as silent and as still as a statue. I listened for her breath but it was held. They walked along the landing, their footsteps within only a few feet of us, and went into the bedroom. Catherine's grip on my arm was painful. Her breath came now, but it was short, hesitant.

I waited for her to say something, for her to make a move of some sort. Was she angry? Or was this just a further reason to continue with our plan? Would she want to confront him now? I was dumb next to her, but all these thoughts ran through my mind. Did she know the woman? Had she recognized the voice?

Laughter came from the bedroom. Laughter and more charming words.

Catherine moved then. She reached for the door and slowly pulled it open. She hushed me again when I tried to speak, pushing me away from her. She slipped her shoes off and stepped out onto the landing. I watched her disappear into the dark, creeping silently towards her bedroom. I was scared now, the surprise wearing thin and leaving me cold. I had thoughts of fleeing. I realized how ugly things could now become. But I was so close to having Catherine. So I also removed my shoes, then followed her.

She was standing outside her bedroom door. The bedside lamp had been switched back on and she made sure the light it cast couldn't reach her. But she still had a clear enough view of what was happening on her bed. I didn't know whether to touch her, whether she needed comforting. I stood there and watched. I didn't know what else to do.

The woman, a blonde, short, busty, was lying back on the bed being stripped by Anthony. He seemed quite rough with her, his hands fumbling, drunken. His clumsy fingers ripped her white blouse in their haste, but the woman only giggled at this. So he laughed too, and ripped it completely, popping the buttons all the way down the front. This had the woman in a fit of hysterics. She struggled with her laughter and the arms of her blouse at the same time. She was wearing a white, shiny camisole top underneath. Anthony was rubbing her belly and chest through the silky material. Then he stood up and moved over to the dressing-table, started searching through drawers. He returned to the bed with a pair of nail scissors and snipped the thin shoulder straps of the top, one then the other. The woman laughed harder and harder. She threw her arms around Anthony's neck and kissed him on the lips. He pulled the camisole down to reveal the milky skin of her chest and belly. He groped at her, kneading her big, malleable breasts.

I tried to put my hand on Catherine's arm, I wanted to lead her away, surely she didn't want to see this. But she shrugged me off nastily. I couldn't see her face, I couldn't imagine how she'd be feeling. She was standing still and solid, her arms by her side. I was feeling slightly nauseous; I think it was fear. I wanted to walk away, part of my mind was telling me to, but I couldn't leave Catherine. I wouldn't leave her alone, not now.

Anthony didn't bother to remove the woman's skirt, he hoicked it up around her waist. Her knickers were scarlet, lace, see-through. He didn't even seem to care about taking his own clothes off; he was still wearing his shirt and jacket, his trousers and briefs were pushed as far down as his knees. The woman tugged on his erection. She lifted herself up from the bed, raising herself up on her elbows, and spoke into it like a microphone. I couldn't hear what she was saying but both she and Anthony suddenly burst into laughter again. He held the back of her head with both hands when she took him in her mouth, she held his arse.

I was flustered and distressed. I was disgusted with myself for feeling aroused. What I was watching had no care or sensitivity. There was only lust. It was not the way I would ever want to make love to anyone. It was not the way Catherine and I made love.

Anthony turned the woman over onto her belly. She didn't complain. He lifted her backside into the air so she was on her elbows and her knees, her breasts scraping the bed. He pulled the crotch of her knickers to one side, bent and kissed her on the fanny, just the once, then stood up again and entered her from behind. She gasped, sucking in her breath, then squirmed against him. He had hold of her hips and he withdrew completely, then stabbed at her with a grunt. He watched himself as he did this again and again. The woman tried to raise herself up onto her hands, but was knocked back down with Anthony's thrust.

He moved onto the bed behind her. He straddled her like a dog, gripping her shoulders. His movements got quicker, stronger. She let out a little, tight sob. Then another. They got louder and harsher. The two of them slammed against each other. He got faster and faster. Thrusting, ramming into her. Her sobs got louder. She couldn't keep up with his rhythm. He pulled on her shoulders, forcing her back against him harder and harder. She pushed her face into the bed. His face was contorted, biting on his lip.

And it was all over very quickly. She yelped into the bed sheets. He sighed loudly, blowing the air out of himself in a big gush of breath. His knees buckled and for a moment he almost fell backwards from the bed.

They were still and quiet for a few seconds, both panting, sweaty; a sinful tableau against the subtly flowered wallpaper of the room. Then he pulled away from her and let himself sprawl outstretched across the bed, and she rolled over next to him. She dug in his trouser pockets and retrieved a crumpled packet of cigarettes and a lighter. But she didn't light up. She lay and stared up at the ceiling. She was flushed, exhausted. Her fat breasts heaved as she tried to catch her breath.

'Catherine . . .' I whispered close to her ear. And she started, turning on me sharply as if she'd forgotten I was there. Although I still couldn't read the look on her face. I took hold of her hand and gestured that we should leave. She didn't acknowledge me but she let me lead her away. The woman in the bedroom was playing with Anthony's penis, wanting him again.

We retrieved our shoes and the suitcase and silently moved downstairs. Catherine walked awkwardly, she wouldn't look at me. I put the suitcase on the back seat of her car and we both sat in the dark, neither of us speaking. I was sure I should have been comforting her, telling her that at least now she knew she was doing the right thing by leaving him, but I didn't know how to say it. She sat quiet and still, unmoving. I kept glancing over my shoulder in case they came out of the house.

'I can't believe he'd do something like this,' she said suddenly. She stared at her hands in her lap. 'It's just not the Anthony I know.' She turned and looked at me. 'He hasn't touched me in months. And yet there he is, with her . . .'

'Come on,' I said. 'Let's go. We ought to just get away from here.'

'What's she got that I haven't got? She's no better than me.'

I took hold of her hand. 'We'll go back to my flat,' I told her.

But she shook her head quickly. 'No. No, I'm going back to Anthony.'

'You can't, that woman's there.'

'I'm not letting her steal my husband.'

'You said you were leaving him, you said you were coming to be with me.'

She shook her hand free of mine. 'He's my husband.'

It felt as though my insides were crumbling away. I tried to take hold of her hand again, I tried to kiss her. 'But I love you. I can take care of you. I love you, Catherine.'

She pushed me away.

But I grabbed at her again. 'Don't go back to him. Stay with me tonight, think about what you're saying.' I hated the desperate sound of my voice, but I could do nothing to change its pitch; the way it seemed to be getting higher and higher, more childish. 'I could take care of you. You'd never have to worry about me leaving you, I love you so much. I can get a bigger flat. I'd always be there for you. Always. We could marry. I adore you.' But even as I was speaking I knew it wasn't what she wanted.

She gently pulled her hand free of mine. She didn't speak to me. She stepped out of the car. I followed quickly, jumping out of the passenger seat, wanting so desperately to speak to her again, but she hushed me with a small glance. We stood staring at each other over the roof of her car.

She'd found me because she thought Anthony had turned into a passionless man, a safe man. I was her affair, her danger. But I was talking like a husband; I was talking like the man she believed Anthony had become. The man Anthony had suddenly proved himself very much not to be.

WHAT MIGHT HAVE BEEN

Elizabeth Kay

'HELLO,' she said, 'my name is Misha. I am to be your guide to our culture. I study English, and I hope to make you understand the things that I say.'

He smiled very slightly, not a pleasant smile. Then he sat back on the broken cane chair, folded his arms and watched her. His sleeve was torn, she could see the fuzz of apricot hair on his arm and the blue flesh underneath it, bruised.

She cleared her throat. 'I have been sent here to ask you some questions about your thoughts. I have to fill in a document – here – ' she showed him the sheet of paper, with the symbols all down one side and spaces for the answers. He glanced at it, but he made no move to take it.

'You were captured six weeks ago. Your injuries happened before that.'

He raised one eyebrow, sarcastic. His gaze was level and steady.

She looked down at her lap, flustered. 'I have been sent here to educate you,' said Misha. 'To make you see things from our point of view. Then you will be sent home.' She glanced up. He was so ugly, she hadn't been prepared for it, no one had warned her. His skin was like alabaster compared to hers, pale, unhealthy.

He made some slight derisive movement with his head. It was obvious that he didn't believe a single word.

'It is true.' She lowered her eyes again. He had a very direct way of looking at her, and she wasn't used to that sort of eye contact. 'I am to come to you once a week for six weeks,' she told him, 'and we are to talk. You too can ask questions. This is not easy for me, you are my first prisoner. I am sorry if I offend you in any way.'

He didn't say anything. Water dripped off the corrugated roof outside, timing his silence. His breathing was slow and even, like a cat in the sun. A fly buzzed around his head, but he made no attempt to brush it away.

'All right,' she said. 'If you are not going to speak to me, I shall tell you about myself. It is what I have been instructed to do.'

He stretched out his legs on the sandy floor. He was barefoot, and she could see that one of his ankles was swollen as well. He would be tall, if he stood up. Much taller than her.

'My name is Misha. I am twenty years old, and when I finish my studies I shall do three years of service before I marry. Then I will make a house, bear one child, and have my five years of motherhood. I am looking forward to that very much. When I met my own mother last year she told me it was the most . . . the most . . .' She bit her lip, temporarily at a loss. 'There is no English word for it,' she said eventually. 'We have a word that means the feeling you get when you do a duty, and it gives you pleasure.'

He suddenly seemed to decide that she was of no interest. His eyes left her face and became distant, unfocused, as though he was trying to count the specks of dust caught in the sunlight that came through the tiny window above them. She talked about her English course, how wonderful it was that her country had made these things available to women, and how much she wanted the opportunity to practise her skills. He was looking at the ceiling now; she could see him counting the bats that hung there, huddled together, small enough to come and go at will. She told him how she loved to cook, when she could get the ingredients; she asked him if he too liked locusts, quick-fried with cinnamon, but she could get no response from him at all.

She tried looking where he looked, up to the token square of sky that served as a window, a sky striated with bamboo bars. As she watched a skein of geese flew past, honking the gossip. 'Look,' she said, 'it is a good omen. Seven geese, one leader, three either side. You will live to be seventy, for the geese are evenly spaced and they have chosen your window as a picture-frame.' She saw his eyes flick to the window just for a moment. Then a lizard caught his attention, glued to the wall by suckered feet, the toes spread out like demon's fingers.

When the guard came to get her she felt like a failure, and she knew that her supervisor would not be pleased. She said goodbye, but he didn't even look at her as she left the room.

'Think about him,' said her supervisor, 'try to get into his mind. You are inexperienced at this, you are young. I am prepared to give you another chance, but you must get something out of him next week.'

She bowed, and went away to think.

Daniel had been very surprised when Misha had come through the door, although he hadn't shown it. Such a pretty girl, small, slight, her black hair plaited round her head and tied with a piece of string. He'd been expecting a beating, not a politically correct lecture from a little wisp of a thing with dark eyes and a quiet voice. He didn't think she would return. And then he began to wish that she would, for there was only so long you could spend counting cockroaches, or composing tunes that synchronized with the rain. And how it rained. Day after day, exactly the same, a cloudless morning, a sultry afternoon, thunder by the evening. And then the inevitable, as though the weather had decided to wash the slate clean and start again. He tried to imagine what Misha would look like naked, but it didn't seem appropriate somewhow, and he let it drop.

She spent her week as her supervisor had suggested, thinking. Her prisoner would have been trained to give nothing away, but she didn't want military details. She wanted his background, his home, his family, his life. She wanted a complete picture that she could make him dissect, piece by piece, until none of it remained intact. She could then replace it with something else. She had been taught to destroy, and then rebuild. But she began to wonder whether she had to build before she could destroy. If he would give her nothing, she had to give something first. And he had been totally unmoved by her rather straightforward and factual account of her activities.

He was sitting on the same chair, quietly defiant. The swelling round his eye and down the side of his jaw was subsiding, and the hair on his face was now some way between stubble and beard.

'Hello,' she said.

He nodded.

It was an acknowledgment. She brightened, and fumbled in her trousers for the pawpaw she had brought him. She knew this was dangerous; but she needed to offer him something to gain his trust. She placed the fruit on the stained wooden table between them.

Naive, he thought, she is so naive. He didn't take it. He had become so comfortable with his hopelessness, he had been preparing himself for death in a gradual fashion, anaesthetizing himself; he didn't want the process reversed.

'Don't you like pawpaw?' she asked.

He smiled slightly. He hadn't eaten anything but rice and beans for six weeks. And he knew that suddenly he was losing, for her simplicity was awakening something in him again.

She reached out to take it away again, for it would never do for the guard to see it. As her hand closed round it his hand closed round hers. She became aware that one of his fingers was the wrong shape, twisted. His grip was gentle but firm. The slight smile again, and a brief shake of the head.

'You must eat it now,' she said.

There was no knife. He had to break the skin with his teeth, and then dig into the fruit with his thumbs and pull it apart that way. He was economical in his movements, self-controlled. He watched her as he ate but he didn't rush, and he wiped his mouth with the back of his hand when he'd finished. The black blood had gone from his lips and she could see a scar, pink, new; he wasn't quite so ugly any more.

'What is your name?' she said.

He thought for a moment. Then he said, 'Lazarus.'

It was the first time he had spoken. His voice was surprisingly soft. She wanted to hear him say something more, and she wondered which question to try first. The faint smile was back, and for a moment she had the feeling that he knew exactly what she was thinking. That he'd played games like this before, and won them.

'Lazarus,' she said, savouring the sounds. Her supervisor would be pleased.

Suddenly he seemed to make up his mind about something, and he said, 'How old did you say you were?'

'Twenty.'

'Married?'

She laughed. 'Nobody marries before the age of twenty-five.'

He looked surprised, then amused. 'What do you all do before that?' he said.

'We study.'

'I didn't mean that.'

Her brows drew together in confusion. 'I do not understand.'

'Do you have a boyfriend?'

'No, of course not.'

He shook his head, as confused as she.

'You must be married,' she said. 'You are old.'

'I'm thirty-three,' he said, 'I'm not *old*. And no, I'm not married.'

'Why? Did you commit a crime?'

'What?'

'Did you do something wrong?'

'No,' he said, 'I'm a palaeontologist. Palaeontologists don't do anything much except dig things up and sit in museums identifying them. And straying across borders, apparently.'

He could see that he'd lost her. A look of incomprehension crossed her face. 'Please,' she said, 'I think we change the subject. Tell me about your country.'

He started to talk, slowly at first; he hadn't used English for several months. He described his home, aware that he was embellishing things, enlarging the garden, putting in a patio, digging a pond.

'You keep fish in it?'

'Some.'

'To eat?'

He laughed. 'No. To look at.'

'Why?'

'Because they're beautiful,' he said, and he began to describe his imaginary fish, giving them personalities and family trees. He became more and more outrageous until his fish performed astonishing feats of synchronized swimming and came to him when he called them, and he gave them outlandish names, Darwin and Copernicus and Schopenhauer.

She told him about her glow-worms, how each one had a slightly different brilliance and chose the same resting place each day.

His smile widened. He hadn't expected her to enter so quickly into the spirit of the thing. Then he wondered whether she was, in fact, being perfectly serious. Her face was impassive. There was no way he could tell.

'Do you breed glow-worms?' he asked her.

'So sorry?'

'Breed them. Mate them. Get baby ones.'

The confusion had returned. 'They do it themselves.'

He laughed. It was the first time she had heard him laugh, and it made him less alien, more like her.

'There are two sorts,' she said. 'The one that is like a beetle and the one that is like a centipede.'

'Male and female.'

'No, two different kinds.'

'The glow-worm *is* a beetle,' said Daniel, '*Lampyris noctiluca*. They're sexually dimorphic.' He knew he was going to lose her this time, and he enjoyed it. 'In both *Photuris* and *Lampyris* the luminosity has a sexual significance.' He let her puzzle for a bit, then he felt cheap. 'The man is different from the woman,' he finished lamely.

'Oh,' she said.

'Like I am different from you.'

'Not so very. You are bigger, and you have hair on your face.'

He was about to say, I don't have breasts; but she was so slim that he wasn't really sure whether she did either, under the shapeless grey cotton, so he didn't say anything. But thinking about the differences between them was surprisingly inflammatory, and he didn't want to stop. He hadn't slept with a woman for over six months; fear and lack of food had taken his mind in other directions.

'And that's the only difference?' he said, smiling.

She looked at him, not understanding. 'Yes. Of course.'

She meant it. The smile left his face. 'Who were you brought up with?' he asked.

'My sisters.'

'What about your father?'

'We do not see our fathers after the age of five,' she said. 'They go off to fight.'

'Did you have male teachers? At school?'

She laughed. 'Don't be silly. All teachers are women.'

'And the students?'

'My sisters.'

He realized that it was a generic term. She didn't mean blood relatives at all. 'What about the boys?'

'They have their own schools, houses, teachers. We meet together to worship. I know what a man looks like.'

'Without his clothes on?'

She flushed deeply.

'You don't, do you,' he said. 'My God. And they want to take over the world.'

'Sorry?'

'Your lot, the bloody . . .' He stopped. Invective wasn't going to help. He didn't expect to live too much longer, and taking it out on this total innocent was not the last action he wished to commit. A small matter, but small matters become important when there is nothing else to think about. 'Tell me,' he said, 'what sort of man do you think you will marry? Or have you met him already?'

'Of course I haven't,' she said. 'He will be shown to me the day before. We are fatalists. What happens, happens. We do not dwell on the past, or what might have been. I hope he will be kind. That is all.'

'So do I,' said Daniel.

She looked at him, and she knew he was referring to something else. 'How strange,' she said, 'there is something you know about marriage that I do not, despite the fact that you are not married yourself. And I thought I was here to teach you.'

'Moving on from the glow-worms a minute,' he said, 'to people. What do you know about making babies?'

She flushed again. 'When they are married, the man and woman lie next to one another. And after that, the seed begins to grow.'

'Lie next to one another.'

'Yes.'

'Jesus Christ,' he said.

'Lazarus,' said Misha, 'I have let you down somehow.'

He shook his head. And then the guard came in, and took her away.

For the next week he couldn't get her out of his head. He pursued his exercise routine with his usual conscientiousness; it was something to do, but it didn't stop him thinking about her. It wasn't a sexual craving, it was the urge to mean something to her, for when he was gone he knew there would be another prisoner, and another. He was only the first in a long line. The compound was full of them, he just never saw them. He heard them instead; the crying at night, the pleading, the sudden crescendos of swearing. There had been shots, as well, outside in the courtyard. He had observed everything very carefully on his way through, more as a final setting than an escape route. A sun-baked square of dirt, hemmed in by barbed wire and wooden buildings, huge birds raking through the rubbish in one corner like pterodactyls, a single water-pump, a washing-line strung between one of the huts and the rough post that stood in the centre. There was a dark stain around it on the sand.

He wondered at the brutality of a regime that could hang its washing from a place of execution and send an untutored girl to interview someone who could have been a psychopath. He could have told her the facts of life in a particularly nasty way, got off on it if he'd been that sort. Then he wondered whether it was actually a very subtle psychological ploy; if she knew nothing about sex she wouldn't flirt. She would appeal to the potential father in him, he'd want to protect her by giving her information. The trouble was, he didn't have any. He wasn't a mercenary, he was an academic who'd hired a bum guide and gone the wrong way. And the guide had killed two men before he had died himself.

'*Lazarus*,' said Misha's supervisor to her, smiling. 'I don't think so. Lazarus is a character from their holy book, a man who rose from the dead. I think he was having a joke.'

'You mean he lied.'

'Don't get too downhearted. First of all he wouldn't speak. Now he will, but he deceives you. It's a step forward. Now you must try to get the truth from him. Has he criticized his country in any way?'

'No.'

'Has he said anything positive about us?'

'No.'

'Choose one subject. Is there anything about which he has been willing to talk?'

'Marriage,' said Misha.

'That is forbidden,' said her supervisor. 'You must find something else.'

She sat alone in her tiny room that night and wondered what gave him pleasure. He hadn't reacted when she'd talked about the pleasure of duty. It was going to be difficult; she would have to ask him.

The swelling on his face had gone completely by the next meeting. The skin was still coloured oddly, purple and yellow patches, red lines and blotches, but the shape was symmetrical once more.

'Hello Misha,' he said, as soon as she entered the cell. He sat opposite her as usual, one hand resting lightly on the table, the other on his thigh. The fuzz on his face was now a proper beard, and she didn't like it. It made him look too different from her. This time she had brought him some dried fish and a banana, and he ate as before, slowly, thoughtfully, watching her.

'I wish,' she said, 'that you would shave.'

He smiled. 'Tell them to give me a razor, then.'

It was easier to meet his eyes. The resentment that had been there initially had gone. 'My supervisor says you have lied to me,' she whispered. It was a terrible thing to say to anyone.

'Yes,' he said, quite unapologetically. 'My name is Daniel. Doctor Daniel Murray. I am a scientist, I am thirty-three and I have never fired a gun. I want to go home, but I know I never will. I know nothing about military installations. There is no more information I can give you.'

'There is,' she said. 'I want to know what you dislike about your country.'

He laughed. 'Everything.'

She stared at him. 'Everything?'

'Apart from one thing.'

'What is that?'

'Oh Misha,' he said, 'I shouldn't be the one to tell you.'

'Is it something to do with marriage?'

'It's something to do with life itself.'

'Oh,' she said, 'that's all right then. I was only told not to discuss marriage with you any further.'

He put both his arms on the table and rested his head on them. He hadn't meant to get round to this subject again. It just seemed to happen, it was such a fundamental lack of understanding between them that he couldn't see how they could talk about anything until it was resolved.

'Tell me,' she said, 'what it is that I don't know.' Somehow she knew that he would tell her the truth, and the truth was what her supervisor wanted. If he could tell her the one thing that was better where he came from, then they could get onto the things that were worse. He was probably mistaken, anyway. She had been told that prisoners had a very subjective view of their own culture.

Daniel wondered where on earth to begin. What a totally ludicrous situation. In the end he started with the pawpaw, and the little black seeds in the middle. They moved on from fruit to frogs. It had been perfectly obvious to her that when frogs lay next to each other, they produced frogspawn. He explained what really happened, and she seemed to accept it without too much difficulty.

Things got more emotive when they dealt with mammals. Initially he chose sheep, as it appealed to his sense of humour. Again, she had just assumed that the ram brushed against the ewes. When he asked her whether she'd ever seen a ram mount a ewe she said, oh, you mean when they play together.

'They're not playing,' he said.

'They seem quite happy,' she replied.

He wanted to laugh very badly, but he held it in. He asked

her whether she had ever noticed any physical differences between the ram and the ewe. She only cited the horns, as there was too much wool in the way to see anything else.

'Don't you have dogs?' he asked, getting desperate. They did have dogs. And yes, the dogs played too. And then, finally, at last, yes. A dog had bits under his tail, and bitches had nipples with which they fed their puppies. Nipples didn't seem to be a problem.

He explained what the dogs were doing when they were playing.

Her mouth dropped open and she stared at him, aghast.

He felt he'd tackled it too clumsily, and silently castigated himself for it.

And then, to his astonishment, she made the mental leap from dogs to humans without him saying another word. He saw her eyes open very wide, and drop to below his waist. But the table was in the way, and as she raised her eyes his eyes met hers.

'I'm sorry,' he said, 'I did that very badly.'

She just stared at him.

'How can I put this,' he said, 'it's not a horrible experience, Misha. It's the most beautiful thing in the world.'

She shook her head.

'Believe me.'

'I can't. I thought you were the same as me. But you're not. You've got . . .' Her eyes wandered; once more the table was in the way. She pursed her lips. 'Show me. I want to see for myself.'

'What?'

'Show me.'

It was his turn to look aghast. He hadn't forseen this at all.

'You are obliged,' she said simply. 'It is your duty, as my teacher in this matter.'

Daniel stood up. Yes, he could refuse, but what was right

under other circumstances wasn't right on this occasion. He'd brought it on himself. He stepped back from the table. He was wearing nothing but a pair of cotton trousers and a shirt. He could imagine himself standing there in just the shirt, thinner than he'd ever been and with everything dangling, and the image was ridiculous. He took the shirt off first.

She sat very still and watched him. She could see the golden hairs on his chest, the muscles just evident beneath. The veins down his arms and the scars. There were scars everywhere. He untied the string that held up the trousers, and let them drop to the floor, and then he was quite naked. Her eyes travelled all over his body, noting the differences. His hips seemed to sink inwards, she could see the bone. She looked hardest at his genitals, but she couldn't quite make out what went where. She stood up and went over to him for a closer look.

He closed his eyes and his brows drew together, as though he was thinking a complicated thought. She put out a finger and touched his penis, very gently, right on the tip. It jerked, and began to grow larger.

'Misha,' he said quietly, 'if you do that I'm going to get an erection.'

'I just wanted to touch it. Did I hurt you?'

He took a deep breath. 'No.'

But he couldn't will the erection away, and he didn't dare to open his eyes because he didn't think he could look her in the face. He tried to think about something else, the insect bites on his legs, the itching each night, but he couldn't keep the thought coherent. He knew she was going to touch him again, he could feel her proximity, hear her breathing, knew how fascinated she was, it was only a question of when. The anticipation made things far worse, and he knew that by now he had one of the stiffest hard-ons he'd ever had.

'Can I hold it?' she said.

Oh God no. But he couldn't speak. Her fingers closed round him. She just felt him for a few moments, establishing form and texture, and then she ran her hand down the shaft. He *had* to speak. 'You mustn't,' he whispered, and she let go immediately. He opened his eyes. Phrased that well, didn't you, he thought. Prat.

'It gives you pleasure, doesn't it,' she said.

'Yes. A great deal. You have no idea.'

'Have you done it? With a woman?'

'Yes.'

'More than once?'

'Many times.'

'But you are not married.'

'You don't have to be married,' he said. 'You do it for fun.' Then that sounded far too trivial, and he cursed himself again. He put his clothes back on, jerking the string tight around his waist.

'Why should it be fun?'

He didn't need to ask her if she'd ever touched herself. He knew she hadn't. There was a sort of translucency to her, a fragility, a something not yet broken. 'Because you would feel the same sort of pleasure as well,' he said. 'If it was done right.'

She looked thoughtful, went back to her chair and sat down again. He sat down as well. The table was between them once more. 'So this is the thing you have,' she said, 'that we don't.'

'I don't know,' he said, 'I don't know how your society works. Arranged marriages can be very successful.'

'Or not,' she replied. 'If it isn't done right.'

He felt like the snake in the garden of Eden. He'd tried to explain, and all he'd done was to sow seeds of doubt and dismay. He wanted to beat his head against the wall. When the guard came to take her away he was relieved.

* * *

Later that evening, when the rain came, he cried. He felt as though he'd deflowered her, without her understanding what he was doing, and therefore, without her consent. And later still he masturbated, thinking of how it could have been if he hadn't stopped her.

He remembered saying *you mustn't*, and the inadvertent admonition implicit in it. He wished he'd found a better phrase. Then he deleted it from the encounter and let her carry on, imagining himself standing there, naked, instructing her, being her teacher in this matter. He told her how to touch him, how to move the foreskin, how to run her finger delicately around the glans. In his head he heard his voice stumble and crack as he explained things; his hand acted out the scenario, becoming hers, exploring himself and his responses as though he was doing it for the very first time. The tension built and he fought it back, not yet, not yet. He told her how it felt to be inside a woman, how wet it was, like saliva; watched her put her hand to her mouth and lick her fingers, licked his own fingers, felt the fingers close round him again, slipping, sliding, simulating, stimulating. He saw her face watching his, learning his reactions, her pleasure growing with his, intensifying, accelerating. He pictured himself shutting his eyes and telling her to do it faster, faster, heard his voice become rough and urgent. Felt his muscles knot and heard himself groan as the moment approached. The trickle of sweat at the back of the neck, the exquisite ache spreading from his loins, the thrill of knowing that, in a moment, he would lose all sense of self.

Then suddenly he saw himself as she would see him, no longer the calm collected foreigner with the gentle voice but a male animal, in the grip of something she didn't yet understand, and he faltered.

He tried to tell the Misha in his head that it was all right, this was how it was for everyone, this focusing of consciousness before the ultimate release. That it was so physical it could not be contained within decorous behaviour, he wanted to scream, to point his head at the moon and howl, and he wanted her to hear him. And he wanted to be inside her.

Just the thought was enough to carry him to the point of orgasm; he became her once more, and her hand became oddly expert. When he ejaculated he didn't know who he was.

And then he was ashamed of himself.

'We need something specific, Misha,' said Misha's supervisor. '*Everything* tells us nothing. He hates everything about his country. Get him to tell you what. You have him speaking honestly now – you are doing well. But I want a list.'

'Can he have a razor?'

'No. But if you find him offensive, I will arrange for him to be made presentable.'

She bowed.

Misha had withheld information for the first time in her life. In the end, everything Daniel had said had related to marriage, and that topic was forbidden. She kept looking at the dogs in the street, but she didn't see any of them doing it. She also found herself watching the outline of men's bodies rather more closely. It wasn't easy, for they all wore the same shapeless cotton trousers she did, but just once in a while . . . She couldn't believe that she'd never noticed anything before.

When she was taken to his cell for the fourth time, she saw that he had shaved. His clothes were clean, and his face was back to the right colour, if a little pasty; he was almost beautiful. He looked pleased to see her, but wary. She gave him a mango and some sheep's cheese.

'I have to have a list,' she said, 'of the things you hate. Specific things.'

'Okay,' he said. 'If we get through that, can we talk about other things after?'

Get through the list? She couldn't believe it. She licked her pencil.

'Too much traffic, too much pollution, corrupt government, inequality . . .'

'Wait,' she cried, 'wait.'

He watched her scribble furiously, let her catch up before he resumed his tirade. And it was a tirade. He was fulminating against a government that would do nothing to secure his release, one that had consistently cut his funding at home, one that saw the rich and the poor as two separate species, the environment as a financial resource. He spat out one thing after another, and she wrote them all down. When she reached the bottom of the page she looked up at him, her eyes shining.

'Thank you,' she said, 'thank you so very much.'

He smiled. He had given her something at last.

'You need to sign,' she said.

He signed. He would be dead before long, what did it matter. But he'd meant it. Meant every goddam word.

She put down the pencil and smiled at him. 'What do you want to talk about?'

'You.'

'I am not very interesting. I am very average.'

'I've done you an injury.'

'No, you have not.'

'I have,' he said. 'I should never have told you all that last week, it wasn't my place to do it, I've spoilt things for you.'

'No,' she said. 'I am glad you opened my eyes. Perhaps . . .' she looked at him. He could see her struggling with something. 'Perhaps there are other things, too.'

'Perhaps.' But he didn't want to destroy anything else.

'What do you like about our culture?'

'I don't know anything about your culture.'

She began to list things.

'Ssh,' he said, putting his fingers to his lips, 'that's for next time.'

'So what are we to talk about now?'

'I want to tell you . . . this is difficult . . . I want to explain . . .' The words wouldn't gel. He wanted to make sure she knew what she was aiming for when she did get married. That she got something out of it herself. And the more he thought about it, the more he wanted to dispense with words altogether and just show her. He reached out across the table and took her right hand. It was small and dainty, but it had known hard work. The skin was rough and calloused and a couple of the nails were broken. He turned it over and ran his finger across her palm, between her fingers, up to the inside of her wrist. She didn't pull away.

'You need to know,' he said, 'that certain things . . . can give you pleasure.'

She simply smiled, and placed her other hand on the table, palm upwards. He wanted her very badly then. But he traced the same design on her left hand, and stopped at the wrist.

'It's nice,' she said, as though she was talking about a new recipe.

'How long have we got?' said Daniel. Was he really saying this? Had he thought any of it through?

'I don't know. Five minutes, maybe.'

'And next time, for how long?'

'Two hours.'

'Can you come for longer?'

'You want me longer?'

Jesus Christ, thought Daniel. '*Yes*.'

'I will ask. Now do something else to me that gives me pleasure.'

'Stand up.'

She stood up. He walked round the table and put his hands on her shoulders. 'Can I kiss you?'

'Like children do?'

'No,' he said, 'not like children do at all,' and he started to show her, very gently at first, forcing himself to keep his hands on her shoulders. He felt her resistance to begin with, then a gradual relaxation. She heard the guard's footsteps before he did, and she pulled away. He went back to his chair, and they said casual goodbyes.

Daniel spent the next week going from anticipation to dread and back to anticipation again. It was a manic cycle – he wanted to make love to her, knew he shouldn't; then he would remember that next time would be the last time he'd *know* he was going to see her again. He tried to think of other things but it was hopeless, he could find her face in every shadow, hear her voice with every gust of wind outside. He knew he ought to stay on the other side of the table, make small-talk about war and society, but he didn't trust himself to do it.

Misha's supervisor was very pleased with her. He granted her the extra hour she requested; she was a credit to her teachers, her enthusiasm had been noted. She was very aware that she was perverting the truth by her silence, but her loyalties were beginning to change. She asked what would happen to him after she had finished with him. 'He will be released, of course,' said the supervisor – but now that she had herself seen how easy it was to lie she didn't know whether to believe what he said, despite the fact that he was so much older than her. A sadness seemed to descend over her, and it stayed with her until she saw her prisoner again.

* * *

He was very self-controlled when she arrived. He'd argued it out with himself, taken different parts, been different people, explored other points of view. Supposing he got her pregnant. The thought was horribly exciting, and utterly appalling. It was quite possible that they'd just shoot her. He wouldn't do it. He sat on the other side of the table, legs crossed, arms folded, holding himself together. She was wearing a dress today, a simple cotton shift that reached her instep. He could see the form of her body quite clearly where it caught between her thighs.

'I have to fill in the form.'

He nodded. 'Make it up. I'll sign it. Anything you like. Just do it.'

She started to say things out loud, and to write them down. He nodded at every one, but the phrases began to sound false to her. 'Every child has a happy life at Citizenship School.' She had been told she had a happy life. But had she really? Hadn't touching another human being reawakened memories of a time before, when someone had held her close, and bedtime didn't mean fifty little girls doing their devotions in unison? She began to slow down.

'Come on,' said Daniel, 'what's the matter?'

She looked at him, on the edge of tears, and he realized what he'd done.

'You don't believe any of it any more do you,' he said, 'I've taken that away from you as well. Fill in the form, Misha, you have to.'

'A marriage arranged with guidance is the best basis for a family.' She wrote it down through a haze of tears, and went on to the next.

When she'd finished they just sat and looked at one another.

'It's no good pretending I don't want you,' said Daniel. 'I do. But . . . oh God. I'm the one with the experience, I ought to be able to decide what's best. And I mean what's best for you, not me. I'm a dead man, Misha, and I don't want to haunt you.' He laughed suddenly. 'Listen to me,' he said, 'God's gift to women. What an ego.' But he knew he could arouse her, and he knew that if he did it would be cataclysmic for both of them.

'You believe they will kill you, don't you,' she said.

'Yes.'

She bit her lip. 'My supervisor says I am doing very well. I am not searched as thoroughly as I might be. I could bring you a knife.'

'I don't know if I could use one.' He knew that when it came to it, he would hesitate for far too long. He could handle a scalpel, no problem, he'd dissected many creatures in his time – but they'd been dead. Slicing up living tissue was a different matter. He could see himself imagining the first incision, picturing what would happen, calculating the thrust, the twist, the withdrawal. And preferring to die himself.

'Let me bring you one anyway.'

'Be careful.' If it gave her pleasure then so be it.

They talked for a while about general things. He found that she knew nothing of evolution or the origin of man; it had never occurred to her to query why things were as they were. He talked about his job, the museum, his colleagues, the places he had been. She had no idea of geography, and she knew no history except that of her own country. She was a very good mathematician, and she loved music. She had been trained in both armed and unarmed combat, and she knew the language of flowers.

'What happens after the kissing?' she asked suddenly, as though she was in the process of learning a strange new ritual and she wanted to get it right.

She saw him glance at his mattress, a thin wedge of straw in a cotton cover on the floor in the corner. She stood up and walked over to it. Then she knelt down, and went onto all fours, hitching her dress around her thighs. 'Like this? Like dogs?'

She hadn't the faintest idea what she was doing to him. 'Sometimes,' he said.

'How else, then?'

'On your back, on your side, on your stomach . . . oh, Christ, every which way.'

'How long does it take?'

She realized that he was sitting very still, as though the slightest movement might hurt him.

'Depends,' he said.

'Ten seconds? Two minutes?'

'Longer.'

She looked surprised. He didn't move, but he was watching her with an intensity that made her feel slightly uneasy. 'Have you got an erection?' she asked, pleased with herself for remembering the right word.

'Yes.'

'That means you want to do it, doesn't it?'

'My body wants to.'

'But not your mind.'

He didn't answer.

'How do I know if my body wants to?'

'You start to get wet,' he said, 'between your legs.'

'You mean my bladder leaks?'

He laughed, glad of a way of releasing some of the tension; then he wanted to hold her. He gripped the tops of his arms with his hands. 'No Misha, it comes from the other place.'

'Oh.'

And then she simply pulled up the shift, bent over and looked at herself. He felt the most acute pang of desire he'd ever known, and he turned away.

'What's the matter?' she said. She was sitting up again, looking at him. 'I didn't see anything.'

He swallowed. 'Touch yourself,' he said. 'You will be able to feel it.'

She looked horrified. 'That's unclean.'

'No,' he said, with a slight shake of his head.

'Another lie?'

'Another lie. Really.'

Very tentatively she lifted the shift again, and put her fingers between her legs.

'You need to know your own anatomy too,' he said.

She had an expression of faint surprise on her face, but she hadn't taken her fingers away. He sat there, aching, watching her. It would be an honourable solution. Teach her to do it herself. And then do it himself, blindly, desperately, once she'd gone. Hold out, he pleaded silently, you can wait. But he wasn't sure that he could.

'If you rub a little bit,' he said, 'you will begin to feel the same sort of pleasure I felt when I . . . when you touched me.'

She tried it, watching him. He saw a blank look come across her face as the sensation took over, heard her breathing quicken slightly. Then she stopped.

'If you carry on,' he said, 'you will reach a climax. After that you will feel very relaxed and happy.'

'Do men do this as well?'

'Yes.'

'Show me.'

He hesitated. He felt that there was a fundamental flaw in this compromise solution, but he couldn't work out what it was. Perhaps it was that she would finally see his defencelessness. He had shown her no vulnerability so far, he didn't want her pity, or any of the other emotions that might follow. But at the moment of orgasm she would see another side to him. He shook his head.

She stood up and paced the room, restless. One more thing

he'd made her want. He felt as though he kept on making the wrong decisions, and he wanted to scream. And then the thunder rolled in the distance, and the rain started, and instead of being a refreshing sound it reminded him of his captivity, and what they'd have done if it had been a different time, a different place. He hit the table with his fist and she turned round and stared at him. It was the first violent action she had ever seen him perform.

'I think,' she said, 'you could use a knife if you had to.'

'Bring it,' he said. 'Next time.' But he knew that the only person he could use it on was himself.

She told him about the countryside around the compound. Mainly jungle, with occasional clearings for villages and a little agriculture here and there. She told him how to find the river that would take him to the sea – he could work his way up the coast and reach the capital, where he could contact his embassy. He played along with it, establishing escape routes, learning the names of villages that would help him, memorizing landmarks.

Suddenly she stood up, looked at him, paced up and down the room as she had earlier and then stopped. She was staring at his face with a new intensity. He felt his stomach contract. 'What is it?' he said, his voice a little unsteady.

'I want you to kiss me again,' she said, 'it was nice.' She walked over to him and sat on his lap, putting her thin arms round his neck.

It was hopeless; her body was pressed against his, he could feel every part of her. His mouth found hers and he began to kiss her with more passion than before, and when she responded he felt his self-control begin to slip. He put his hand on her thigh and started to stroke it, slowly moving from the outside of her leg to the inside. She squirmed against him and sighed; then her tongue was touching his again, and her breasts were against his chest, and he was losing it, second by second. He felt his erection between them, and then her hand was there and she was feeling him through the cotton, very gently, very tentatively. He remembered lying on his mattress a few days earlier and wanting to howl; he wanted it now. His whole body was consumed with desire, and he kissed her with less restraint than he would have liked. Her hipbone was digging into his stomach; they had got into an awkward position. He slid her off his lap, picked her up and carried her over to the mattress. *No*, said a voice inside his head. He knelt down beside her, took a deep breath and said, 'We mustn't. We really mustn't.'

She looked perplexed, then she opened her legs and felt herself with her fingers. 'Why not,' she said, 'I am wet.'

He put his arms round her and held her close. 'No,' he said. 'It's not right.' They sat like that for a while, not saying anything, and then they resumed their former positions at opposite sides of the table.

And suddenly the guard came back, and she was gone. He'd had his extra hour and he hadn't made love to her. He wanted to feel proud of himself, but he didn't.

He looked at the scars on his arms, the misshapen finger that they'd broken and he hadn't been able to set. He counted his ribs, and the bones in his feet. He ran his finger across the burn on his back that wouldn't heal, and he knew that there would be no happy ending. One more visit, and sometime after that it would happen.

He reviewed his life, the small discoveries he had made, the friends he had left behind, the women he had loved. Their sophistication, their erudition, their expertise in bed. None of them had ever moved him the way Misha had done. He wished he had made a bigger contribution in his own field, discovered something important. Was the corruption of a young girl all he was to leave behind? He tried to imagine her dressed Western-style, drinking a gin and tonic and making small-talk about the weather. It didn't work. She was part of something else, she didn't fit; she would hate the small deceptions that were part of everyday life, the lack of direction, the obsession with trivia. He lay on the mattress, staring at the ceiling, listening to the rain. He didn't masturbate.

'Well done, Misha,' said Misha's supervisor. 'You completed the whole questionnaire in five weeks instead of six. You are to be congratulated.'

Misha froze. It hadn't occurred to her that by doing her job too well she might forfeit the last week with Daniel. 'Is there nothing else you wish me to ask him?' she said, hoping she had kept both her face and her voice expressionless.

'Oh yes,' said the supervisor. 'Now we really get to work.'

She looked up at him, uncomprehending.

'You have gained his trust,' said the supervisor. 'Now you must ask him about the military installations.'

'He's a palaeo . . . palaeonotologist,' she said. 'He's a scientist. He digs up the bones of dragons. He's not a mercenary.'

'You are wrong, Misha,' said the supervisor. 'He killed two of our men.'

'No.'

'I repeat, you are wrong. He knows where the arms dumps are, on the other side. Now you must get him to talk. I will explain how you do it, what his reactions are likely to be, how you can catch him out. Remember Misha; he would kill you without thinking twice, if he had the means.'

She left the supervisor's hut in a daze, and crossed the courtyard. For the first time she wondered about the brown patch on the sand, by the post. When she helped in the kitchen that evening she stole the knife she'd been using to chop the celery, but she didn't know whether she would give it to him. She took it home with her. The walk back took an hour and a half, along a jungle path thick with flowering creepers and the erratic humming of insects. She fingered the knife all the way back, feeling the edge, touching the point. She imagined him piercing her with it.

He noticed a difference in her the moment she walked through the door. There was a distance, a formality to her, and when she sat down opposite him she didn't meet his eyes. He waited.

She put another piece of paper on the table. 'I have been instructed to ask you,' she said, 'the location of the arms dumps on the other side.'

'What?'

'I have been instructed to ask . . .'

'I heard you,' he said shortly. 'I just didn't believe it.'

'You killed two men,' she said, her voice flat and lifeless, 'you lied to me.'

'No. My guide killed two men.'

She glanced up at him. He was absolutely motionless, his eyes fixed on her face.

'My *guide* killed two men,' he repeated, with emphasis.

'They told me to expect you to say that.'

He smiled, the nasty smile she'd seen on the first day. Then he leant back in his chair, folded his arms and stared at the floor. She tried every method her supervisor had suggested. She told him they would send his signed document to the newspapers in his country. It was quite apparent that he didn't care. She told him how many people would die if they couldn't locate and destroy the weapons. He didn't react. And finally, she forced herself to tell him how bad it would make her look if he didn't answer her questions. He didn't raise his eyes. Then she passed him the knife, covertly, under the table, opening his fingers and pressing the wooden handle into the palm of his hand.

He closed his eyes, but he took the knife. They sat there,

not speaking. Then she said softly, 'Think of me. When you are free.'

Again he marvelled at her naivety, for even if he could escape the compound the chances of him reaching the coast were very slim. He wondered whether she had donned her ideology again as a defence, whether she'd realized that she could not stay where she was without it. Then he wondered if someone was listening.

The door opened, and Misha's supervisor walked in, flanked by the guard. Misha stood up immediately and bowed. Daniel stayed where he was. The guard jerked his gun at Daniel, indicating to him to get to his feet.

Daniel didn't move. The guard drew himself up to his full height. There was a fleeting impression of bulk, with little brainpower behind it – the face was memorable mainly for its bad teeth and its sinister eyes, one milky-white, the other blue-black.

The supervisor smiled, picked up Misha's notes and glanced at them. He was a middle-aged man, grey-haired, he had the bearing of someone of importance. He raised his eyebrows and looked at her in admonition.

'Nothing,' he said, waving the sheet of paper at her.

Misha said something in her own language, but it was too fast for Daniel to snatch any sense from it. He'd learned a few phrases, but not enough.

'No no,' said the supervisor, 'we will all speak English. It is polite.' He turned to Daniel. 'Allow me to introduce myself. My name is Lin-Dah.'

Daniel suppressed a smile. He wanted to say, that's a girl's name, but he knew it wasn't advisable.

'You say you are a doctor,' murmured Lin-Dah.

'Not a medical one.'

'Ah. So you cannot prove it by making the blind see?' He

smiled in the direction of the guard, who grinned despite the fact that he obviously didn't understand a single word.

'No. I am not a surgeon.'

'You are a soldier,' said the supervisor.

'I am a scientist.'

The supervisor shook his head, amused. 'I know that Misha has explained to you what we wish to know. I strongly suggest that you tell me.' His English was fluent, impeccable, his accent faint.

'I am not in any army,' said Daniel slowly. 'I *cannot* tell you what you wish to know.'

'You held out very well against the torture,' said Lin-Dah, 'you have been well trained, my friend.'

Daniel saw Misha look at the supervisor in disbelief, then horror. Her eyes flicked to the scars on Daniel's arms and then the broken finger, and a sort of numbness seemed to creep across her face.

'Admirably trained,' the supervisor continued. 'But you are not yourself any more, are you. Look at you. Thin, weak, ill, maybe. No one will blame you for talking.'

'If I had known anything,' said Daniel, 'believe me, I'd have told you last time.'

'I don't believe you,' said Lin-Dah.

He nodded at the guard. The guard seized Misha by her hair, and dragged her to the mattress. She screamed out; he clamped a hand across her mouth, and knelt over her. Then he looked up at the supervisor, waiting. He still had the gun in one hand.

Daniel was on his feet and moving forward when the gun swung in his direction. He stopped.

'Sit down,' said Lin-Dah.

Daniel stood there, undecided.

'Sit down,' repeated the supervisor softly, and he nodded

briefly at the guard. The guard hit Misha across the face, and looked at Daniel.

Daniel sat down.

'It's a wonderful method,' said Lin-Dah. 'The breaks between the visits are particularly important, time to fantasize a little . . . or a lot. And she is totally innocent, she had no idea we'd be prepared to kill her to get you to talk. Obviously. So – I'm listening. First her virginity, and then her life; they are both in your hands.'

'I don't know anything!' shouted Daniel. 'God Almighty believe me, I'd tell you. *I would tell you.*'

He saw the guard push Misha's dress up to her waist. The supervisor was smiling. The guard pulled down his own trousers, one-handed, his other hand still across her mouth, holding the pistol. Daniel glanced at Lin-Dah. He did not appear to be armed, and his smile was getting wider. His hand went into his trouser pocket.

Jesus Christ, thought Daniel, he's getting off on it. 'You total bastard,' he hissed, 'jerking off to *that.* She's one of your own.'

The supervisor laughed, but he didn't look at Daniel, he was watching Misha. 'All regimes screw the populace,' he said, 'one way or another. There are many more where she came from. We have a population problem, she will be doing her country a service, there will be one less mouth to feed. Unless, of course, you tell us what you know.'

'I don't know anything,' said Daniel desperately, and he realized that this, in many respects, was true. He hadn't seen it coming, hadn't second-guessed them.

'Come and stand next to me,' said Lin-Dah, 'I want you to watch. You told her all about fucking, I presume? It goes about fifty-fifty – half the prisoners do tell the girls, half of them don't. A few of them try to show them. Not many.

Torture appears to have a rather paralysing effect on the necessary equipment. As I said, it's a good system.'

'I didn't tell her it could be an act of violence,' said Daniel. He felt the knife press against his thigh as he stepped out from behind the table; he was dreading what he might have to do. The guard was smiling up at them, waiting for a signal. Lin-Dah had a distant look on his face, he appeared to be jiggling something in his pocket. It's hardly likely to be loose change out here, thought Daniel, astounded that he could come up with something like that at a time like this.

He heard a slight sound above them, a rustle perhaps, and even though he knew it was probably the bats he couldn't help glancing upwards. The snake fell from the rafters like a piece of brown ticker-tape, twisting this way and that; the thud as it landed on the floor reminded him of his mother making dough, a sort of low-pitched slap. The guard leapt backwards as though stung – he was visibly shaking, and he started to babble something incoherently, pointing with his finger and pulling his trousers back round his waist with his other hand. The snake reared up, defensive, its tongue flickering; the guard backed away to the door and fled, leaving it open. His pistol was the only part of him that remained behind, dull and black on the floor. Misha lay there, very still, the snake a few inches from her head, swaying gently. But the lidless golden eyes weren't looking at Misha, they had noticed the movement of the supervisor's hand in his pocket. The man was as still as stone now, staring at the snake. Petrified, Daniel thought, I never really appreciated the meaning of the word before. There was absolute silence as the reptile slid towards Lin-Dah.

Misha got to her feet, smoothly, silently, held out her hand to Daniel for the knife. He gave it to her. She moved very slowly behind the snake, bent down, picked it up by the tail and cracked it like a whip. It was almost certainly dead before it hit the floor, but she decapitated it with the knife, presumably to make absolutely sure. Then she picked up the guard's pistol.

Lin-Dah took a deep breath. His face had gone yellow, and there was a stippling of sweat on his forehead. Misha levelled the gun at him and said something, too fast for Daniel to understand. The man opened his mouth, then closed it again. There was something different about him, his whole bearing had changed, he sagged like a plant without water. He started to speak, softly, miserably. Daniel watched their faces, trying to guess what they said to one another, but apart from a few puzzling words about ancestors and obligations it was impossible. Misha kept pointing at the dead snake. Eventually the supervisor bowed his head.

Misha said to Daniel, 'You must walk before him as though you are his prisoner. He will tie your hands behind your back. I will walk five paces behind, as is proper, but I will carry your shirt, and the gun will be under it. It is very unlikely that he will try anything, but if he calls for help I will kill him, and then it would be best if I killed both of us as well. I have explained this to him. Take off your shirt.'

Daniel took off his shirt, and handed it to Misha. She ripped off one of the sleeves, and gave it to Lin-Dah. The material was very thin, and Lin-Dah tied Daniel's hands with it as Misha instructed. Daniel expected there to be at least one vicious jerk, but there wasn't. It was as though the man had acquiesced to something for reasons beyond Daniel's understanding.

'Once we're outside,' said Daniel, 'what then?'

'We find the river,' said Misha.

He marvelled at her optimism, but he went along with it. They were both the walking dead.

As they passed from one barbed-wire fence to another he watched her self-composure with astonishment. She spoke quickly and easily to every official, and they let her through. Lin-Dah said very little, and his face was expressionless. When they reached the last enclosure, where the vehicles were kept, the supervisor went over to one of the drivers and demanded the keys to a jeep. The man seemed inclined to argue until Lin-Dah said something rather sharply, and then he handed over the keys without another word.

'You will drive,' Misha said to Lin-Dah, and they climbed in. She kept the gun levelled at his heart.

As they drove out of the compound and away down the dirt track, Daniel was convinced he was dreaming. It had all been so ludicrously simple.

'We need to get rid of this vehicle, and cut through the jungle,' said Misha. 'There are many swamps. We will leave it in one of them.'

'What about our driver?'

'We'll let him go.'

'Misha . . . why did he just agree to all this? He hasn't even tried to fight back.'

'Oh,' said Misha, 'it is difficult for him, you see. Because of the snake.'

'I don't understand.'

'The snake. The snake that falls from the sky is very bad omen. This is why the guard ran away. Then the snake chooses my supervisor instead. He must have offended an ancestor by his actions, and he must try to put it right. So he helps us. He does not like it, but he has to do it.'

And when they stopped, an hour or more later, Lin-Dah climbed silently out of the jeep, bowed to both of them and walked away without a backward glance.

She took over. He did everything she said, blindly, automatically, knowing he was functioning on adrenalin alone. He remembered her making him put on a pair of boots, giving him a rucksack; he remembered them changing their clothes. He remembered watching the jeep sink into green sludge and disappear. They had been walking for a long time when she finally said, 'Here. This is the cave I told you about. We can sleep.'

He lay down on his bedroll and slept, deeply, dreamlessly.

When she woke him the sun was shining, the way it always did in the morning. There was a profusion of butterflies, beetles, orchids, a sensory overload of life itself. She showed him the way to a stream and there was a pool beneath a waterfall, moving patterns of turquoise, sapphire and jade. He took off his clothes and went for a swim. She sat on the bank and watched him for a while, then she turned her back towards him and took off the shirt and trousers. He caught a glimpse of her, tiny, naked, and then she was in the water as well and he swam over to her. They touched very tentatively at first, and then the water pushed their bodies together and he felt the whole length of her against him. He turned her round and floated with her on his chest, his hands on her breasts. When they climbed out of the water and sat on the bank once more he knew he was going to make love to her. It was inevitable.

He reached out and took her by the wrist, repeating the design he had drawn on her palm three weeks earlier. She smiled, opened his other hand with hers and drew the same design. He felt a shiver run through him.

'Sometimes,' he said, 'it can hurt a little. Just the first time. And not for long.'

'I am not frightened,' she said.

He had expected her to be; after all, she had nearly been raped the previous day, a violent side to the sexual act had been introduced with no warning whatsoever, no explanation, no preparation. He had seen himself as a healer, someone to slowly overcome the damage that must have been done, someone patient and gentle and understanding – but even here he was wrong. He realized very quickly that she wanted him as badly as he wanted her, and he was astonished at her resilience.

He spread his clothes on the ground, amongst the flowers and the butterflies, and laid her down on them. However badly he wanted her, he wasn't going to rush this. She was watching his face expectantly, as though he was about to perform something magical and rare, a mystery. A bird called from the jungle, eerie, distant, arcane, a perfectly tailored soundtrack. He started to kiss her forehead, her eyelids, her neck, her shoulders, working his way down, systematic, skilful, very very gentle. The bird called again, a thin, extruded cry, he kissed her hips, her thighs, the backs of her knees. The deliberate delaying of his own gratification heightened everything to a pitch he had never experienced before; just the taste of her naked skin was enough to drive him to distraction, and fighting off his desire was the most exquisite of agonies. He worked his way back up again, counting her ribs with his tongue, touching her nipple, licking it, rolling it round in his mouth, feeling her press herself against him. His hands moved to her waist, across her belly; he traced the line to her groin with his thumb, moved her legs apart and opened the folds with his fingers, stroking as lightly as he could and noticing almost immediately the evidence of her arousal. He began to rub, building the pace, feeling the tension increase, finally entering her with his finger. But rather than drawing back she pushed against him. He heard her gasp, then there was no more resistance and she pulled him to her as though she was frightened he would dissolve, evaporate, disappear. They held each other very tightly for a few moments, and then he kissed her on the mouth and rubbed the tip of his penis against her, feeling the wetness, wanting to thrust, holding back. Her whole body shuddered, the tendons in her neck tightened, her stomach muscles clenched; she held her breath for long moments, then released it convulsively and held it again. He knew she was on the edge, and then he wasn't thinking at all, he was inside her and totally lost.

Misha separated the two events quite easily in her head. The threat from the guard the day before had nothing to do with what Daniel was doing to her today. She had always been able to compartmentalize things; it was the only way to exist – from mother to Citizenship School, from there to college, from college to service and from service to marriage. She relegated the guard to an irrelevant past and gave herself up to Daniel completely. For once they were speaking the same language, fluently and in depth. Her body amazed her; she had not realized it was capable of such pleasure. His fingers were like fire, and wherever he touched her she melted. She felt a coalescence that was completely alien to her, the idea of becoming one with another person was not a concept that had ever entered her head. Part of her was leaving to live in him, and part of him to live in her; they were exchanging pieces of their identities, it was the strangest and most wonderful thing that had ever happened to her. She didn't want it to end, and when it did it was with a violent beauty that stunned her to silence. They lay there for a long time, not speaking.

'What are we going to do?' he asked her later, knowing he sounded weak and indecisive, but too drained to sound any different. He was shaken by the intensity of what had happened between them.

'Find your embassy,' she said, 'and go to your country.' It was all so simple to her.

'You wouldn't like my country,' he said, '*I* don't like my country.'

'I thought – I thought you were making all that up. To please me.'

'No,' he said, 'I meant every word.'

'Then . . .' She looked at him, her eyes wide.

'We find somewhere else,' he said, knowing that there was nowhere. There wasn't a single state that wasn't on one side or the other – and most of them were on *his* side. She would be nothing, unacceptable, just another immigrant sponging off the taxpayers.

They walked for many days, following a stream, knowing it would join up with the river eventually. They met nobody, and he began to believe in luck.

She watched him as they walked. He was so beautiful to her now, with his shock of straw-coloured hair. He would have been conspicuous anywhere.

They were travelling along a wide shallow river criss-crossed with weathered areas of bedrock. They skittered from one stepping stone to another and walked along the bank when they could. She was ahead of him; he had stopped to wring the water from his clothes. When he looked up there were two of her. He blinked, and wiped his eyes. Now there were three. Three figures dressed in grey shirts and trousers, talking animatedly and glancing towards him every so often. He stood there, not knowing what to do, an empty feeling in his chest. Misha was gesticulating, arguing, the other two were shouting back, not aggressively but urgently, as though there was something she didn't understand. Then all three of them turned to look at the far side of the clearing.

The figures that came out of the jungle were like ghosts against the darkening sky and the relentless sheets of rainwater, and they were wearing the wrong uniform. Daniel saw one of the soldiers raise his gun, and two of the grey figures turned and ran. After a few paces one of them stopped, went back for Misha and pulled her along with him. A warning shot whistled over their heads. Daniel moved directly into the line of fire and just stood there, waiting, offering them a target. There were no more shots. After a few seconds of eternity the three grey figures vanished into the green mess of the jungle.

'Hey,' called a voice, 'Doctor Murray! Doctor Daniel Murray! Hey, fellers, we found him! Doc, we're on your side!'

It wasn't what he wanted.

BERENICE

Edgar Allan Poe

MISERY is manifold. The wretchedness of earth is multiform. Overreaching the wide horizon as the rainbow, its hues are as various as the hues of that arch, – as distinct too, yet as intimately blended. Overreaching the wide horizon as the rainbow! How is it that from beauty I have derived a type of unloveliness? – from the covenant of peace a simile of sorrow? But as, in ethics, evil is a consequence of good, so, in fact, out of joy is sorrow born. Either the memory of past bliss is the anguish of today, or the agonies which *are* have their origin in the ecstasies which *might have been*.

My baptismal name is Egæus; that of my family I will not mention. Yet there are no towers in the land more time-honoured than my gloomy, grey, hereditary halls. Our line has been called a race of visionaries; and in many striking particulars – in the character of the family mansion – in the frescoes of the chief saloon – in the tapestries of the dormitories – in the chiselling of some buttresses in the armoury – but more especially in the gallery of antique paintings – in the fashion of the library chamber – and, lastly, in the very peculiar nature of the library's contents, there is more than sufficient evidence to warrant the belief.

The recollections of my earliest years are connected with that chamber, and with its volumes – of which latter I will say no more. Here died my mother. Herein was I born. But it is mere idleness to say that I had not lived before – that the soul has no previous existence. You deny it? – let us not argue the matter. Convinced myself, I seek not to convince. There is, however, a remembrance of aerial forms – of spiritual and meaning eyes – of sounds, musical yet sad – a remembrance which will not be excluded; a memory like a shadow, vague, variable, indefinite, unsteady; and like a shadow, too, in the impossibility of my getting rid of it while the sunlight of my reason shall exist.

In that chamber was I born. Thus awaking from the long night of what seemed, but was not, nonentity, at once into the very regions of fairy-land – into a palace of imagination – into the wild dominions of monastic thought and erudition – it is not singular that I gazed around me with a startled and ardent eye – that I loitered away my boyhood in books, and dissipated my youth in reverie; but it *is* singular that as years rolled away, and the noon of manhood found me still in the mansion of my fathers – it *is* wonderful what stagnation there fell upon the springs of my life – wonderful how total an inversion took place in the character of my commonest thought. The realities of the world affected me as visions, and as visions only, while the wild ideas of the land of dreams became, in turn, – not the material of my everyday existence – but in very deed that existence utterly and solely in itself.

Berenice and I were cousins, and we grew up together in my paternal halls. Yet differently we grew – I ill of health, and buried in gloom – she agile, graceful, and overflowing with energy; hers the ramble on the hillside – mine the studies of the cloister – I living within my own heart, and addicted body and soul to the most intense and painful meditation –

she roaming carelessly through life with no thought of the shadows in her path, or the silent flight of the raven-winged hours. Berenice! – I call upon her name – Berenice! – and from the grey ruins of memory a thousand tumultuous recollections are startled at the sound! Ah! vividly is her image before me now, as in the early days of her light-heartedness and joy! Oh! gorgeous yet fantastic beauty! Oh! sylph amid the shrubberies of Arnheim! Oh! Naiad among its fountains! – and then – then all is mystery and terror, and a tale which should not be told. Disease – a fatal disease – fell like the simoom upon her frame, and, even while I gazed upon her, the spirit of change swept over her, pervading her mind, her habits, and her character, and, in a manner the most subtle and terrible, disturbing even the identity of her person! Alas! the destroyer came and went, and the victim – where was she? I knew her not – or knew her no longer as Berenice.

Among the numerous train of maladies superinduced by that fatal and primary one which effected a revolution of so horrible a kind in the moral and physical being of my cousin, may be mentioned as the most distressing and obstinate in its nature, a species of epilepsy not infrequently terminating in *trance* itself – trance very nearly resembling positive dissolution, and from which her manner of recovery was, in most instances, startlingly abrupt. In the meantime my own disease – for I have been told that I should call it by no other appellation – my own disease, then, grew rapidly upon me, and assumed finally a monomaniac character of a novel and extraordinary form – hourly and momently gaining vigour – and at length obtaining over me the most incomprehensible ascendency. This monomania, if I must so term it, consisted in a morbid irritability of those properties of the mind in metaphysical science termed the *attentive*. It is more than probable that I am not understood; but I fear, indeed, that it is in no manner possible to convey to the mind of the merely general reader, an adequate idea of that nervous *intensity of interest* with which, in my case, the powers of meditation (not to speak technically) busied and buried themselves, in the contemplation of even the most ordinary objects of the universe.

To muse for long unwearied hours with my attention riveted to some frivolous device on the margin, or in the typography of a book; to become absorbed for the better part of a summer's day, in a quaint shadow falling aslant upon the tapestry, or upon the door; to lose myself for an entire night in watching the steady flame of a lamp, or the embers of a fire; to dream away whole days over the perfume of a flower; to repeat monotonously some common word, until the sound, by dint of frequent repetition, ceased to convey any idea whatever to the mind; to lose all sense of motion or physical existence, by means of absolute bodily quiescence long and obstinately persevered in; – such were a few of the most common and least pernicious vagaries induced by a condition of the mental faculties, not, indeed, altogether unparalleled, but certainly bidding defiance to anything like analysis or explanation.

Yet let me not be misapprehended. – The undue, earnest, and morbid attention thus excited by objects in their own nature frivolous, must not be confounded in character with that ruminating propensity common to all mankind, and more especially indulged in by persons of ardent imagination. It was not even, as might be at first supposed, an extreme condition, or exaggeration of such propensity, but primarily and essentially distinct and different. In the one instance, the dreamer, or enthusiast, being interested by an object usually *not* frivolous, imperceptibly loses sight of this object in a wilderness of deductions and suggestions issuing therefrom, until, at the conclusion of a day-dream *often replete with luxury,* he finds the *incitamentum* or first cause of his musings entirely vanished and forgotten. In my case the primary object was *invariably frivolous*, although assuming, through the medium of my distempered vision, a refracted and unreal importance. Few deductions, if any, were made; and those few pertinaciously returning in upon the original object as a centre. The meditations were *never* pleasurable; and, at the termination of the reverie, the first cause, so far from being out of sight, had attained that supernaturally exaggerated interest which was the prevailing feature of the disease. In a word, the powers of mind more particularly exercised were, with me, as I have said before, the *attentive*, and are, with the day-dreamer, the *speculative.*

My books, at this epoch, if they did not exactly serve to irritate the disorder, partook, it will be perceived, largely, in their imaginative and inconsequential nature, of the characteristic qualities of the disorder itself. I well remember, among others, the treatise of the noble Italian Cœlius Secundus Curio, *De Amplitudine Beati Regni Dei*; St Austin's great work, *The City of God*; and Tertullian, *De Carne Christi*, in which the paradoxical sentence, '*Mortuus est Dei filius; credibile est quia ineptum est: et sepultus resurrexit; certum est quia impossibile est,*' occupied my undivided time, for many weeks of laborious and fruitless investigation.

Thus it will appear that, shaken from its balance only by trivial things, my reason bore resemblance to that ocean-crag spoken of by Ptolemy Hephestion, which, steadily resisting the attacks of human violence, and the fiercer fury of the waters and the winds, trembled only to the touch of the flower called Asphodel. And although, to a careless thinker, it might appear a matter beyond doubt, that the alteration produced by her unhappy malady, in the *moral* condition of Berenice, would afford me many objects for the exercise of that intense and abnormal meditation whose nature I have been at some trouble in explaining, yet such was not in any degree the case.

In the lucid intervals of my infirmity, her calamity, indeed, gave me pain, and, taking deeply to heart that total wreck of her fair and gentle life, I did not fail to ponder frequently and bitterly upon the wonder-working means by which so strange a revolution had been so suddenly brought to pass. But these reflections partook not of the idiosyncrasy of my disease, and were such as would have occurred, under similar circumstances, to the ordinary mass of mankind. True to its own character, my disorder revelled in the less important but more startling changes wrought in the *physical* frame of Berenice – in the singular and most appalling distortion of her personal identity.

During the brightest days of her unparalleled beauty, most surely I had never loved her. In the strange anomaly of my existence, feelings with me *had never been* of the heart, and my passions *always were* of the mind. Through the grey of the early morning – among the trellised shadows of the forest at noonday – and in the silence of my library at night, she had flitted by my eyes, and I had seen her – not as the living and breathing Berenice, but as the Berenice of a dream – not as a being of the earth, earthy, but as the abstraction of such a being – not as a thing to admire, but to analyse – not as an object of love, but as the theme of the most abstruse although desultory speculation. And *now* – now I shuddered in her presence, and grew pale at her approach; yet bitterly lamenting her fallen and desolate condition, I called to mind that she had loved me long, and, in an evil moment, I spoke to her of marriage.

And at length the period of our nuptials was approaching, when, upon an afternoon in the winter of the year, – one of those unseasonably warm, calm, and misty days which are the nurse of the beautiful Halcyon, – I sat (and sat, as I thought, alone) in the inner apartment of the library. But uplifting my eyes I saw that Berenice stood before me.

Was it my own excited imagination – or the misty influence of the atmosphere – or the uncertain twilight of the chamber – or the grey draperies which fell around her figure – that caused in it so vacillating and indistinct an outline? I could not tell. She spoke no word, and I – not for worlds could I have uttered a syllable. An icy chill ran through my frame; a sense of insufferable anxiety oppressed me; a consuming curiosity pervaded my soul; and sinking back upon the chair, I remained for some time breathless and motionless, with my eyes riveted upon her person. Alas! its emaciation was excessive, and not one vestige of the former being lurked in any single line of the contour. My burning glances at length fell upon the face.

The forehead was high, and very pale, and singularly placid; and the once jetty hair fell partially over it, and overshadowed the hollow temples with innumerable ringlets now of a vivid yellow, and jarring discordantly, in their fantastic character, with the reigning melancholy of the countenance. The eyes were lifeless, and lustreless, and seemingly pupil-less, and I shrank involuntarily from their glassy stare to the contemplation of the thin and shrunken lips. They parted; and in a smile of peculiar meaning, *the teeth* of the changed Berenice disclosed themselves slowly to my view. Would to God that I had never beheld them, or that, having done so, I had died!

The shutting of a door disturbed me, and, looking up, I found that my cousin had departed from the chamber. But from the disordered chamber of my brain, had not, alas! departed, and would not be driven away, the white and ghastly *spectrum* of the teeth. Not a speck on their surface – not a shade on their enamel – not an indenture in their edges – but what that period of her smile had sufficed to brand in upon my memory. I saw them *now* even more unequivocally than I beheld them *then*. The teeth! – the teeth! – they were here, and there, and everywhere, and visibly and palpably before me; long, narrow, and excessively white, with the pale lips writhing about them, as in the very moment of their first terrible development. Then came the full fury of my *monomania*, and I struggled in vain against its strange and irresistible influence. In the multiplied objects of the external world I had no thoughts but for the teeth. For these I longed with a frenzied desire. All other matters and all different interests became absorbed in their single contemplation. They – they alone were present to the mental eye, and they, in their sole individuality, became the essence of my mental life. I held them in every light. I turned them in every attitude. I surveyed their characteristics. I dwelt upon their peculiarities. I pondered upon their conformation. I mused upon the alteration in their nature. I shuddered as I assigned to them in imagination a sensitive and sentient power, and even when unassisted by the lips, a capability of moral expression. Of Mad'selle Sallé it has been well said, '*que tous ses pas étaient des sentiments*,' and of Berenice I more seriously believed *que toutes ses dents étaient des idées. Des idées!* – ah here was the idiotic thought that destroyed me! *Des idées!* – ah *therefore* it was that I coveted them so madly! I felt that their possession could alone ever restore me to peace, in giving me back to reason.

And the evening closed in upon me thus – and then the darkness came, and tarried, and went – and the day again dawned – and the mists of a second night were now gathering around – and still I sat motionless in that solitary room; and still I sat buried in meditation, and still the *phantasma* of the teeth maintained its terrible ascendency as, with the most vivid and hideous distinctness, it floated about amid the changing lights and shadows of the chamber. At length there broke in upon my dreams a cry as of horror and dismay; and thereunto, after a pause, succeeded the sound of troubled voices, intermingled with many low moanings of sorrow, or of pain. I arose from my seat and, throwing open one of the doors of the library, saw standing out in the ante-chamber a servant maiden, all in tears, who told me that Berenice was – no more. She had been seized with epilepsy in the early morning, and now, at the closing in of the night, the grave was ready for its tenant, and all the preparations for the burial were completed.

I found myself sitting in the library, and again sitting there alone. It seemed that I had newly awakened from a confused and exciting dream. I knew that it was now midnight, and I was well aware that since the setting of the sun Berenice had been interred. But of that dreary period which intervened I had no positive – at least no definite comprehension. Yet its memory was replete with horror – horror more horrible from being vague, and terror more terrible from ambiguity. It was a fearful page in the record of my existence, written all over with dim, and hideous, and unintelligible recollections. I strived to decipher them, but in vain; while ever and anon, like the spirit of a departed sound, the shrill and piercing shriek of a female voice seemed to be ringing in my ears. I had done a deed – what was it? I asked myself the question aloud, and the whispering echoes of the chamber answered me, '*What was it?*'

On the table beside me burned a lamp, and near it lay a little box. It was of no remarkable character, and I had seen it frequently before, for it was the property of the family physician; but how came it *there*, upon my table, and why did I shudder in regarding it? These things were in no manner to be accounted for, and my eyes at length dropped to the open pages of a book, and to a sentence underscored therein. The words were the singular but simple ones of the poet Ebn Zaiat, '*Dicebant mihi sodales si sepulchrum amicæ visitarem curas meas aliquantulum fore levatas*.' Why then, as I perused them, did the hairs of my head erect themselves on end, and the blood of my body become congealed within my veins?

There came a light tap at the library door, and pale as the tenant of a tomb, a menial entered upon tiptoe. His looks were wild with terror, and he spoke to me in a voice tremulous, husky, and very low. What said he? – some broken sentences I heard. He told me of a wild cry disturbing the silence of the night – of the gathering together of the household – of a search in the direction of the sound; – and then his tones grew thrillingly distinct as he whispered me of a violated grave – of a disfigured body enshrouded, yet still breathing, still palpitating, still *alive*!

He pointed to my garments; – they were muddy and clotted with gore. I spoke not, and he took me gently by the hand; – it was indented with the impress of human nails. He directed my attention to some object against the wall; – I looked at it for some minutes; – it was a spade. With a shriek I bounded to the table, and grasped the box that lay upon it. But I could not force it open; and in my tremor it slipped from my hands, and fell heavily, and burst into pieces; and from it, with a rattling sound, there rolled out some instruments of dental surgery, intermingled with thirty-two small, white and ivory-looking substances that were scattered to and fro about the floor.

THE PLAIN BROWN ENVELOPE

Lyn Wood

THAT'S quite some paintjob, thought Sophie. Someone had designed the lorry as an enormous brown envelope – one of those heavy-duty ones, with a slight grain to the paper. The illusion only worked if you were sideways-on of course, but it was a clever idea, with the company's name and address placed exactly where it should be, a little over half-way down. And the stamp was a first-class job – in every respect.

Sophie had never hitch-hiked on her own before, and she wouldn't have been doing it now if she hadn't decided that it was the only way to research an article she was writing. She told a colleague what she was planning, arranged to ring her by a certain time to say she was all right and wore her straight black trousers – no point in being unduly provocative. She buttoned up her raincoat and bundled her hair under her hat so that she looked as masculine as possible. Act forcefully, she said to herself, be in control. Don't look like a victim and you won't become one. At the same time an impish little voice inside her head said, how far are you prepared to go with this, Sophie? You're suggesting that being picked up by a lorry driver is one of those universal female fantasies, aren't you. Another one of your raunchy articles on make-believe. To be screwed senseless by someone you'll never meet again, a quick bit of rough. How thorough are you really prepared to be? And then the plain brown lorry stopped and she suddenly felt very nervous.

'I'm going all the way to Manchester,' said the driver. He was wearing a tatty T-shirt and jeans and he hadn't shaved for a couple of days. Dead scruffy really, but he had nice blue eyes and he was rather good-looking underneath the dark stubble. She'd started to hope that he'd be sixty, with bad teeth and one eye, and then she'd have had a good excuse to back out.

She took a deep breath, said 'That's where I'm going,' and climbed up into the cab beside him. He cleared away a few papers and sweet-wrappers, and apologized for the mess. She watched him as he pulled away. His easy domination over the huge machine was . . . well, sexy. She reprimanded herself and tried to think more objectively. They drove for a little while in silence, then as they turned onto the motorway he asked her her name.

'Sophie,' she said. 'What's yours?'

'Jeff.' It seemed like the sort of name a lorry driver ought to have. He asked her what she did and she started to lie about herself, saying she worked in a supermarket and inventing a flat in Brixton and a cat called Albert.

'Boyfriend?' he said.

'Peter,' said Sophie, although she'd split up with Peter a couple of months back. It might be wise to keep him in existence for the duration of the journey. She talked about him for a while, his obsession with Manchester United, his disastrous attempts at plumbing. Plumbing was a nice safe topic, second only to diseases as a sexual deterrent. She was chickening out.

It started to rain, then the rain turned to sleet and the traffic grew heavy. They slowed down, a long succession of red tail-lights in front of them, the wipers sluicing away the slush from the windscreen with an irritating little squeak. Another lorry passed them, bearing the immortal words: *Get a slice of the action with Paolo's Pizzas*.

'What are you carrying?' asked Sophie.

He glanced at her, and hesitated.

'Surely you *know* what's in the back,' she said. It sounded more patronizing than she'd intended.

''Course I do,' he said.

'What then?'

'You really wanna know?'

'I'm asking, aren't I?' She was trying too hard to be forceful, and had only succeeded in sounding rude.

'All right,' he said, 'sex aids.'

Her eyes widened and her mouth dropped open.

He laughed. 'You did ask.'

'You could have lied.'

'True.' He grinned. 'Aren't you interested, then?'

'What in?'

'What I've got in the back. Most people are, when they find out what I do. They act shocked; after a moment or two they snigger, then they ask the odd sly question and before you know it you've sold them a couple of magazines and a tube of KY jelly.'

'Oh,' said Sophie. 'Really.'

'You're not a prude, are you?'

'No.'

'It's just a job.'

She looked uncomfortable.

'Oh come on,' he said, 'lighten up, do you seriously think a rapist would travel around in a lorry carrying what *I'm* carrying?'

'No,' she said, 'I suppose not.'

'Good,' said Jeff. 'That's got that out of the way. Have a peppermint.' He grinned again. 'Or don't you accept sweets from strangers?'

She laughed and took one, and she began to relax. The sun had suddenly come out in the cab, although it was now snowing outside. They laughed quite a lot for the next fifty miles.

There was little traffic left now; the snow was getting heavier all the time. She peered out of the window at the side – the fields were white, and there were drifts building up on the hard shoulder. Then the road began to change colour as well, and Jeff slowed right down. Five minutes later the lorry snaked from one carriageway to the other, and Sophie clutched at her seat, white-knuckled.

'We'd better stop,' he said. 'They'll have the snowploughs and the gritters out before long.'

She nodded. There really wasn't any other alternative. He pulled over, and for a while they sat in the cab with the engine on so that the heater kept them warm, drinking the tea from his flask and eating biscuits. But it soon became apparent that the heater wasn't really powerful enough for the extreme conditions.

'I think I can turn it up from the engine,' he said, and he grabbed a flashlight and got out of the cab. She heard him moving around outside, and then the engine cut out completely. The cessation of tepid air from beneath the dashboard was like a blast from the Arctic. After a couple of minutes he clambered back in, shaking his head.

'What are we going to do?' asked Sophie, wondering if he'd done it deliberately.

'Get in the back. There are boxes of clothes, bed linen, a couple of rugs, we can use them as blankets. Sort of.'

Again, there didn't seem to be a sensible alternative.

He scribbled a note saying that Jeff and Sophie were in the trailer, and left it on the dashboard. She was impressed with his forward thinking, and glad he had advertised her presence by using her name on the note. She smiled at her own paranoia, for it wasn't the first time she'd regretted her actions in pursuit of a story. Journalists were inclined to see sinister motives behind everything. She glanced at her watch, but she didn't need to phone her contact for another hour and a half.

There was a bottle of something called Boukha in a plastic bag behind him – he took that, the cup from the thermos and the rest of the biscuits. Then they got out, waded through the snow, unlocked the doors at the back and climbed in.

Jeff swept the flashlight round the interior, and then hung it from a metal strut. The light swung back and forth, stretching the shadows first in one direction, and then the other. There were a lot of cardboard boxes, ropes to tie things down and some dustsheets. A bed stood to one side, covered with plastic in which she saw reflections of the swinging light, little flashes of yellow like eyes in the night. The bed was an extravagent fourposter with lots of carved bits and a bolster at one end.

'It's a display item,' said Jeff. 'For the red satin sheets and the sheepskins.' It was so cold in the trailer that Sophie could see the white mist of his breath. She shivered. 'Have a swig of this,' he said, 'whilst I get something organized.' He handed her the Boukha; she took a mouthful and her throat went numb.

'We need to think igloo,' he said, 'the smaller the space, the warmer we'll be.'

'The bed, you mean.'

'Mm.' He pulled the plastic off the mattress and started to hang the dustsheets over the frame, turning them into curtains. 'Open some of those boxes,' he said, 'there's a quilt somewhere, and masses of sheets. Should be some pillows, we'll make a sort of nest. Pile things up against the side of the van, and the bedends. Then we're enclosed on three sides.'

She started opening boxes. The first one was fine; black satin sheets and pillowslips. The next box was full of flavoured condoms, and the third one was packed with jars of chocolate body paint. They wouldn't starve, then. She found the quilt and the pillows underneath the dildos and the Mould-a-Willy kits. So this is what you get, she thought, when you open a plain brown envelope.

When the igloo was completed it looked like an Aladdin's cave. One side was piled high with sheepskins, some of them white and fluffy, some of them dyed, silky greens and blues and purples. He'd put the red satin sheet on the mattress, matching pillowslips on the pillows and a pile of garments against one end. They were all costumes; frilly white aprons and little black numbers for chambermaids, royal-blue staff-nurse dresses, a toreador suit of all things – the brocade glittered in the flashlight, and the sequins danced like fireflies as he scrunched the clothes up to one end and said, 'Do you mind taking your shoes off? I can do you some harem slippers.'

They sat cross-legged on the bed, smothered with sheep-skins, and Jeff pulled the makeshift curtain across. It was curiously intimate, and they ate the rest of the biscuits and drank some of the Boukha, but they still shivered from time to time. Eventually by tacit mutual consent they snuggled up to one another, and after a while the goosebumps subsided.

'What you have to second-guess in my line of business,' he said, 'is the private bits inside people's heads. Doctors and nurses, schoolboys and matrons, supermarket checkout girls and lorry drivers . . .'

She stiffened slightly, rope and rape going through her mind. He laughed. 'Some fantasies are perennial, Sophie. For lorry driver substitute blacksmith, or gamekeeper, or turf-cutter. The cashier becomes the wheelwright's daughter, or the parson's wife. Mind you, we had a run on inflatables after the junior health minister gave us all that free publicity.'

'You seem to know a lot about the business side,' she said. 'I thought you were just a driver.' And there it was again, the subtle put-down.

'You're a bit of a snob, aren't you,' he said.

She didn't reply.

'Aren't you,' he repeated, turning her head towards him.

'You just aren't quite . . . what I expected.'

'And what did you expect? This?' He pulled her head towards him and kissed her, quite hard and deliberately. Sophie started to respond without thinking; she had drunk more than she'd realized. Then the little imp voice inside her head said, *good fun, eh*, and she thought – what on earth am I doing? She pulled away from him rather abruptly.

'So,' he said, 'what does your fantasy dictate I do now?'

'What do you mean, my fantasy?'

'Don't you have any?'

She glared at him.

He raised an eyebrow and waited.

She felt oddly cornered. To deny the truth (which involved all sorts of people from Arab sheiks to film stars) was to admit to a total lack of imagination, and her pride wouldn't stand for it. On the other hand, the conversation had got quite dodgy enough. The trouble was, she had a horrible feeling that she really fancied him. He'd certainly known what he was doing when he kissed her. So – if she offered him a fantasy as proof of her creativity (why did she care so much what he thought of her?) she had to make it good. Not something pedestrian like a checkout girl and a lorry driver.

'Some guy way out of my league, no doubt,' he said, watching her. 'What turns you on? Power? Money? Designer jeans?'

'Togas,' said Sophie, thinking, *yes*. Good one. Then *no*,

total bummer. Anyone can make a toga out of a sheet. He seemed to follow her train of thought, for he laughed. Half an hour earlier she'd have expected him to ask her what a toga was. Now she didn't quite know what to think.

'Not even a sneaking hankering after a bit of rough?'

'A centurion, maybe,' said Sophie.

'All right.'

She stared at him. 'What do you mean, all right?'

'There's a costume in one of the boxes,' he said. 'How good's your Latin?'

'*Amo, amas, amat*,' said Sophie, remembering her schooldays and forgetting that she was trying to sound uneducated.

'*Amamus*,' he said. 'Won't be a tick,' and he took the flashlight, pulled back one of the dustsheets and disappeared.

She sat there in the dark thinking, this can't be happening. How ludicrous can life get. Stuck in the snow in the back of a lorry with a lorry driver who thinks he's a Roman soldier and speaks Latin. Something pleasurable flickered in the pit of her stomach, for his roughness had a strange sort of gloss to it. Maybe it was the Boukha. Or maybe it was him. He was a bit of an enigma.

He seemed to be gone for ages, she could hear him rifling through the boxes, little thumps as he moved things, soft rustles and clinks. She was feeling sleepy, the warmth of the sheepskins and the strength of the alcohol were having a powerful effect. She closed her eyes and lay back.

She must have fallen asleep, because what happened next seemed like a dream, although somewhere inside her she was aware that it wasn't. She suspected vaguely that she had woken up at some point and drifted from dream to reality, only the strange thing was that the two were the same.

She had been standing in a market-place; the scene had been very vivid, bright sunlight, crates of scrawny chickens, baskets of figs, women in long dresses, a man in white picking his way carefully through the rotten apples scattered on the ground. She could smell the over-ripe fruit as well as baking bread and spices. A horse whinnied and someone jostled her, and it was an old man with bad teeth and one eye. She had no idea what she was doing there; perhaps she was lost. She glanced round.

A soldier in a plumed helmet caught her eye, haggling with someone over an oil-lamp. He hadn't shaved for a couple of days, but he had nice blue eyes and he was rather good-looking. He glanced in her direction, said something to the trader and walked towards her. She stood there, not knowing what to do. He spoke to her, but she couldn't understand what he said. She felt the panic begin to rise. He repeated himself, louder, but his words made no sense. He shook his head, slightly annoyed, seized her by the wrist and pulled her into a wine shop. The proprietor pointed to a door at the back of the premises; the soldier dragged her through and into a tiny room. There was a thin straw mattress on the floor, and some blankets. He put his arms round her and kissed her roughly, and she felt very small and insignificant and powerless, and at the same time she began to feel very excited. He slipped her dress off her shoulders and felt her breasts, his eyes never leaving her face. She swallowed. There was something about being an object that made her want to dissolve rather wimpishly at his feet. He picked her up, carried her over to the mattress and lay her down on it. Then he stood back and looked at her, his face expressionless. She said something; he obviously didn't understand. Then the blankets seemed to turn into fluff, and she felt the cool slickness of a satin sheet.

He unfastened his breastplate, and laid it down carefully next to him. Then he took off his sandals and his tunic and knelt beside her, quite naked. He put his sword on the bed beside them, and the leather scabbard touched her thigh, reptilian, strange. The room had shrunk, and it was hung with curtains.

He didn't speak. She watched him as he unbuttoned her shirt, his face in shadow, his shoulders lit by a lamp somewhere. He was slow and unexpectedly gentle, and she didn't resist. As he removed each garment he savoured it, smoothing it against his body, fingering it as if it was something unfamiliar and strangely arousing. When he finally slipped off her rather practical white cotton knickers he wrapped them around his penis as though they were made of French silk. Then he took hold of her hand, and she felt him through the thin material, hard and yet softened by the fabric.

He bent over her, and touched the tip of her nipple with his tongue. She felt it stiffen, and her hips moved automatically in response. She knew she was awake now, but it was so strange, so surreal, so erotic. The velvet of his skin, the softness of his lips, the delicacy of his touch. She wanted him.

His hand slipped between her legs, and she felt him separate the folds and run his finger around the inside of her labia. The feeling spread outwards like wine spilt on a tablecloth. The white cotton knickers slid onto the sheet, and she could feel his penis against her for the first time. He was wearing a condom. It was a sudden shock of the present; but like a cold shower in the tropics the effect was short-lived. He began to rub himself against her, very slowly and deliberately, and the winestain reached her fingertips. He hadn't kissed her at all; it made the whole episode seem very theatrical, a shadow-play, figures on a screen. Then suddenly he gripped her by the shoulders and she felt him enter her, and the gentleness had gone.

She let her muscles tense against his; they were riding a storm together, out on some ocean, higher and higher with each wave, salt on her tongue, a pounding in her ears. It was the most exhilarating thing she had ever done, her eyes were shut tight, the way they always had been when she rode a switchback as a child, drunk with sensation, scared and ecstatic.

He's a lorry driver, said a voice in her head. A lorry driver.

I don't give a damn, came her own response. But she opened her eyes, and he was watching her, a slight smile that tightened with each thrust. She was so near; she felt herself pull at him, she wanted it as hard as he could do it.

The smile widened. '*Nil desperandum*,' he whispered, '*et quid pro quo*.' And as they went over the top of the seventh wave she lost all sense of where she was or who she was or who he was, and it was the most intense orgasm she'd ever had.

After a while she said, 'Who are you?'

'Whoever you want,' he said.

She shook her head. 'Who are you really?'

'I told you,' he said. 'I'm a chameleon.'

'With an HGV licence.'

'Yes.'

'Do you own the business?'

'Nope.'

The sheepskins were piled over them, it was almost too hot. She pushed a couple of them away and looked at him. He made no attempt to avoid her gaze. There were no clues on his body, no tattoos, no scars, no jewellery. He was muscular, but not overtly so.

'So you're just a driver,' she said, 'who happens to speak a bit of Latin.'

'A pleb,' he said, and he started to kiss her. She knew there was something she had to do, something connected with rope . . . or was it rape . . . She couldn't quite remember, for what he was doing to her seemed to produce a sort of temporary amnesia . . .

Some time later it occurred to her that kissing was an

excellent way of stopping her asking any more questions. She pulled away.

'No,' he said, 'I'm not having any more of the third degree. The night is still young. What comes after a Roman centurion?'

'Certainly not your slave-girl,' said Sophie, thinking, *phone call*. I didn't make my phone call.

'Slave-girl, eh,' he said, smiling, 'so that's what you were.'

'What about you?' said Sophie. 'What's your fantasy?'

'Being whatever you want,' he said.

'All right,' she snapped, annoyed with his evasions whenever she asked him anything about himself, and she said the first thing that came into her head. 'A polar bear.'

He bit her on the shoulder, not too hard but hard enough. She pushed him, and he cuffed her round the side of the head. Again, it didn't really hurt, but it wasn't gentle. She wriggled away from him. He growled and pounced on her, making claws of his fingers. They rolled across the sheepskins, scratching and biting, until they fetched up against the end of the bed and there was nowhere left to go. He spread her legs and licked her like an animal, rhythmically, single-mindedly, accurately. Then suddenly he turned her round and mounted her from behind. This time he fucked her slowly and frustratingly, holding her in position, not letting her move against him. She tried to twist away; he hauled her back. She snarled at him, and he withdrew. It wasn't what she'd meant; then she realized he was perfectly aware of that. She turned to face him; he bared his teeth at her. Then he slid off the bed and handed her a white sheepskin jacket, which he made her put on inside out. He put one on himself, and picked her up. Then he carried her to the door, leant on the handle and kicked it open.

The blizzard swirled around them like feathers. The snow was up to the top of the lorry's wheels, and there wasn't another vehicle in sight. It was a drop of about three feet; he jumped, and they both fell into the drift. 'At the risk of stepping out of character for a moment,' he said, 'this had better be quick.' Then they were polar bears again, and they tussled and tumbled until they were some way from the road, and surrounded by bushes, their hair frosted with white, the fur of their coats becoming bearskins, their breath as visible as the breath of dragons. It had all been so energetic that Sophie didn't feel the cold, and she thought briefly of Scandinavians dashing naked through the snow after a sauna. Metabolisms were funny things. He cornered her against a tree, and the branches trembled and showered them with white. Finally he forced her onto all fours, bit her neck and penetrated her from behind, holding his fists against her like paws. It was brief and fast and violent, and it was fantastic. And very soon after that they both started to shiver, and they scrambled back to the lorry as fast as they could.

It took them rather longer to get warm this time. Sophie's teeth chattered most unbecomingly until Jeff handed her the bottle of Boukha, and she anaesthetized her entire digestive tract with it.

'Look,' she said eventually, once she could speak again, 'I may as well come straight out and say it. I don't believe you're who you say you are.'

'Ditto,' said Jeff. 'You're no checkout girl, are you.'

She was shocked. She thought she'd played her part rather well.

He smiled. 'Tell me the procedure for cashing up an electronic till.'

She didn't say anything.

The smile widened. 'You're a journalist, Sophie. I looked through your bag whilst you were asleep, I've even read things you've written. The piece about the five housewives who shared an Italian waiter?'

'Oh God,' said Sophie. Then, angrily – 'You went through my bag? Whilst I was asleep?'

'I was curious,' he said. 'Although I was kind of hoping you'd turn out to be what you said you were.'

'You'd rather I worked in a supermarket than for a magazine?'

'On this occasion.'

'Why – worried I'm going to write about you?'

'No,' he said. 'Because I don't think you will.'

'Don't bank on it.'

'What was it going to be – my night of passion with the lower classes?'

She stared at him.

'Rough and ready at the roadside? He can grease my nipples any time? And just wait till I tell you about the size of his camshaft, readers?'

'All right,' she said, 'I do write some garbage sometimes, but that's what they want. I'm working on a novel.'

He had hysterics.

Suddenly she was absolutely furious with him, and she noticed his jeans lying next to her on the bed. There was a small wallet in the back pocket, and she leant over and grabbed it. She turned her back towards him, so that he couldn't see what she was doing, and thumbed through the contents. There were the usual credit cards, in the name of Jeremy Thomas. The name rang a faint bell, but she couldn't place it. She glanced at him over her shoulder; he was lying back on the pillow, his eyes closed and a silly smile on his face.

She smoothed open pieces of paper. A receipt for a fencing foil, of all things, some stamps, a season ticket to a gym, some raffle tickets – *and an Equity card*. Jeremy Thomas. He was an actor, he'd been in some sit-com her mother watched, although Sophie had never seen it herself.

'Bloody hell,' she said, 'Jeremy Thomas.'

She turned round and looked at him. He wasn't smiling any more.

'I'll deny it,' he said.

It was her turn to smile.

'My agent will tell me to sue.'

She laughed out loud. 'Tell me,' she said, 'is this what they call *resting*?'

'No,' he said shortly, 'it's research. I've got a part coming up as a lorry driver.'

'And you wanted to shag a checkout girl to see what it was like. Bad luck. Try the next services.'

'You wanted to get laid by a lorry driver.'

They looked at each other, and then they both started to giggle.

'Bit of a waste of time, wasn't it,' said Jeremy eventually.

Sophie's expression darkened.

'I didn't mean it like that,' he said.

'No. You meant, what am I going to write about now.'

He shrugged.

'I'll make it up,' said Sophie. 'Like I usually do. What about you?'

'I'll pretend,' said Jeremy. 'Like I usually do.'

They grinned at one another.

'You don't have a mobile phone, do you?' said Sophie. 'I was meant to contact a journalist friend to tell her I was all right.'

He shook his head. 'Actually,' he said, 'you could write one hell of an article, as long as you didn't mention me by name. There's an awful lot of stuff to try out in those boxes. And we could be here for some time.'

She forced herself not to sound too incredulous. 'You've made it twice already,' she said, 'do you eat a lot of spinach or something?'

'I didn't mean me,' he said. 'I have electronic devices

beyond your wildest dreams. And remember – I can be anyone you want me to be.'

Sophie took another swig of the Boukha. The flashlight swung from the highest strut of the fourposter, and the grey dustsheet curtains bore a fleeting resemblance to the metallic interior of a spaceship. 'Okay Zard,' she said, 'ravish me the Filtergropian way.'

He stood up and put his hand on the flashlight. 'For real authenticity,' he said, 'we'll do this one in the dark. But before we start – and rather in reverse to the way these things usually work – allow me to ask you if I can see you again. I do feel we have a quite remarkable working relationship, and I'd hate to pass up the opportunity to capitalize on it further at some later date.'

'You mean you want me to play the checkout girl?'

'That sort of thing.'

'Okay,' she said, 'on one condition.'

'What?'

'I get to do an article on you. The real you.'

'All right,' he said, 'but make it reasonably clean.' He wrapped himself in a kimono, and went off to sort through more boxes.

'Pure as the driven snow,' Sophie called after him, with as much sincerity as she could muster, thinking – *no chance.* Then – if I spill the beans I won't get to see him again. And after that – I could write a whole series on fantasy, and I could research every one with him. He was humming to himself, and she could hear him opening plastic bags and carboard cartons. She lay back on the red satin sheet, and began to plan out her opus in her head.

Zard switched off the light. Everything went completely black and some strange ethereal music started to play, quietly, repetitively, minor keys and odd discords. After a while she felt something move across her belly, a hand and yet not a hand, the texture was too smooth and silky, like rubber. Another touch – a finger, a claw, a tentacle – she had no idea. It moved down her body to between her legs, left her for a moment, and then returned, cool and very wet. She felt it slide back and forth, smearing her with something gelatinous, and then she heard a faint hum, like a wasp trapped in a jam jar.

The touch of Zard's alien penis was like an electric shock it was so suddenly and violently arousing. He hissed softly as he moved it around and around until she tried to follow it and trick him into putting it in the right place. He avoided her clitoris with consummate skill, nearly driving her to distraction, and then suddenly, somehow, he was licking both her nipples at once – at least, that's what it felt like. Her body arched upwards for a moment, and she felt his forelimb, cool and smooth, amphibian almost, and she heard him make some sound in his throat, inhuman in its cadence. She couldn't concentrate on all the sensations at once, she had to think about them one at a time. The strange penis shivered against her clitoris for a few seconds, taking her right to the edge, then drew away again and circled as before. She heard herself groan, heard him hiss dramatically in response. Once more he took her to the brink, and then slid away again. She was nearly screaming with frustration. When he touched her there the third time it was enough. As she started to come he laid the full length of his extra-terrestrial organ against her, and the vibration travelled right from one orifice to another. The whole world seemed to contract like a collapsing star; then it expanded again and went on contracting and expanding for a very long time.

She was so blanked out by it that she didn't hear the knocking on the side of the lorry, nor did she hear the voice say, 'Hello? Hello? Anyone there?'

That's quite some paintjob, thought the policeman, as he

paused to listen for a reply. Someone had designed the lorry as an enormous brown envelope – one of those heavy-duty ones, with a slight grain to the paper. Clever.

'Give it another go, constable,' said the sergeant, stamping his feet and rubbing his hands together to ward off the cold.

The constable took a deep breath and shouted, 'Oy! You in there! This is the police. If you don't answer we're coming in, someone's reported a missing person called Sophie.' He put his ear against the icy metal. Still there was no reply, although he fancied he could hear a faint buzzing, like the sound of an angry wasp.

The sergeant shook his head. 'They could have frozen to death in there. I think you'd better open that envelope constable. God knows what we'll find.'

Acknowledgments

The publisher is grateful to the following for permission to reproduce copyright material from:

'An Outside Interest' by Ruth Rendell, reprinted by permission of the Peters Fraser & Dunlop Group Ltd

'The Undead' by Robert Bloch published by permission of Eleanor Bloch, C/o Ralph M Vicinanza Ltd

'The Birds Poised to Fly' from *Eleven* by Patricia Highsmith. All rights reserved.
Copyright © 1993 by Diogenes Verlag AG, Zürich

'Colette's Column' Copyright © 1996 by Andy Harrison

'Elvara Should be Easy' Copyright © 1996 by J. K. Haderack

'Angel' Copyright © 1996 by Philip Robinson

'Old Times' Copyright © 1996 by Alick Newman

'What Might Have Been' Copyright © 1996 by Elizabeth Kay

'Plucked' Copyright © 1996 by Frank Finch

'Catherine Would' Copyright © 1996 by Sidney Gray

'The Plain Brown Envelope' Copyright © 1996 by Lyn Wood